SUCH IS LIFE

Gianni Franco

GFP Productions

ISBN-13: 9781736621769 (Paperback)
ISBN-13: 9781736621776 (E-Book)

Cover design by: Domenico Colaprete
Library of Congress Control Number: 2025904986, 1-10820015151
Printed in the United States of America

Life is fleeting. That last embrace, that last I love you, that last phone conversation, that last smile, that last laugh, that last cry, is worth more than a lifetime.

GIANNI FRANCO

GIANNI FRANCO

CH 1

May 13, 2030

Not my ideal Friday afternoon in May, especially the 13th, but to be fair, for us Italians, the number represents good luck. Pollen flitted within the warm breeze like a cotton ball blizzard, stifling each breath as I rushed to my doctor's appointment. Bus 28, late again. This time due to traffic, last time it was a flat tire, and the time before that, it just didn't show. The driver missed the drop-off at South Avenue and Bellevue Drive by several hundred feet. Exiting, I slipped along the grated stairs, and if not for the stranger who caught me from behind, I would've cracked my knees against the pavement. I stumbled along the inclined cobblestone path of Doctors Drive to the Highland Hospital Physician Group like a drunkard on a catwalk with stilettos, finding a bit of reprieve and several breaths as I leaned against the slivered, wooden door labeled *ENTRANCE* in faded red, the letters flaking and peeling. Today, its handle heavier than the boulders I lifted during a stint in construction.

"Greetings, Mr. Romano. I hope you're having a great day," Miss Penelope howled as I limped to the check-in counter, passing a swath of empty chairs in the large waiting room. "No need to sign in. No need, Mr. Romano. Go ahead and take a load off," she said, waving towards the chairs.

"But, I'm here now. I made it. Can't I just si—?

"Nope. No need. I took care of everything for you, Mr Romano. You didn't have to walk all the way up here," she said with a smirk.

"Fine. Thanks for telling me after I passed all the seats," I mumbled, trekking to the waiting area.

I plopped onto a teal, vinyl chair, the cracks and creases digging into my thighs. An instrumental of "Spirit in the Sky" by Norman Greenbaum played through speakers mounted on various sections of the walls and ceiling, which time had stained yellow. Latex and rubbing alcohol lingered throughout the windowless room, wringing my lungs further. Across from me, an ornery child occupied his purple seat cross-legged sans shoes and missing a sock. Between each sniffle, his mom, or nanny, blotted the dripping snot, giving him an opportunity to leer. I smirked. He frowned. Kitty-corner, an older woman straddling a green chair dangled her bruised arms over the backrest. Every few moments, she stretched her feeble fingers towards the wall ahead of her, and with each attempt, she missed. Giving up, she propped her thin chin atop her bony shoulder. She gurgled, coughed, and swallowed with each breath, lapping her lips like a thirsty dog. I tapped my boot atop the faded carpet, hoping my future wasn't as grim as hers. The red door leading to the patient area creaked open. The doctor leaned into its space, curled his finger in my direction and nodded.

I rose, then my legs faltered. Stumbling, my thighs slammed into the armrests and I flopped onto the chair sideways. I waved for him to loan me a minute and he obliged, meeting me halfway to help me up and walk. Lurching, he guided me with his hands, one at my elbow, the other steadying my back.

"Weird, Doc. All of a sudden I couldn't breathe or walk."

"Well, you shouldn't have missed all of your

appointments this past year. They were important, Mr. Romano," he scolded.

"I was busy with things," I said with a weak chuckle.

He firmed his jaw and shook his head. I skipped the visits more for fear than anything else, but one can't run and hide forever.

"Perhaps, if you would've come, we'd have better news for you today," he said, followed by a sigh. "It's alright, Nico. We'll chat when we get into the room."

"Okay. Just a bit of advice, I think you need a filter system. The air is stale in your waiting area. That's what probably caused my mishap." I turned towards him and smiled, but he didn't reciprocate.

"We'll talk in the room," he said, monotone. "A few more steps. Third door on the right. The blue one."

I'd been treated by Doctor Robert Gordon for many years. What he lacked for a sense of humor he amended with extensive knowledge. I gathered his seriousness was due to doctor stress. Then again, I didn't know him outside work. It's possible at the black-tie galas he pranced around the dance floor with a bottle of scotch and a megaphone.

He closed the door and asked me to sit upon the table. The bright white walls, opposite those in the waiting room, contrasted the charcoal linoleum and cabinets like day and night. He ran the typical tests and checked my pulse on various regions of my body, twisting his lips and squinting. I found it odd, but I'm just the patient. I'm certain he wanted to be accurate as all good doctors do. He retrieved the blood pressure cuff from a drawer, and cycled through the pump-and-release procedure several times as if trying to get a perfect score. I don't believe he did because he stepped back and grimaced, throwing the cuff atop the counter. Silent, he scanned me from head to toe, then stroked the salty scruff on his chin.

"Well, Nico…" He paused and grabbed my file sitting next to the cuff.

"What is it, Doctor?"

"I understand you haven't been feeling well. And, we've been dealing with your health issues for years. I am repeating myself, but those appointments should not have been skipped. The checks I just performed confirm the reports we've been monitoring and the new ones we received. You—"

"Come on, Doc. I didn't come here for more bad news. Haven't I had enough?"

"Nico… Let's just—" He flipped through the chart, glancing at me with sullen eyes. His placating West Indian accent couldn't mask the negative aura in the room. "Time isn't on your side anymore. I'm sorry for the bad news. I didn't want to tell you. I'm not good at this part of doctoring, but—"

"What the hell does that even mean?" I bit my lower lip and slapped the table. My hunch from his repetitive checks proved correct. I knew at some point during my lifetime this statement would arrive, but not today, not now. It's too soon. It's Friday, the start of the weekend. I have so many things I still haven't accomplished.

"Mr. Romano," he shouted, snapping me from the daze.

"Yes… Doctor."

"Obviously, you're upset. We can talk through this dilemma and find some resolve, some stable ground to set our feet."

"It's quicksand, not ground. I think if what you say is

true, then we should address it head-on." I lied. I didn't want to deal with it from any angles.

"Agreed. That's the best option to take with end-of-life scenarios."

"Whatever you say, Doc, but I no longer want to."

"You must address it. There's no other way. You can call me Robert, considering. Ask me anything. I'm here to help as best I can," he said with a soothing tone.

"Alright, Doctor. I mean… Robert. Time. How much time? What is time anyway? Can't you be wrong?"

He folded the file under his arm, adjusting the stethoscope around his collar. "It's difficult pinpointing an *exact* time. We recently acquired a new, experimental program called iLifeCheck, which is used to predict length of life. Your information is inputted and the Artificial Intelligence and algorithms compute the time. In my opinion, it's as accurate as Punxsutawney Phil on Groundhog Day, fifty-fifty. But, at a recent conference, the software company explained the program has been updated. I still don't trust it completely. That being said, whatever the estimated time, I suggest you get your affairs in place."

"What affairs? I'm poor."

"I'm sorry." His gaze circled the floor, then the ceiling.

"I don't believe it, or you. Any of this." I flicked my wrist. "I feel fine. It'll pass. There's no reason for it to happen now or any time in the future."

"Come on, Nico. Did you forget I helped you walk into the room?"

If I would've tried harder, I could've made it without assistance. Of course, I couldn't tell him. His response certain to shoot down my suggestion. He opened the folder and scanned it again. I think he did it more for effect, then continued with the medical diagnosis.

"Well… during and after your hospital stay last year we completed a series of tests. We explained the primary illness is Heart Failure, Stage D: hypertensive and atherosclerotic cardiovascular disease. You must've understood the issue. You signed the forms and nodded the whole time. Come on, Nico. Work with me here."

"Doc, I thought you were kidding. You know… exaggerating like most people do."

"No, Nico. Not at all. I'm a doctor, not a comedian."

"I understand, now. I guess." I sighed, then swelled my chest. "But, I feel strong, not sick. At least not ill enough to die."

"I'll further explain, Nico. We're all built different, so the symptoms we exhibit aren't always similar. Some have none and some have more than average. Compounding the situation was a severe bout of pneumonia and the lasting effects from COVID-19 in 2020. If you recall, we placed you on a ventilator for almost a month. These illnesses did irreparable damage to the heart muscle as well as the mitral and pulmonary valves, which were already weak. We compared chest x-rays to confirm. Additionally, your BNP and hemoglobin levels are high."

"This BNP thing, can it be reversed?"

"Unfortunately, no. The B-type natriuretic peptide is released by the heart in response to the strain from blood volume. The only way to fix your situation is with a heart transplant and that option is impossible as well."

"Why?" I swiped the dribble upon my lip and sniffled.

"I understand this is difficult, Nico. Yours is a complicated case and the time, whether two days, two weeks, or two months, doesn't give us the ability to find a donor heart. The list is long." He lowered his head and sighed. "The labs haven't yet perfected creating an assembly line of hearts from scratch. And, even if we had a heart, surviving the major surgery might be difficult as well."

"What's my time frame? What's that stupid program say? What do you say? Why, why, why… Tell me, please." I said, hoping for a positive response.

"My personal opinion is you have between two and six months. A small percentage of people in your situation can last twelve. The program, well, it's not as optimistic. As I stated, its accuracy is about fifty percent, a coin toss. We submitted all your blood tests, x-rays, body scans, and genetic profile to the AI simulator and ran the prediction sample several times with the same results, between two and thirty days, give or take a few hours. I want to reiterate it's not a hundred percent accurate."

"Dammit. Either way, I lose. Funts and cuckers. *Che fregatura. Ma perche a me? Non e giusto. Sono gentile.*" I jumped to my feet from the exam table, tearing the paper covering.

"Excuse me, but what does that even mean?"

"Means nothing, but maybe if I stop swearing in English or speak more Italian, I'll be cured. I'll be saved. Right?"

"That's not how it works, Nico."

"Fine, but it's worth trying."

"Let's get back to reality. The years of risky behavior and unhealthy habits didn't help, but there *is* one positive. At least you know there's an expiration date." He flipped his wrist and looked at his watch. "The exact time is not important."

"That's not a damn positive. It's the end of it all. This is ridiculous. I think you need to check the plastic machine again and review your notes. One of its microchips must be shorting, or its electric brain is misfiring. I'm not sick like all the other people in your manuals. I'll be fine. For years, even. You're all wrong."

"It's not the case. I'm sorry, Nico. We, as humans, are limited by our organs. Until they discover a way to replicate our organs in a lab, then we're stuck with our fates."

He stretched his hand towards my shoulder. I stepped out of his reach, abutting the wall behind me. He tried once more. I stood stern, shaking my head like a child refusing to take a dose of medicine.

"I know how you're feeling. This is expected from patients who receive this kind of news. If you'd like, I can send you to another office so you can talk to one of our counselors. They can offer comfort, as well as walk you through the final stages of this process."

"You don't know how I damn feel." I slammed my palm against the wall. "You'll be alive, whereas I'll be a corpse burning at the local processing plant we call a funeral home. There's no way this can be happening. And to me of all people. I'm too young. Every day in the news they talk about people living until a hundred or more."

"Well, that's just not you. I understand how you feel. I'm a doctor. My job is to help you the best I can within my capabilities. I, nor any of my colleagues, can control the way illnesses progress."

I tilted my head towards the lamps above and their glow

tunneled my vision. Blinking didn't resolve the issue. The more I stared, the darker the surroundings. A muffled, angelic voice echoed.

"Are you alright, Nico? It's going to be okay. I promise."

Silence followed. The seraph appeared, cradling my head in its hands. As my eyes crept open, I soon realized none of it was true. I moved away from Doctor Gordon's shoulder, the thick threads from his lab coat imprinting my face. Shocked, I leaned against the examination table, juddering to regain focus.

"You just had a mild cardiac episode. The severity will increase with time. You'll need assistance. We can offer you a hospice home. I didn't mention it earlier because I figured you weren't interested."

"You're right. Screw that option. No way am I sitting in a death house with all those dying people. I'd rather have my demise arrive on the street or in an alley."

"Good point. I'd probably do the same as well." He paused and scrunched his brow. "Well, on second thought, not on the street or an alley. At home, surrounded by family and friends is a more suitable environment." He noticed the anxiety stamped on my face and changed the conversation. "Anyway… enough about my choices for the future. Do you have any other questions about the process?"

"Yes. Can—you—" I cleared my throat and firmed my stance. "Can you give me anything to keep me going? Keep the heart pumping? Give me time. Like the pills you gave me before?"

"You didn't get the refill extended?"

"No. I didn't want to bother you, plus I was feeling

better."

"Oh, Nico. You're supposed to call us. We advised you as such. I'll write a new script."

"No. Not now. I don't have time or money for the pharmacy."

He tapped his finger on his chin and narrowed his eyes for several moments. "Great idea," he blurted, breaking the eeriness. "I have a bunch of free pills the pharmaceutical rep dropped off." He reached into the cupboard above the sink and retrieved two, enormous pill bottles. "And, no, they aren't opiates. One is nitroglycerin mixed with two experimental drugs called Tolvaptan and Cuorica, the other aspirin. Both are high dosage." He handed me the stash. "Take them when your chest tightens and you're short of breath. I don't recommend chewing or crushing the pills. If you do, then the results will be immediate and you may not be able to handle the effects. Also, they may damage your stomach lining and possibly cause you to bleed internally, so be careful. There are enough pills to fill a sixty-day script. And, don't forget to keep taking your other heart medications as well. We'll save you time and call in the script for those. Do me a favor and pick them up."

"Okay. Thank you, Robert. Means a great deal to help me. This whole thing, it's just not fair."

"You're welcome and I know. Life is sort of bad cliché. We can sit and chat for a few more minutes, or you can wait until I'm done with all the patients and talk longer. What do you think?"

I ran my fingers through my hair, down to the nape of my neck, pondering his offer.

"No. We don't have to chat any longer. You've done all

you can. I do want a few minutes to myself. Of course, if you'll allow me to stay in this room. Is it free or is another patient scheduled?

He shrugged. "No, you're fine. Take all the time you need. If you're here long enough, then we can talk without being rushed."

"Time is something I no longer have and rushing is the only option remaining. I'll make it quick and try to find you on my way out."

"Make sure you do, Nico," he said with a pleasant smile.

He stretched for a handshake, and when I met it, he surprised me with an embrace, followed by several strong pats on my back. He took a deep breath, offered a forced smile, and marched towards the door, fumbling the handle, then shutting it with care. His designer shoes clacked the corridor, then they paused and he bellowed, "How are you today? So glad to see you." Hopefully, their experience wasn't as bad as mine.

I surveyed the room for the last time, admiring the elongated swabs stuffed in the glass jar alongside the tonsil sticks and latex gloves. I wanted to take one of each as a souvenir, but at the last moment decided those mementos served no positive purpose. Less sinning equals more living. I exited the room not bothering to look for Doctor Gordon. A final goodbye too depressing for my psyche and probably his. At the front desk, I stopped to pay the receptionist.

"Oh..." She coughed. "Mr. Romano. It's your lucky day. I've been informed by Doctor Gordon that we're waiving today's fee."

"I'm not sure it's lucky. I'll pay. It's fine. The least I can do for all the Doctor has done for me."

"No, sir. I'll get in trouble by Robert if he knows I collected money from you. Let it slide and have a great rest of your day and week."

"That's a moronic statement," I mumbled.

"What did you say, Mr. Romano? You were whispering and the fan on the desk is blowing too hard at my face.

"I said it's ironic I don't have to pay, Miss Penelope. Thank you for your service. I doubt my week will go well. Give the Doctor my regards and wish him a good day."

"Will do, Mr. Romano."

"Thank you." I offered the peace sign with my hand and exited the office.

CH 2

An attempt at a deep breath caused me to hunch with a hacking cough. I regained my composure and walked across Alpine Street, then down Reservoir Avenue to Highland Park. A misnomer since neither the park nor Rochester resided in a mountainous region. I visited after each appointment, but today it meant more than any other. An empty, wrought-iron bench, flaking orange specks from its legs, greeted me. The splintering, wood seat provided me a place to ponder my options for my finite life, whether in hours, days, weeks, or months. Not an easy task, but one that needed to be addressed as soon as possible.

I spent over an hour thinking about nothing, drawing varying lines and dots against the blackboard within my mind, awoken from time to time by skates etching their signatures atop the paved path, and bicycles swooshing past, their tires whirring like a swarm of hornets. In the distance, along Highland Avenue, cars honked, screeched, and rumbled with the fluctuating pace of traffic. I could do without their pollution. I believe some of the drivers would agree, although they busied themselves hurling vulgarities out their windows like concrete spitballs instead of pondering their individual insignificance.

The passersby, unlike my prior visits to the park, intrigued me today. Their loveliness untethered to my doomsday psyche. Like a cop on a stakeout, I observed their gaits, facial expressions, and clothes, eavesdropping on conversations some had with their partners, themselves, the sky, and animals, while others sang along to a tune. I was guilty of the same detached communications on more than one occasion. Every so often, I'd catch a whiff of a cigarette, bringing back memories of a vice I missed. Its aroma more appealing to breathe than the lasting stench it glued to my fingers and clothing. Even though a single stick would be certain to kill me on the spot considering my state of affairs, I would partake if offered by a congenial walker. Nothing to lose when everything is lost.

Beside me, a tall elm provided partial shade to the bench and path. Gazing upward, I caught sight of a peculiar squirrel teetering upon a branch no thicker than a fishing pole. Its pelt, striped like a skunk, glistened as the sun warmed it. It spun midair, then landed and hopped each uneven rung jutting from the trunk. Within seconds, it reached the base of the tree and scampered towards the bench. At my feet, it craned its small head and blinked. I believe it wanted a nibble to fill its empty belly.

"I don't have anything," I said, splaying empty hands.

The squirrel paused, tilted its neck, and exposed its buck teeth. Perhaps it was their way to protest and show disappointment with my lack of resolve.

"Little friend, if I knew in advance, I would've brought you a piece of bread or a handful of nuts. My day isn't going well. I hope you understand."

Batting eyes and an upright tail suggested it accepted my reasoning for failing to bring a morsel of food. It twirled its body like a ballerina and scampered up the tree. I never paid much attention to their perspectives, rather took them for granted. I fed and loved animals as most do, but not until today did I understand their plight without speaking their language. It's no different than mine or any other human. Search for food, a place to sleep, and stay alive. Without the latter, nothing else is possible. I hoped the squirrel could understand the universe threw me a curveball, which I couldn't catch with a mitt as big as a cloud.

The countdown to the rest of my life had started and it was something I'd never contemplated. Sure, I knew it'd arrive one day, but planning ahead for death and deciding who to visit and where to go is not for the fainthearted. Vague ideas darted about the mind, and as they entered, I flushed them out with a firehose. I didn't own a car, nor could I afford one, so driving through this city or to another was impossible. I'd made it this far in life without the need because everything was within walking distance from my apartment. I checked my watch and realized another thirty minutes had passed pondering nothings.

"Come on. Get with it, Nico," I shouted towards the sky. A man pushing a stroller ahead of me jumped, then glared and sped off. I'm sure he would've understood my dilemma, if I had a chance to explain. My body couldn't afford to chase him, even if purchased on a discount.

I rose from the bench, deciding best not to be present if he returned with the park police. Jail time not an option with my time constraints. I stopped at the tree, scanning the trunk and branches for the squirrel, but it had disappeared. It probably set off to the neighboring trees and I couldn't search them all. I tapped the bark and wished it the best of luck in its quest for survival. I checked the path and seating area once more, and no one had returned. Relieved with the thought of no confrontation, I headed to Lily Pond centered in the park.

The elusive squirrel brought an idea to mind as I strolled across the lush and manicured hundred-acre lawn. It climbed and pounced from tree to tree with friends and family, then returned home. I bet it never left its earthly confines. The plan as plain as day; visit those I hold close to my heart and give them a proper send-off within a couple days. If I don't do it now, then I may never. Keeping my corporeal countdown secret, so as not to upset them, paramount.

I stood at the edge of the water with amazement. Glistening goldfish and minnows shimmered below small, rippling waves reflecting the rays from above. Ducks paddled and dipped their bills between tall reeds and oversized lilies. In the distance, a flock of geese roared to flight like military jets, cawing their mates into formation.

On occasion, when I wasn't working and younger, I'd come to the park and feed the birds, fish, and squirrels with my first love, Beatrice. She actually introduced me to Highland Park. A first-generation Italian, who was born in the United States and, unlike me, didn't need to carry a green card. Those damn permits always created a problem. Without one, a human didn't exist in the States.

Just out of high school, I acquired an opportunity to work at a major factory for one of the big-three automakers. A friend, of a friend, of a friend, finagled an interview for me. I walked into the office wearing a pressed shirt and tie. The pleated slacks and dress shoes were the best I could afford at the time. I still have them in my closet today. Strutting with a smile towards the interview room, I thought how amazing

America had been to offer me such opportunities. I carried the pizzazz to the padded chair ahead of the interviewer.

"Good morning, Mr. Martin," I said with a strong Italian accent. To this day, I haven't been able to shake it to meld with those around me. I think his first name was Rex, Brett, or Buford.

He winced, then flashed a fake smile and a nod. "Mr. Rom —ano. Thanks for your interest in this here company. We *likes* your kind. In fact, almost loves. Y'all make great p—izza." He chuckled like a neighing horse. "You's a hard working group. You I—talians. Never complain no matter how tough the job like good ole boys and girls." His accent not from Rochester, rather southern like those from the Westerns.

I didn't like what he said and knew what he meant. I'd been trained by the Italian community to accept it or you'll never get a paycheck. Desperate for one, I gave the best response I knew. "Okay, great." Then, I grinned as wide as the American flag hanging in the corner of the room.

He shuffled the paperwork upon the desk, scanning multiple times, then grunted. "Odd, you forgot to check the important box."

"Which one, sir?" I said, confused with a hint of trepidation.

"You'sa citizen, Mr. Nicola Ro—ma—no?" His drawl accented the consonants instead of the vowels.

We sat in silence, he drumming the table awaiting my response. "Well, almost Mr. Martin, Mr., Sir. I'm legal resident. I have green card." I patted my pockets, searching for my wallet to show him proof.

"Don't bother, boy." His welcoming mood changed

without notice. "I don't want to see it. We have a saying in this country: almost doesn't count, except in horseshoes and hand grenades. You's people need to follow the goddamn rules in this here U-S-of-A."

"Scusa? I mean excuse me?" I didn't understand what he meant. Grenades kill you and horseshoes don't. I just wanted a job. I follow rules.

"It means come back to see us when you get your citizenship. Otherwise, we *are* closed to your kind and business." His condescending scowl meant more than the words.

"But I just wanted to—" Pointless to plea, I paused. "Okay," I said, then mumbled, "*bastardo, testa di cazzo.*" I rose with my held head high and shoulders stern.

"While you's at it, best learn some damn English too, boy," he shouted as I approached the door.

"Vaffanculo," I said, then slammed the door shut behind me.

From that day forward, I learned my place was always at the back of the line. Italians only a convenient ethnicity when cooking, or being jibed on national television, or slurred, or being portrayed as mobsters, or gold-chain-wearing loudmouths, or cartoons, or video games, or hanged in a New Orleans square. My love for America never faded, although I detested its corporate entities, racist sects, and narcissistic clowns holding the highest office in the land. I couldn't blame the country as a whole. Perhaps it did afford me some luxuries I wouldn't have had in Italy and the advice from the moron during the interview, priceless. I read hundreds of books, even studying the dictionary, and became enamored with the

English language.

I didn't need a corporate gig, finding a multitude of comfort working for other Italians and immigrants around the neighborhoods. I sliced meats, built mountainous hoagies, and flipped burgers at Nacca's, the local delicatessen, for many years. The paychecks didn't afford me an extravagant lifestyle, but they paid the rent, allowing for sporadic excursions to the cafes, and later in life to the bars.

Beatrice, on the other hand, sat at the front of the line on a plush, leather chair, usually supplied by a bank. It was fine, her luck better than mine. Beatrice and I met during grammar school at Saint Theodore's, lost touch, then revisited each other during high school. Our innocent curiosity led to intimate discovery and love. Our dates began at Café Gino, sipping espresso or a cappuccino. We'd stroll East Avenue, a thoroughfare encompassing eateries from all ethnicities in Rochester, sampling drinks, foods, and deserts, then walk along the Genesee Riverway Trail.

One Friday evening, the exact date I can't recall, after a quick bite, she tugged me to Highland Park. She led me over the lush expanse, crossing several gravel paths, one of which had a group of kids from our high school smoking cigarettes and drinking, listening to "Never Say Goodbye" by Bon Jovi. We arrived at the pond's edge and sat upon a grassy mound where she pointed out the birds and fish. I stroked her hand while she caressed my hair and nape with her long, manicured nails painted a violet hue to match her summer dress. My body warmed and tingled. I've always wondered if hers did as well. We leaned into each other, her breath cooling my lips, and as we closed our eyes, we kissed for the first time. It lasted no more than a few seconds but meant more to me than life itself.

Today, I stand in the same place we stood decades ago, and my gut tells me to visit her before my time expires. I believe she still resides at 818 Mulberry Street, only a few blocks from Highland Park. I'm certain time has changed her as it has me, but nothing will complete me more than to look into her eyes and swim within their gaze one last time. A chance to talk, just to utter my final goodbye would make my final days palpable. Perhaps we'll have our last walk around this park holding hands and hoping for a better future; mine definite and mediocre, hers unbounded and notable.

An hour later, I arrived at my one-bedroom apartment at 103 Audubon Street. I opened the aging laptop, which took several minutes to boot. Beside me sat the white pages in the remote case the Internet couldn't connect or find the information. Google linked me to various services who provided her address, and much more, if I decided to pursue the stalking route. I passed on the latter. She hadn't moved. My journey began with the first stop to visit with my first love. I hoped to find her home, opening the door with a sensual kiss and loving embrace.

CH 3

I buttoned the best dress shirt I owned, which I'd bought at Matthew's Closet, a five-and-dime offering an eclectic selection of clothing and furniture donated by wealthy east-siders. The corporations never hired me, but I was able to wear a slim selection of their attire, albeit at a discount. Without those options, I'd probably be walking the streets in ragged clothing. Pleated slacks may have been more impressive for Beatrice, but I didn't bother changing my jeans. I owned the single pair for years, washing them only a handful of times as not to destroy their aura. They'd been through the trenches, protecting me like armor. Although, today, their powers failed me.

Inside the bathroom, I gazed at the reflection in the mirror. It told a dire tale. My once vibrant, hazel eyes are now surrounded by a faint and peculiar yellow. The dark, curly mane, resting below the shirt collar, had greyed at a rapid pace within the last year. The winding creases and crevices along my face more pronounced. Sighing, I shrugged with heavy shoulders and a sore chest, steadfast to avoid a tragic ending.

I spun the faucet open with a weak hand, then struggled to splash my face, styling my hair with dabs of water. The malaise certain to pass soon. It'd been a long day and the news from the doctor knocked me down several rungs on the ladder of life. Stepping back, I tilted my head and engaged the mirror once more, hoping a different angle equaled a better outcome, but it didn't. Trembling, I raised my fist to strike it, then retreated, grabbing the edge of the sink.

Bawling, I beseeched the reflection to listen. Doctor Gordon is wrong. The stupid, plastic box filled with microchips and wires must've made a mistake. iLifeCheck had to be inaccurate. Those programs are always incorrect. Well, maybe not always, but sometimes. He must've inputted bad information and that's the reason for all the erroneous results. Or, perhaps the computer was confused with another of his many patients. It agreed with no further debate. Elated, I organized myself for the trek through the city.

Beatrice lived several blocks away. I doddered along the sidewalk on Audubon Street, huffing the floating aromas from the Park Avenue bistros: tomato sauce, fried chicken, hamburgers, pizza, and curry. Years ago, we walked the streets of the Corn Hill and Park Avenue Neighborhoods hand in hand. She'd break free from me and dance ahead, twirling and jumping like a bonfire flame. I'd flick my cigarette into the street and chase her down, scooping her up with the strength of a gladiator, then nuzzle her forehead. Cradled in my arms, she stroked my hair and kissed my lips, all the while people in cars cheered us with blaring horns, and those walking beside us smiled with envious eyes. Those days as breathtaking as the rays from the setting sun painting the sky sienna in the distance.

We dated for a few years, and then, two days after our last Christmas together, she ended our relationship without even a phone call. She had tucked a note into my mailbox. It said it's time for me to go. I can no longer be with you. She shared her love and signed off with a heart and smiley face below her name. I hope she remembers because an explanation is well overdue.

I pressed my moistened palms the length of my jeans, attempting to remove any evidence of nervousness as I stood at the steps. I circled my finger around the doorbell several times, uncertain if she wanted to see me or even answer. At the door, a child shuffled away and snickered. Holding my breath, I pressed the button. A chime ensued similar to an orchestral overture.

"Who is it?"

I coughed, then grunted, "Nico."

"I'm sorry. I didn't hear you."

"John Smith. RG&E. Rochester Gas and Electric."

"Okay. I'll be right there… Put those toys down, Mateo. One moment, please. I'm coming."

Her youthful and sultry voice hadn't changed since we dated. Hopefully, God nor the angels counted the minor fib against me. The locks jangled and the door swung open.

Mouths agape, we stood silent, staring. "Hi—hi Beatrice," I said with a trembling voice, harkening to the virgin version of myself when I first met her. Perhaps I had erred in visiting. "Beatrice…" My cheeks warmed like a child meeting their crush.

Her lips parted, but she didn't utter a word. Uncontrollable blinking followed as her brow rose, then fell, then rose again. "Is that really—"

"Yes, Miss Russo." I nodded with surety and winked. A veneer while I mused screaming, crying, or laughing. None occurred as I hesitated a bit to regain composure and prevent a potential doorstep heart attack. "It's me. Nico. Not John Smith from RG&E."

"Obviously. I see that, John." She paused with a smirk, then chuckled. "Wow. What are you doing here?"

"Not sure, yet," I said with a bit of hesitation and slight stutter.

"And, double wow. You're still using that nickname? I always preferred Nicola. Your real name has a much better ring to my ears."

"But, you're the one that gave me the nickname. I think during our third or fourth date. Seems like only yesterday. You said Nico was cooler and easier to say."

"If it only was yesterday. I don't remember. If I said that, then I'm sorry. Maybe it's because the white people were making fun of you. Anyway, what brings you to my doorstep after all these years? Are you dying or something?" She guffawed.

I couldn't tell her yet, so I did what anyone would do. I ignored the question and lied, adding to the fib tally. "I wanted to see you again. It's been a long time. I've missed you."

"Well, you didn't miss me after we broke up. You never did chase after me."

"Chase? Beatrice, you broke up with me and only left a silly note. Why did you do it that way? What did I do to you?" I implored.

She sighed. "Well, I had no choice. It just wasn't working between us. Do you want to come in? I can't leave the door open with this damn heat during spring. The air conditioner has been non-stop."

"Of course. Thought you'd never ask."

I crossed the doorway and the dam of memories broke, the waves flooding my mind, shivering my being like I had stepped into another dimension. Basil and bay leaves rose from the simmering sauce on the stove while her father stirred the pot and monitored the boiling spaghetti. Her mother kneaded the meatball mix, rolling them into perfect spheres as big as billiard balls. The sauce never too thin or thick and each bite of the meatball melted in my mouth like cotton candy. After dinner, we'd sit on the couch beside her parents watching the nightly news followed by *The Tonight Show*. They'd sip wine or liquor while we ate various Italian cookies from a plate upon the coffee table. Between them, full glasses of cold milk. I'd leave her house filled with a sugar high, which dwindled as I walked home.

"Come." She waved me towards the kitchen table. "Have a seat. I just put Mateo to bed. Boys are always acting naughty. We'll have time to chat. I've been meaning to contact you and tell you—never mind. Would you like some coffee… espresso?"

"Tell me what?"

"It's not important. Don't worry so much. Maybe we'll talk about it later or another time."

My chest tightened without warning. I forced the ensuing cough back into my lungs by holding my breath and squeezing my fists. I couldn't expose my illness, let alone ruin this exquisite moment.

"Are you okay, Nicola?"

Damnit. She noticed my welling eyes. Clenching my jaw, I inhaled through my nose, willing a temporary reprieve to the pain. "Yes. Just a throat tickle." A quick gasp transitioned to normal breath. "Probably the air conditioning. It'll be fine. And yes, you always knew how to make a good espresso."

"Yup. The key is not to use the machine. Have to do it

the old-fashioned way with the Moka pot on the stovetop. And, never, ever pack the grounds tight."

"Yeah. Your mom always used to say that. And, you're right. In Italy we couldn't afford espresso machines. The first one I ever saw in a home was when I came to America. Makes sense. They have everything here. Italy had nothing but poverty and war."

"Being poor isn't bad. Italians make the best of any situation. We can survive on anything like stovetop espresso, polenta for dinner, and the luxurious meal called bread dipped in wine."

She laughed and spun the aluminum canister, separating it into three pieces. From a sealed container in the refrigerator, she retrieved the espresso grounds and filled the bottom half of the Moka pot.

"These are your favorite. I do remember some things."

She set a large plate upon the table and filled it with Spumetti, Savoiardi, and the classic Rainbow Cookie, which mirrors the Italian flag.

"Back in those days, you could eat twenty of each."

I nodded with the same wanting eyes, but refrained, refocusing on my mission. Plus, I didn't know if gorging would cause me to choke or have a stroke.

"How are your parents?" I asked.

"Dad passed away a few years ago. A couple months later, Mom died. Some of the superstitious Italians call it a broken heart. I call it failing organs, but in either case, she, they're gone. May they rest in peace." She completed the sign of the cross and looked to the ceiling.

"Yes. May they rest in peace." I paused. "Good you had a

partner to help you through that time."

She rolled her eyes, waved her hand, and bit her lower lip. "He wasn't there. We ended our relationship."

"I'm sorry, Beatrice. I didn't mean to assume there was someone else. I didn't know. Well, we know what happens when I assume. Two shoes aren't enough to stuff in my mouth."

"No big deal. I should've been more honest with him, and likewise, he. We divorced because—" She cleared her throat. "—because…" With fists curled, she raised them towards her face. The fear in her eyes confirmed the horrors. "Such is life, Nico. We choose our destinies and have to live with them. Amen."

"Oh… my… What the hell? Is there anything I can do, Beatrice? That's horrible, reprehensible," I said, my stomach roiling. "If I could, I'd take care of him for you."

"It's okay, Nico." She winked. "I mean, Nicola. Violence doesn't resolve anything. Only begets more."

"You're right. And, what is an old man like myself going to do anyway? I'm useless. Good thing you were able to leave him. Those situations are quite difficult mentally as well as physically."

"Yes, they are. I worked through it with some help from friends and a therapist. Luckily, I lost nothing in the divorce, for obvious reasons. I didn't gain anything either because he's a deadbeat. I ended up inheriting the house from my parents. Rather than selling, and since money was tight, I moved in. Better for the kids and myself. Enough about me." She gazed at me, tilting her head. "You haven't changed a bit, Nicola. Always relaxed without a care in the world."

"I think it's more of a depression with too many cares than I want to deal with. I wanted to see you because I always wondered what it could've been like if we, you know, stayed together. Love, and a family, and a home."

"Well, I know one thing for sure…"

"What's that?"

"Even with your hot temper, you wouldn't have raised a hand to me or the kids." She wiped her eyes and sniffled.

"You can bet the house on that."

"I know and I would. Let's move on. I don't like to think about that situation. How's life treating you?"

"Life…" I slid my fingers through my hair, then picked up a Savoiardi cookie and inspected it. "Life's like this sweet, chocolate-covered goodness. You enjoy it while you're chewing, then before you can appreciate it, you've swallowed a hint of sweetness and it's all gone."

"You could just grab another one." She smirked while twirling her long, black, curly hair.

"Eventually, they all disappear. Nothing is as good as the first taste."

"That's awfully pessimistic."

"Realistic, not pessimistic. Anyway, you're correct. Let's talk about something more positive. You! You haven't changed a bit either. Just as beautiful as when we first met. Those eyes as mesmerizing as the nighttime sky. I always used to think I was a star in their reflection."

"You were and always will be."

Her cheeks reddened as they rose. She extended her hand, placing it atop mine, squeezing it like she'd done so many times in the past when I'd run away from home during the frequent, raucous quarrels. She'd hug and hold me at this same table, telling me everything would be fine. Today, I knew that nothing would be okay and all that remained was dwindling like a burning wick.

"Thank you, Beatrice. That means more than the world to me." I regarded her, rubbing my forehead. "I have something to tell you and I don't know how."

"Ditto. So do I."

"Well, we have more than one thing in common." I tittered, offering an uncertain grin. "Do you want to go first?"

"We should draw straws." Her quick smile gave way to firming lips. "You're not going to like what I'm about to tell you."

"Likewise."

"On second thought," she shrugged, "you might accept my admission with open arms."

"Unlikely with mine, but you may be indifferent. Shall we do the straw draw?"

"Sure. I'll get some."

"No. Wait. Maybe we can play rock-paper-scissors or cards or—"

"Okay, Nicola. Enough with the playing. We obviously can come up with many games. Go first." She tightened her grip atop my hand. "We haven't seen each other for years, but I'm here for you."

I furrowed my brow. Tense eyes trickled a few tears. I wiped them with my sleeve, then cleared my throat. "I've been given bad news today."

"What is it," she said with consternation.

I hung my head. "Doctor Gordon told me that I have

days, weeks, or months to live. The time is not as important as the finality of it all." I said, crackling each word.

"What—the—hell." Nonplussed, her eyes darted.

"They ran all the tests even using that stupid iLifeCheck program multiple times with the same results."

"Oh my…" She released my hand, cupping her mouth. "No. This can't be." Her voice muffled. "Is there anything they can do? Or I can do."

"Unfortunately, no." A sigh escaped with a gurgle.

"What's the actual diagnosis?"

"My heart is beyond repair. Literally."

"Can't they change your blood and give you meds and a transplant?"

"No luck on those options either. He gave me some pills, but those are more for keeping the blood flowing so I can put my affairs in order."

"In this day and age they can't figure something out for the disease? For chrissake." She pitched her voice with disgust and flailed her hands. "What's wrong with those doctors?"

"I know. I wish there were other options."

"You weren't exaggerating, then again, I should've known something was up when I answered the door. You wouldn't show up out of nowhere, if it wasn't important, plus you look tired."

"Well, you've always been smarter than me."

"Not smarter. Just more aware."

"Whatever you want to call it. You're up. What's your big news? Doubt it'll be worse than mine."

She folded her hands as if to pray. "I assure you, it'll be close," she whispered. "I don't want to tell you because I don't know how you're going to take it, especially now with your news about the illness." She paused and tilted her head towards the ceiling. "Actually, on second thought, I really shouldn't tell you. It's not appropriate at this sensitive time."

"Remember. You said no games, so stop playing. I can handle whatever you tell me. Anyway, I'm dying. It won't be, can't be any worse than that."

"Are you positive, because this is big?"

"Yes. Be straight with me."

"Fine. I'm going to be blunt, even though you're going to get upset. Keep in mind I didn't want to tell you."

"Okay..." I said, addled.

She sipped her now cold espresso, placing the cup on the saucer, and held a blank stare.

"We have a... son. I broke up with you because of him. I had mixed up the birth control pills and it was my fault. I didn't want to ruin—or make your life harder, so I kept him from you. There was no way we could've raised a family at that time either. You weren't ready. You weren't working or able to find a job."

"What the cucker, Beatrice?" My chest tightened and I wheezed, attempting to find a breath.

"Are you okay, Nicola?"

"No! How can I be?"

"Wait... what does cucker mean?"

"I'm trying not to sin or swear." I eked out a grin, then returned to sternness.

"Anyway, I'll get some water." She rushed to the faucet. "Do you want some medicine or something?"

"No. I have pills."

I swiped the glass from the table as she set it down and slipped an aspirin into my mouth.

"They say it's better to chew them when you have heart issues. And, I warned you about the secret. I shouldn't have told you, but you have the right to know, considering."

"Why didn't you tell me sooner? You've had years to figure this out."

"I wanted to, but all that time passed like a blink of an eye. I had other children, the divorce, and my parents dying. My life hasn't been easy either."

"Was our son one of the reasons you ended up getting divorced? I can't believe I just uttered those words, *our son*."

"Yes, that was part of it. He couldn't forgive me for having a child by another man, but that didn't add to his violent tendencies. He was broken from the get-go."

"This kid. Does he know?"

"*Our son*. Yes, he knows all about you and understands the situation. He's just like you, laidback, a hard worker, and smart. He's obviously older. Mature and responsible. Trying to get by in life."

"What's his name? Where is he?" I slammed the table with my palms and panted. "I want to see him before I leave this world. Why did you do this to me?"

"At the time, it was best for both of us. When I wanted to share it with you, it was already too late. His name is Alessio Nicola Russo. I'll write it down and give you his address. His apartment isn't far from here. You'll be proud. He's a chef at a fancy restaurant."

"Fine! I can't believe you did this to me." My thumping heart echoed through my eardrums as my chest rose and ribs shook.

Calm down. Calmati. Don't die. Not now. Breathe.

"I won't apologize to excuse the situation," she said, patting my hand. "Not telling you was my only option and a decision I pondered many days and weeks. My only mistake was taking so long to tell you. I know that now as I look into your ailing eyes."

"You should be apologizing on repeat, *disgraziata*. How were you able to wake every damn day knowing you kept something so important from me? That is pure evil."

"Don't start with the name calling. It wasn't on purpose."

"Of course it was and I will not stop with the name calling. *Sei una stronza.* You knowingly kept it from me 365 days per year and however many hours go into that year for who knows how many years. What the hell, Beatrice? Good thing we broke up because there's no way I could deal with you."

"I broke up with *you*, Nico. And, it was only because I didn't know how you would help support our family. Don't get this all twisted. I thought it was best for all of us. Do you want his information or not?"

"I'm not twisting anything. At least, I'm honest. I want an apology, considering my bleak future."

She paused, scanning every item in the kitchen but me. "Fine, Nicola. I'm sorry. *Mi perdona?* I apologize for not telling you, but what good is an apology now. It's futile."

We sat silent for a few minutes. "I'll accept it, I guess. I suppose I'll forgive you, considering where I am in life. *Si, ti perdona.* But, I don't do it lightly."

"Fine. Glad you're satisfied. Do you want his information or not?"

"Fine. Give me his damn information. My chest is hurting now."

"Well, try to stay relaxed. Remain strong. I'll be right back."

She arose from the table and walked to the counter, opening a drawer and retrieving an address book. She tore a page and scribbled, returning to her chair, and sliding the sheet towards me. I swiped it, knocking the espresso cup onto its side atop the saucer and glanced at the note.

Alessio Nicola Russo

313 Hemingway Drive, Apartment 1

"Thanks." Dismayed, I shook my head. "On second thought, an apology is as pointless as forgiveness. We're not even. I don't know how to rectify this situation. Is revenge even one of my options?"

"Let's move on. Such is life. Remember?" She straightened my cup onto its base. "Would you like more coffee? It'll de-stress you."

I waved her away without a response, staggering as I stood, balancing my legs against the chair's backrest, my breath escaping like a deflating balloon. As I regained it with quick puffs, I realized for the first time the doctor's diagnosis may hold validity. Hunching, I contemplated Beatrice. Marching into a tirade crossed my mind, but that wouldn't end well for either of us. More wasted energy I didn't have to expend. I took the simplest road, making sure we both remained civil.

"It's time for me to leave. Thanks for telling me about

Alessio. It was a pleasure to see you again after all these years. I'll abjure all the clichés because we both know they don't exist in real life, only in books and movies. It was an honor to have met you and share that time in my life with you. I wouldn't trade it for anything."

"Neither would I." She enveloped me with her eyes. "May I hug you?"

I nodded. She approached with outstretched arms. We embraced without exchanging a word. She caressed my back, stroking my hair and nape as she did when we were young. She kissed me on the cheek, and I, her forehead, then stepped away from each other. I walked to the door and paused at the exit.

"Stay strong and well, my beautiful Beatrice," I said with a raspy tone.

She remained silent with quivering lips, then bowed her head, a stream of tears trickling upon her blouse. I couldn't lay blame. I ended our pain by shutting the door behind me. Sitting upon the steps, I cupped my hands over my face and implored myself not to sob. Any additional stresses certain to flare my symptoms. My emotions overrode my mind, soaking my palms for several minutes.

GIANNI FRANCO

CH 4

The geyser gushing from my eyes tapered and dried, the jeans imbibing the saltwater from my hands, leaving a set of smeared and chalky handprints. I twisted my wrist and checked the antiquated watch, which still kept perfect time as it had decades ago. I heeded its demand to move forward without disagreement or hesitation. Struggling for footing, I grabbed the handrail edging Beatrice's porch.

Dante Batiste, next on the before-I-expire list. I considered him one of my good friends, although my feelings for him, depending on the day, teetered between love and hate. He, younger than I by six months. We met while working at the Trevi Café and encountered each other on a somewhat frequent basis, but I hadn't disclosed my ailment. My mom taught me not to burden others with my troubles. She always said crosses bear weight that break backs. They had their lives to fret about and didn't need the additional drama on my account. I phoned him. The short, cordial conversation ended with a self-invitation, which he accepted straight away. He resided at 222 South Clinton Avenue, a few blocks from Beatrice and my new child, Alessio.

I decided on the way to Dante's to stop at Alessio's. During the walk, I realized the brevity of Beatrice's revelation. Its consequence could mean he detested or loved me, or worse, he was indifferent. I hoped the blood bond we share to be stronger than the negativity towards an absentee father. Standing on the curb of Hemingway Drive, outside the art deco building, I came up with two nicknames that could coax him into adoring me, little Nico or Nico Junior. Of course, he'll love them. He's my son.

I continued along the concrete path to his porch and stopped, glancing over my shoulder several times, hoping for him to appear and save me the awkwardness, or to never appear and save me from an alien introduction. Either option a loss. With those thoughts arrived a bout of trembling and throbs crawling atop my spine and legs that intensified with each breath. I swooned, gripping the brick corner of the building with both hands, then it ceased. No one had arrived to save me, and, I suppose, that's fair. I regained some poise. The brass knocker inoperable, hanging upside down. While pressing the doorbell my hand cramped. It rang for a full minute with no response. With no luck and no one home, I decided to return at a later time.

***   ***   ***   ***   ***   ***

The short walk to Dante's tiresome, lasting longer than expected, having to chew a set of pills with no water. Doctor Gordon was correct about their potency using this method. They gave me a slight welcoming high, alleviating some of the pain and allowing me to regain breath. At the curb, I adjusted my hair and straightened my clothes, swatting the dried remnants of tears from my jeans. His modest two-story brownstone reduced to a Monopoly piece thanks to the new neighbors. A high-rise apartment complex towered over the home, casting a monstrous shadow, and across the way, the City gorged the greenery for a park-and-ride. Before I reached the entrance, he opened the door and welcomed me. I found it a bit odd, since it took ten knocks and a steady doorbell harassment before he arose from his couch or bed during a normal visit.

"Hey, Nico." His perfect teeth in full display. "How are you?" He leaned forward and we embraced.

"As good as I can be. Just trying to survive," I said. "And you?"

"I'm okay." Coconut pomade kept his chocolate curls tight and glistening, although he stroked his hair every few seconds ensuring not one strand escaped the goo. In all the years I knew him, they never did. "The ex-wife never stops bothering about child support and alimony." He smirked and led me into the lavish kitchen fit for an upscale restaurant. In the background, music shuffled from Diana Ross to Metallica. "There's a light at the end of the tunnel. The kid's finally eighteen."

"Amazing. Already eighteen? I can't believe it. It was only yesterday I cradled her in my arms. "

"Yeah... younger than Ale—" He cleared his throat. "—you want a beer, liquor, coffee? I got them all."

"Younger than who?"

"No one. It's not important. Which drink did you say you wanted?"

"I didn't, but I'll take one of each." I chortled, sliding upon a sumptuous, leather chair at the polished, aluminum kitchen table. Certainly custom made or from Williams Sonoma and not a big-box store. "Is this furniture new?"

"Yeah. Special order. Like I said, the ex is almost paid in full. Once the alimony is officially done, then it's full steam ahead. I'm going to splurge like it's my last day on Earth. How's work?"

"I took a few days off. I don't know if I'm going back. I need a change."

"Change is good, friend. A host on a daytime talk show once said, 'without change we're insane and stifled.' I'm not one for a dictionary, but those two words, insane and stifled, don't gel. Anyway, you get the point. I'm not a professor. I'll get the drinks. Have some of the peanuts in the bowl."

The loose nuts as old as last Christmas, the mold flecking their discolored skin. I envied his extravagance, spending money on women, drugs, and whatever else, rather than snacks, but to be fair, his bulging belly hidden under oversized shirts, suggested he ate well too. Those who couldn't, like myself, stayed thin. Granted, the sickness may have contributed to my weight loss, but I was skinny throughout my life.

He worked as a day trader, supplemented by odd jobs around the city, perhaps IT or some kind of tech. I could never pinpoint the exact type of extracurricular work he did, nor did I press the topic. His vivacious lifestyle and its changes outpaced mine monetarily and physically. Even with some of his deficiencies, I still liked, loved him. Anyway, I couldn't be choosy at this point.

"I'll pass on the nuts. You might want to change them out. I'll have a sip of beer and some liquor. Save the coffee for later."

"Good. Coming right up. I have some cookies in the fridge. My mom dropped them off. Got them from Etna's Bakery."

"I'm all set. I just came to talk. I... forget it. Doesn't

matter."

"Tell me. What's up, Nico? Something bothering you?"

I spun the peanut bowl on the table. "Just bring the drinks over. Maybe we'll talk about it in a minute. It's really nothing." The tennis match of thoughts in my head being played with lobs.

"You want me to cook some pasta. It'll only take a few minutes."

"So that's the secret to how you stay so thin," I said with a sly grin.

He shook his head and set the drinks onto the table. "Whatever... Now, don't you ruin the new table by spilling drinks or smudging your fingerprints all over it."

"I promise not to. Just like a boy scout."

"Problem is you were never a boy scout." He winked with a smirk. "I guess I'd better get the rags. In case you're wondering, it's a regular beer and the best scotch I have."

"Was it aged for a year at the local bodega?"

"Twelve and from a barrel in Scotland. Just enjoy it, man. Don't be difficult."

He sat across from me and raised his tumbler, tipping it forward. I accepted with a nod. We clanged the glasses and guzzled. The liquor shuddered me into a heaving cough. Either it was too strong or my body could no longer handle alcohol. Several minutes passed before I regained composure, breathing through my nose like a marathon runner. Dante stood at my back, burping me like a baby.

"Are you okay, man?" His voice fading from clarity. "Nico. Come on, man."

He helped me stand, leaning my haunches against the

table. My heart rate and breaths stabilized, returning to my new normal. "Don't move. I'll be right back." He returned with a glass of water, which I lapped like a toddler.

"I'm better. Thanks for helping. I don't know what it is. Maybe that scotch is too strong. I need something weaker. Any Sambuca?"

"Yeah, that's what you need," he said with spirited sarcasm. "The drink you can light on fire." He laughed so hard his hip hit the table and shook the glasses atop it. Even the old peanuts found energy to jump from the bowl. "You have to tell me what's wrong, Nico. This isn't like you. Liquor never bothers you."

He hit the mark and hiding my ailment from him harder than I thought. We used to drink every kind of liquor and beer, from expensive to cheap, from flavored to bland. We'd stay up to the wee hours of morning, cooking and drinking, going to bed just before *l'alba*. It wasn't an everyday thing, but it certainly occurred more times than I cared to count. We'd line up shots of Sambuca, light them afire, then guzzle. One night at a bar, I spilled a lit shot the length of my forearm, singeing all the hairs to my elbow, refilled a new one and swilled it. We laughed and continued our night, lighting cigarettes from the flames of new Sambuca shots courtesy of a beautiful barista.

"I'm going to *sip* the scotch this time but feel free to pour me a Sambuca," I said, sliding onto the chair.

"It might make you sicker, Nico. I don't think I should," he said, shaking his head and grimacing.

"Whatever, man. Just pour the damn drinks."

"Okay, but no need to be rude. What's wrong with you? Ever since you arrived, you've had an obnoxious attitude. You have a boulder on your shoulder, not a chip."

"Can't you just get the drinks? Why do you have to be so difficult?"

"I'm trying to be nice. What the hell is going on with you? I didn't invite you to fight." He firmed his lips and scrunched his brow. "Stop acting this way, Nico."

"First of all, I invited myself and you accepted. Second, I don't want to deal with what's bothering me. Just pour the drinks. I don't have all day, let alone… Forget it." I bowed my head and shrugged with a weak sigh.

"We've been friends for many years through the ups and downs of it all. I just want to listen and see if I can help. Talk it out. Like friends, best friends. Come on, man." Compelling eyes complemented his compassionate countenance.

"I'll think about it." I didn't have the courage to express my situation, let alone the moxie.

"Just tell me, Nico. I'm here for you. I can help. I promise." His eyes less captivating and now moistened. "We'll have drinks when the trouble is lifted from your chest. Otherwise, I'm going to withhold the liquor."

"You're actually going to keep the drinks from me like a child? Unbelievable."

"Come on, Nico. Just let go of whatever is bothering you. It'll be fine. We love and trust each other."

We sat in silence for several minutes, he scanning me, and I avoiding him, glancing at various objects within the room. I folded, knowing I couldn't win this soundless game. "Alright. I'll be straight-forward. It doesn't make a difference anymore." I paused again, dreading to divulge the inevitable, then just blurted the news. "I don't have much time remaining… on the life clock, so it's best I try to enjoy it. Do me the favor, man, and pour the drinks already. Okay?" I said, monotone.

"What in the hell, Nico. You can't have drinks now that you told me you're dying. And, you can't be serious."

"Unfortunately, I *am* serious."

He guzzled a shot and thrashed the countertop with his fist. "It can't be… Why, when, how long?"

"It is. I didn't want to tell you. I have days or months, give or take, depending which computer program you listen to. Either way, the clock is ticking. Trying to catch up with everyone, who, well… would be at the funeral, my funeral. I'm doing this like Frank Sinatra, *my way*, and meeting with everyone, since being cremated or a burial won't offer much discourse to the living. The why is because the doctor told me so, plus he used iLifeCheck to further confirm. It's my heart. It doesn't want to work anymore. There's nothing that can be done."

He sat catatonic, then ran his hand through his hair, rearranging the tamed mane into a deranged mess. He jumped from the chair and ran to the cupboard, retrieving the Sambuca. Sitting across from me in silence, he filled our shot glasses and slid the licorice liquor towards me. The corners of his mouth twitched, then he huffed and dabbed his eyes. In all the years I'd known him, I'd never seen him like this. Speechlessness, a once-in-a-lifetime feat for Dante.

He raised his glass and chugged it, followed by a refill. "Damnit. I don't effing believe this right now. You know Beatrice called and told me, but I thought she was exaggerating. I don't believe you either, Nico. This really can't be one of the last times you'll hear me call your name? No—damn—way! I call liar."

"To be fair, Beatrice is a typical Italian and loves to gossip," I said, snickering.

"Don't laugh, Nico. This isn't a joke."

"Such is life. Anyway, it's not a lie. We'd be left with total despair without injecting some humor into this moment. I went to see her for obvious reasons. She was my first love," I said, then knocked back the shot.

"Yeah, man. She's a great woman and was a great girl many years ago. I just didn't want to give much credence to her, especially with the seriousness of it. I still don't. Anyway, what can I do for you to make everything easier?"

"That's why I loved her. You don't have to do anything. You've done enough by inviting me into your home, giving me drinks, and talking to me. I won't hold the peanuts against you. Make sure you get a new bowl." I croaked a deep laugh. "By the way, this Sambuca is amazing. I guess it means more when you don't have much time. The anise seems to be soothing my lungs."

"I don't know what to say. I'm flabbergasted, which doesn't happen too often," he said, studying my face. "Your skin is more pallid than usual. I didn't pick up on the clues these past few months, but it's not like you came around a lot. Figured you're just tired."

"I *am* tired. It's not your job to diagnose or to deal with my problems. It's almost time for me to go to the next stop. Thanks for having me over."

"You're welcome. And if you decide you don't want to go anywhere else you can stay here until..." He broke into a heaving sob, then reasserted himself. "Who's next on the list?" he said with a grating voice.

"I haven't quite decided. There's someone I want to see more than anyone, no offense to you or anybody else. Beatrice told me, rather admitted, something earlier. Sent me for a loop."

"And what was that," he murmured, then sighed.

"Don't worry. It wasn't about you. She told me I—I mean we—have a kid. He's an adult. A chef."

"To be honest with you, considering your situation, I knew about him, Nico. She told me a few weeks after she broke up with you."

"And you never told me? We're best friends. How could you not have told me after all these years?" I slapped the table. "I could've spent time with him when I had it."

"She wanted it kept private. I'm sorry for that and for what I'm about to tell you." He paused, then exclaimed, "Me and Beatrice, after you... we had a thing. It was only for a few months. She told me about Alessio during that time."

"What the hell, Dante." I thwacked the shot glass upon the table, sending it crashing against the opposite wall. It shattered, raining shards onto the hardwood floor. "Why?"

"It wasn't planned. It just happened. She wanted to talk about you, then one thing led to another." He bowed his head and pinched the bridge of his nose. "You have to believe me, Nico."

"How could you do such a thing to me?"

"It wasn't on purpose, buddy. I promise," he said, pleading with folded hands.

"What do you call inserting yourself into her? An

accident?" I shook my head, scanning the table for something else to throw. "And, do not call me buddy. *Bastardo*."

"No," he said, dejected. "It wasn't an accident."

I picked up the bowl of peanuts and chucked them across the kitchen. "Is it possible the kid is yours?" I hoped and despised the potential answer.

"It's not mine. She was already pregnant by you. One of the reasons I got with her was because we didn't need to use protection when we had s—"

"I don't need to hear any more of this *merda* coming from your mouth."

I stood, dizzying in the process, and if not for the chair I wouldn't have regained equilibrium. He rose as I headed to the door but didn't follow, retreating to the counter and quaffing another shot. Weeping with inscribed atonement, he cupped his hands, raising them to his lips, then over his eyes and forehead. Glowering, I admonished his lies and repentance. He could've told me about sleeping with Beatrice and my child many times.

"Thanks for everything, you selfish prick. Have a nice life. Now, I know why I never liked you. *T'odio*," I said, slamming the door, shaking the walls and windows. "*Sei un pezzo di merda.*"

GIANNI FRANCO

CH 5

Standing upon the sidewalk, I scanned the skyline. The cool, evening air wheezed molten steel, exhaust, and gasoline. The distant industrial district and an overabundance of irreparable cars trademarks for this blue-collar city. Above the unseen horizon and the skyscrapers masking the sun, golden halos formed around their tops against the backdrop of a blushing sky streaked with lines of fire. A mirror to my broken soul searching for the reasons they hurt me, but none arrived.

Thirsty for an orange soda and a breather before venturing to the next visit, I stopped at my favorite Italian delicatessen, not the one where I worked, rather the most popular in the Park Avenue Neighborhood, Calabresella's New York Style Deli.

The early-nineteenth-century façade fatigued by time and its own weight. The crumbling bricks and chipping mortar beckoned to be rebuilt, but per the city ordinance not allowed as not to disrupt its historical importance. The vast interior opposite with manicured, plaster walls, sprinkled with mosaics, glistening under an array of pewter sconces and mammoth ceiling fans. The polished travertine floor as pristine as the first day they laid the tile. Concrete arches invited customers to browse each aisle for Italian delicacies while the fragrant tomato sauce enticed them to stop at the sectioned off café at the rear corner of the establishment. It sat no more than ten people at a time and served the same high-end cuisine as the upscale, eastside restaurants.

Domenico DiCaprio, known as Dom D. to most, opened the store well over forty years ago, and just as his two sons and one daughter aged into their teens they joined the Calabresella workforce. By the time they reached their twenties each had a guaranteed position, whether on the retail or restaurant side of the empire he created.

I filled a large Styrofoam cup at the soda dispensary and approached the register. Dom stood on an elevated platform ready to serve. His body twice the size of mine in width and half the size in height, but more healthy than I or a horse. He must've drawn a set of kings and aces while playing the game of creation with the gods while I drew ones and twos.

"How are you, Mr. Nico?" he asked with an accent not as thick as mine. His bulbous, welcoming cheeks puffed and reddened.

"I could always be better." I offered a weak grin.

"You don't look so good," he said, scrunching his pronounced eyebrows. "Have you been to the doctor?"

"The doctors don't know anything except how to take our money. *Sono scemi*."

Heaving his chest and between each gasp, his laughter crescendoed throughout the store. A few patrons standing behind me joined the echoing contagion. I eked out a breathless chuckle, hoping he hadn't noticed my struggle.

"I hope you're okay, Nico. If there's anything I can do, let me know," he said with concern, ignoring the line of patrons behind me.

"Yeah, I'm fine. How much do I owe you, Dom?"

"You know... since you're not feeling good, nothing. It's

just soda, not a bottle of expensive wine." He chortled again and the clientele followed suit, except this time they cheered his name.

"Thank you. My lucky day. If I don't see you, have a great weekend."

"You as well, my friend. *Buona salute.*" He looked beyond me. "Next, please."

Darkness approached with the setting sun. The cool breeze and cold soda providing some reprieve to my burning chest. The sugar returning some of my depleted energy, allowing me to continue the journey about Rochester. I stopped at Alessio's for several minutes, knocking and ringing the doorbell, and once again, no one answered. I should've bought a pen and paper from the store to leave him a note, but it was too late. Returning would be pointless because they'd be closed by the time I arrived. Can't live in the past and must keep moving forward.

I meandered the Upper Monroe Neighborhood and dipped through Chapman Alley leading me to Cobbs Hill Park on Culver Road. A place I frequented with my ex-wife, Jolene Robinson, adding Romano to her name after marriage. I met Jolene while I begged Beatrice to take me back. Had I known about Beatrice's sexual escapade with Dante, I would've focused more on Jolene and nurtured our relationship. Instead, I torpedoed it with multiple missiles and rebuilding the destruction from the explosions impossible.

While staring into the distance of the empty park I popped an aspirin. Using the straw like an ice pick, I broke the cubes into slush and siphoned an icy swig. A violent spasm ensued. Collapsing onto the bench, I pressed my fists against my throat, gasping, stomping the ground in a crazed tantrum, vision blurring.

Don't die. Not now. Breathe through your nose. Slow, Nico.

I awoke surrounded by silence, my breathing somewhat stabilized. I kneaded my damp eyes, and off in the distance, towards the center of the park, the swings swung with no one in sight. It could've been a mirage, but the chills rippling along my arms and over my scalp suggested otherwise. I juddered and brushed my forehead with a sleeve. As I set my hand down, a stranger flumped beside me and nudged my elbow. She wore ragged clothing, mismatched in color and shape. One foot fitted with a muddied boot, and the other, a multi-colored sneaker twice as long with its laces missing.

"Can I help you?" I said, startled.

"Can you help yourself?" she rebuffed. Her mangy mane concealing most of her face.

"Look, lady, I just want some peace and quiet. I have a lot on my mind right now. Can you please find another bench?"

"No. I want to sit with you." She tapped the space between us. "Here."

"Please, Miss…?"

"It's whatever you want it to be."

"I don't want it to be anything. I just want to be left alone for a little while. Can you do that for me?"

"No. I'd like to sit and spend time here."

"Spend your time somewhere else." I pointed into the darkness. "You have plenty of options. The park and city aren't small." Riled, I attempted to keep my heart rate in check.

"I want to stay here. With you," she said, wheezing.

"Fine." My tone harsher than what I intended. "On two

conditions: no more bickering and tell me your name."

"Alright, sir. My name is Sophie. I live here."

"Where?"

"Here, everywhere," she said, splaying her arms towards the sky, then retreating them with haste, tapping the slivered slats of the bench with fingerless gloves.

"Really?" I said, perplexed. "But how do you actually live?"

She didn't respond, instead fingering her hair. She turned towards me, and spread the straggly strands like window blinds, exposing azure eyes. My fixation immediate and conspicuous, intrigued by their beauty. I wanted to know more, delve into the depths of the two unexplored oceans, but refrained from asking as not to make our time together any more uncomfortable.

"Do you like what you see?" She twirled a finger towards her face.

"I can't see much of anything except your eyes, which are breathtaking. You remind me of someone."

I couldn't quite place her. Perhaps she was one of the maundering homeless searching the dumpsters where I worked, or she walked the streets near where I lived.

"Like who?"

"I don't know." I rubbed my temple.

"It's okay. We'll get to it. Guess what?"

"I'm not good at guessing. Tell me, please."

"I know you… Nico."

"How do you know my name? We've never met."

"You haven't changed a bit. Just like when we were young. Same dimples, same olive skin, same Roman nose and hazel eyes."

"Oh, how I wish I was young again." I released an exasperated sigh. "The end is nearer than I want it to be."

"That's too bad, Nico. My days feel like that as well, especially when I have to search for food and drink."

"Life is never easy. So, where did we meet?"

"Junior high. We were each other's first kiss, or at least mine. We dated for a few months and even went to a dance together."

I froze as the memories flooded my mind. She was my first kiss in the coatroom during recess. We were alone while the others played outside. Her laughter always infectious and her coyness cute. We danced to a ballad by Journey. Sophie Barton held her arms tight around me that night and I reciprocated. She knew I struggled with the language and offered to help my shortcomings, even letting me cheat from her exams and homework for most of our classes.

"Yes, Oh my g—"

"You were the best, Nico. You showed me so much love."

"Likewise, Sophie. So, what happened? Why are you here in this park of all places?

"Well, sometimes it's hard to stay on the road when you take wrong turns in life. I've tried to get back in the lane many times. Alcohol, drugs, and failed loves have all made this place my home. I'm lucky to live at Cobbs Hill Park. Some of my friends live under bridges and in cardboard boxes."

"How do you survive?"

"Some restaurants are nice enough to leave us scraps. I'm so thirsty. Can I have some of your drink?"

"Of course." I handed her the cup. She removed the lid,

straw attached, and cleared the hair from her mouth. Parting her lips to sip, she revealed rotten teeth, some missing. "I have to tell you something."

"Yes, Nico."

"I'm dying. I don't have much time to live anymore. I thought you should know since we spent time together."

"That's sad." She shook her head, then gulped. "Life's never fair. Some don't want to die and some wake every morning hoping to die, praying that it will all end and the world will explode. Do you want to know what's helped some of my friends?"

"Tell me, please."

"Light a candle and say a prayer to the man, or woman, upstairs," she said, clasping her hands.

I followed her hand as she pointed towards the heavens, then closed my eyes. Going to church could help the situation, regardless if I rarely attended or prayed to the patrons from the religious smorgasbord. A few minute walk from the park stood the enormous golden steeple for The Church of Glorious Saint Peter. I turned to Sophie and asked her to join me, but she had disappeared, leaving the large cup in the same place she sat. I called into the stillness to let her know she could go with me, but no one responded. I picked up the soda, which oddly hadn't been touched and bellowed her name one more time. Silence. I discarded the contents into the trash, too afraid to sip from it, and headed to church.

***   ***   ***   ***   ***   ***

At the steps of the cathedral, I gazed at the illuminated steeple and shuddered. My experiences with the Church and its clergy had not been good, numbing me for many years. The figureheads sitting on either side of the steeple beamed their villainous eyes, following my every move. Looking away, I stared straight ahead.

The wooden doors to Saint Peter beckoned the Gothic era, carved with inscriptions from the Bible. Its handles like gold javelins roped in pewter. I heaved them open and entered. The doors slammed behind me, echoing throughout the cavernous structure filled with polished, padded pews. With each step, my boots clacked against the marble floor as I ventured towards the altar. Behind it, a colossal Jesus oversaw the Church. His arms stretched and nailed to a cross by iron pins, the crown of thorns gouging his forehead like bloodied talons, wan skin like mine, and bleary eyes searching for life in the final stages of death.

I performed the Catholic sign of the cross like a programmed robot and sat upon the nearest pew to the altar. I raised the leather-bound missal beside me, flipping through its pages to find the *Our Father*. Perhaps a prayer can save me.

Our Father, Who art in heaven, Hallowed be Thy Name. Thy Kingdom come, Thy Will be done, on earth as it is in Heaven. Give us this day, our daily bread, and forgive us our trespasses, as we forgive those who trespass against us. And lead us not into temptation, but deliver us from evil.

I knelt upon the pew cushion, opting for a more familiar approach to gain the attention from one of the anointed, winged beings living in the cosmos. As a child the nuns would say to clasp your hands and pray. He'll hear you if you speak loud enough. They didn't know any better and assumed he wasn't a she or an it. So odd what word-of-mouth does with unproven truths.

"*Nel nome del Padre, del Figlio, e Spirito Santo.* Dear, God, Jesus, Mary, or whomever, whatever. Anyone, anything that may be listening. Even the Holy Spirit. I have something to ask from all of you, or some of you, or anyone that can help. I've been told by my doctor I have days, weeks, or months to live. You're probably privy to my bad news. I need some help. We can make a deal. If you'll let me live, or at least give me a few more years to spend with my newly found son, then I'll devote my life to you or anyone that you choose for my remaining days, whether that be one, two, or five years. I'm open to even more time, if you'll allow it.

"If you're still listening, I have another idea. Perhaps, I can donate a kidney, and in return, you'll renew my heart. I just want to live. I've done nothing wrong to others, or even if I have, it wasn't that bad. I didn't kill anyone. There are many people worse than I who've harmed many and are still alive. I've done my best to care for others. I feed the homeless when I work. I feed the birds and stray cats. I've followed the general teachings and can't understand why I'm now unable to live." My eyes moistened and voice croaked throughout the church. "Please, help me. Please, let me live. Let me befriend my son and spend time with him. He's the only one I have. I'll donate what little money I have to whomever you decide. I have nothing or I would give more to those around me. I'll do more of anything every damn day moving forward. Please, let me live. Please. *Per favore. Aiutami. Aiutami. Aiutami.*"

My heart picked up pace. I retrieved a set of pills and dissolved them between my cheek and gum. Sipping from the holy water fountain for a chaser ill-advised, especially after praying for a second chance at life. I tiptoed to the exit, attempting not to disturb those listening to me from above. Sitting upon the steps, I overlooked the empty courtyard, the crickets accompanying my thoughts, strumming their arpeggios tuned to the symphony of the pulsating stars as evening lost the battle to night.

I needed rest, eyes and calves burning, but continued. Most of those on my list sleeping, except Ravi Chopra. A man I entrusted, who could quell any of my issues while sipping drinks at a local dive bar.

CH 6

Ravi and I's hangout, JD Oxford's Ale and Whiskey, located on Monroe Avenue, not far from Dante's home, who wouldn't be joining us tonight for obvious reasons. I had an affection for the Irish bar because the Irish and Italians shared an almost identical national flag and a love for the drink and family, and that's what really mattered. An oversized leprechaun, drinking ale and reclining against the stalk of a four-leaf clover, greeted tipplers above the front door. Ravi and I usually sat side-by-side at the corner stools, bantering and talking sports, usually soccer, lost loves or those we wanted to love, and about our exciting jobs. He worked at Bombay Palace in Little India as a manager and chef. During his spare time, when not overindulging liquor, he nursed elderly patients in the Indian community at their homes or the local hospice.

I approached him from behind and dug my finger into his back. "Give me all your money. This is a stickup." I leaned forward, nudging his body against the counter.

He inched his broad forehead over his beer and angled it. "If you want money, you better call that damn Italian, Nico. He's got all the connections."

He boomed with amusement and I followed. "I don't have any connections. How come Italians always have to be *connected*?" I retreated my finger, sliding it into an invisible holster.

"Same reason all Indians must be *doctors*. But here we are, and neither of us fit the stereotype." He tapped the stool for me to sit beside him at the usual corner spot. "You want a beer or liquor. Or both?"

"I shouldn't, but I'll have a beer and a shot to sip. I have to take it easy," I said, resting my hand on his shoulder while sliding onto the seat.

"Just waiting for service. Damn Dimitrios does everything but work." The interior hadn't been cleaned in months and once in a while a drunk mouse scampered along the baseboards. "Good you finally showed, Nico. I've waited weeks for you at this stool. I call and get no answer. I would've went to your place, but I didn't have time. Busy with work and whatever. How've you been?"

"A little under the weather. Stress and stuff."

"You don't look so good." His owlish brown eyes followed mine, then drifted, scrutinizing me. "Are you sure you're okay? I may not be a doctor, but in India we learn to recognize things without the degree."

"I'm fine, Ravi. Let's drink for old time's sake."

It's hard to lie with the illness tattooed on my face.

"Alright, friend, but I don't believe you, and understand if you don't want to tell me. Remember, we've known each other a long time and I've always listened."

I changed the topic in a rush. "Hey, guess who I saw at the park tonight?"

"Johnnie Walker on a swing." He snorted with a grin.

"No. I'm being serious. I saw Sophie. Sophie Barton from grammar school. Remember, she kissed me in the cloak room. She's not doing well. It's too bad."

He creased his brow and twisted his lips. "Are you sure? You know what happened to her, right?"

"No, tell me."

"She died a long time ago. It was in the paper. A drug overdose."

"Come on. I just talked to her. Are you sure?"

"Yes, sir. I read the article more than once and each time it shocked me. I almost cried. Like I said, if you need to talk, then I'm here for you. Always have been. Always will. Hope you're not using the same drugs that killed her."

Ravi and I met on the playground while attending grammar school at Saint Theodore's. Our different languages and broken English could've hampered us, but they didn't. Innocence and youthful determination allowed our relationship to flourish and strengthen. We alternated dinners with each other's family. He fell in love with Italian food, and I, Indian. If only there would've been a way to combine both, then I wouldn't have had to work at Nacca's Deli. We could've opened the Ravi and Nico Eatery or the Nico Ravi Diner. We continued to Cardinal Mooney High School and Monroe Community College. The attempt at university only lasted a semester. Instead of reading and doing homework, we spent our time at the arcade and mall trying to meet girls. Luckily, JD Oxford's opened. We christened it as "our bar," meeting three or four days a week for many years, until recently.

"Thank you, Ravi. You're greatly appreciated. I'll think about it. If I decide to tell you, I don't want you upset."

"And the drugs?"

"Nope. I'm not doing drugs. At least not the illegal kind."

"Good. We don't need another overdose in this city."

"Not the way I'm going out," I said with certainty, although since he brought it to my attention, the idea could be a possibility.

"Good. And if you want to chat, I swear not to get riled. I even Irish promise."

The promise no more than lifting a beer and swigging. Dimitrios Khronos, the sole and mostly absent bartender, and probably the only Grecian in this country to own an Irish bar, explained the adage to us one night after he gulped a bottle of Jameson. His Greek accent thickened like pancake batter with each chug from the jug. Ravi later telling me he didn't understand a word, nodding his way through the whole conversation while sipping beer and snickering.

"Irish promise." I blinked with agreement and raised the ale. "Any excitement tonight?" The bar, empty as usual, burbling classic rock on low volume through damaged speakers.

"A morgue is more exciting than this place. Dimitrios has been in and out of the back office. He's taking breaks from the girlfriend-of-the-week to serve drinks."

"Wish I had his problems. I wouldn't mind seeing him tonight to say farewell."

"Farewell?" he said, stunned.

"I mean… hello." Covering up the truth is harder than expected. "Haven't seen him in a couple weeks."

"It's probably been longer since I, we've, seen you?"

"Time flies." Especially when you're down to several days, weeks, or months.

"Sure does, Nico." He raised his glass and drank the shot. "What is it you had? A cold?"

"Well, a little worse than a cold. Don't worry about it."

"Okay. I've learned liquor always cures an illness. At least that's what I keep telling myself. Is it serious?" He sipped his beer, then lapped the rim of the empty, shot glass.

"It's nothing. I don't think the cures are going to work for me anymore," I said with a passive chuckle.

"You have a habit of keeping things to yourself. This cold has lasted over six months. I'm betting it's worse."

"Let's not wager today and just enjoy our drinks."

"Alright, friend. I need another shot and beer. Hey, Dimitrios! Service, please." He turned to me. "Can you believe this guy?" I nodded.

"Get it yourself. Can't you see I'm busy," Dimitrios bellowed from the back office.

"Perfect. Free drinks," Ravi whispered to me.

He sprinted around the bar. With hands as big as baseball mitts, he grabbed several bottles of liquor and beer and slid them upon the counter. My chest tightened for a moment. I snuck a pill into my mouth and chewed, hoping to evade a drunken Ravi. Within minutes, the rising pressure dwindled. We chatted and he continued tipping back beers, mixing shots of vodka and scotch between sips of ale. Each time he gave me one, I lifted the glass and set it aside without drinking. Unfortunately, my luck ran out after his fourth.

"Hey, Nico. How come you're not—"

Saved by an interruption. The front door swung open, its handle crashing against the inside wall. A burly man, with long, blonde hair draping over a black, leather jacket, stumbled through the entrance at full speed. He dragged a petite woman with the same attire and hair as bright as a firetruck. Their bull rush blocked by the edge of the countertop beside us.

"Is... everything okay with you two?" Ravi slurred, then

sipped his beer.

They didn't respond. The man spun and about fell, then caught himself on the woman's shoulder. She screamed, kicked the man in the shin, and grabbed his arm, yanking him towards the open door. He grunted and mumbled gibberish between several expletives as they exited. Ravi rose, shut the door, and returned to his seat, downing a shot and half a beer.

"Nothing ever changes at JD Oxford's. Interesting couple, Nico. I bet they're going to have a better night than us."

I guffawed, which led to a rattle and hacking cough.

"Are you okay, friend?"

I waved confirmation, since my voice had disappeared. He nodded, handing me a napkin, probably noticing my watering eyes. I wiped them dry and stuffed the tissue into my pocket. He swallowed another shot and wobbled to his feet, towering over me like a giant.

"Oh, Nico. You really are sick." The alcohol may have given him a sixth sense because he shocked me with his revelations. "Your lemon eyes and ashen skin. That cough was loud like you have a megaphone attached to your chest. I should've noticed the hints before. Heck, even the drinks. You'd never give them up for free. It's your heart and lungs, isn't it?"

I hung my head. "Time to be truthful," I mumbled. "Yes. More heart than anything else. The outlook isn't good."

He quaffed another shot, and with both hands clumped his luscious hair taut. "Dammit, Nico. Now what?"

"I guess I have to follow it to the end, wherever and whenever that may be."

We contemplated each other while the crackling

speakers provided some reprieve to the moans echoing from Dimitrios' office.

"If only we could be that guy," he said, grinning and flipping his thumb towards the backroom.

"You got that right, Ravi." I sighed with a crooked smile.

"You're my brother, my friend, and all of my heart is with you until that time arrives." He swallowed another shot. "I don't know what I'll do without you in my life." He paused and bit his lower lip. "I love you, Nico. My only option is to drink until I know no better."

"*Bello mio*," I said, overwhelmed.

He stretched his arms around me, pressing his chest onto my frail body, gripping me like a bear. Whimpering, he nuzzled my neck with his damp cheek. It was just yesterday playing soccer on the blacktop or walking with me along the Charlotte Pier to console me after losing a girlfriend. He protected me against bullies and showed me the beaming lights at the end of my many dark tunnels. He convinced me an option always existed, except for today. I loved him with my eyes, turned, and exited without saying goodbye. The stress too much for me.

My eyes dried as I arrived home. I popped a set of pills and set the alarm, hoping to get a couple hours of sleep for the grueling day ahead. Too many people to meet, too many people to miss, too many people to hold, too many people to kiss. And, only one of us in that crowd will die.

CH 7

A dream slithered into my mind not too long after I dozed, paralyzing all, except my eyes. Attached to them, a cardboard kaleidoscope. I'd only held an object like that once. Aunt Rita Ricci, or Zia as I used to call her, helped me assemble a similar contraption when she visited from Italy. Much younger at the time, the psychedelic colors and imagery amazed me through the small toy, focusing and refocusing objects through its narrow oculus. I thought of it as an invention from another world, never experiencing such magic. Stomping towards me and growing in appearance, she'd laugh, calling my name, slipping one hand around my waist while the other stroked my curls.

Without notice, she appeared beside me with elegant makeup applied by a cosmetic artiste, just as I had always remembered. Never gaudy. At times, she went without the maquillage, but when she didn't, she said using all the proper colors of the rainbow accentuated every facial angle.

I tried to wake. She shook her head with a finger upon my lips, humming a brief lullaby, then spoke. "My little biscotti. *Tesoro mio. Mi sei mancato.* It's so nice to see you after such a long time," she said with a low, raspy voice, followed by a kiss upon my forehead.

"Oh my... Zia Rita. *Ti amo.* You as well. How long has it been, twenty years?"

"Maybe more since you visited Italy. Longer for me, *caro mio.* Possibly thirty or forty since visiting America. Time is fleeting. I remember it as if it was yesterday. In Italy, you sat with me almost until the end, holding those hands of mine that had dwindled to skeletons. Your cordialness exceeded my expectations, my little biscotti. *Tesoro*."

"I did it because I love you, Zia. May I ask you a favor?"

"Of course, my little—"

"Please don't use that nickname anymore. You know I don't like it and never did. It's too childish. I'm a man now and have been for many years." I grinned, stroking my chin with surety, although in reality diffident.

"Fine, Nico. And you stop calling me Zia. But, I will still use *tesoro*."

"*D'accordo*. Fair enough."

"Good. So tell me, how have you been?"

"I have bad news Zia—I mean… Rita. The doctor told me I'm dying." I followed with a guttural sigh. "I don't know what to do."

"I know all too well what you're going through. I remember when they told me about my illness. It was a hell of a roller-coaster ride. The injections and hair loss unbearable. *La sofferenza. Gli dolori.* Running from it impossible. The disease caught up to me after a couple years and multiple surgeries. By the time the end arrived, I was ready. How long do you have?"

"I don't know. The Doctor says it's my heart and I need to prepare for the end."

"How do they know?"

"Something to do with the iLifeCheck program, plus the lab tests during and after hospital."

"A program?"

"Yes. I guess they're using computers to try and predict death outcomes. The Doctor said not to listen to its prediction. But, how can I not? He should've never told me."

"Nothing you can do about it now. Technology can be beneficial, yet so cruel," she said with a dismissive sigh. "Are you ready for what's to come, *tesoro*?"

"No, Rita. I'm scared, sad, and angry. I want to fight it, even knowing I'm going to lose the battle."

She rose and spun with remarkable *en pointe*, arms cupping the sky, her full, auburn locks defying gravity, whisking atop her cheeks when she stopped mid-turn a spin. Between the strands, a welcoming smile and tranquil gaze greeted me.

"You'll be fine. Once it passes, peace will envelope you. All negativity will flow from you like a river escaping a dam. What remains is love and happiness. Say goodbye to those who mean most to you, and when those last breaths arrive, it will be easy. You won't even know it's happening. If you have the ability, pick somewhere comfortable and enjoy the final ride."

"Will you come lay with me again? Please..."

"Of course, my lovely *tesoro*."

Nuzzling against her bosom, she kissed my cheek, then embraced me, patting my back. She repeated it'll be okay as her nails grazed the nape of my neck, creating a wave of chills along my body. As I curled into the fetal position and hugged her waist, the alarm blared, rousing me. I had overslept. Rushing to rise, my heart palpitated. I collapsed onto the bed, tucking a set of pills under my tongue, calming the hurricane within my chest. Dawn broke from night's reigns, sending subtle hints of light through the blinds, instructing me to rise. I guided my legs with care over the edge of the bed and searched for energy to stand.

"Thank you, Rita, wherever you may be enjoying serenity. *Ti amo tanto.*"

Time unapologetic with my life or those around me. I trooped to the kitchen, debating a cup of coffee or water. The caffeine certain to spike the heart, but important to jumpstart the important day that lay ahead. I compromised with a thinned version of the java, adding a sacrilegious splash of water to the coffee while apologizing to the Italians and the world for the sin. Back in the day, it would've been three cups of espresso and five cigarettes. The water reserved for the afternoons, which disappeared by the evening after a couple beers and shots of either scotch or vodka, whichever was free or cheapest.

I struggled through a quick shower and brushed my teeth with a trembling hand, then doused the same outfit from the prior night with Versace, my only cologne. It may or may not have been a knockoff, considering what I paid for it at the local perfumery, but it's better than nothing and always did its job masking odors, never once hearing a complaint from anyone.

I brought the coffee outside and sat upon the steps planning my first stop. Beckoning the eastern light, crows cawed and robins whistled sinfoniettas. The horizon listened and set the sun free, its warming rays escaping between the rows of skyscrapers resembling bars in a prison cell, providing me the energy to proceed. I formulated a mental list of all those that remained, including the ones I loathed. What they did unforgivable and unfathomable, hindering my development, inflicting mortal, mental wounds, and yet remaining unscathed. They, too, deserve to see me before my time expires. Hopefully, they weren't dead yet.

I returned inside and surveilled each room, remembering all the interactions I had within them: making wine in a nook next to the entrance, watching soccer matches on the television with Ravi upon the tattered couch, cooking dinner for girlfriends and friends in a kitchen with barely any space to maneuver, nights of overindulgence, and others alone in the darkness. Making my bed, I thought back to all the times I'd slept on it, all the dreams, the nightmares, and the outlandish sexual positions I learned with my partners. As the years passed, I took it for granted, exploiting it without ever paying homage. The importance of the bed only evident now. I hoped to return for another nap upon its comfort, huddled under the duvet, hugging the pillows. Peeping into the bathroom, I realized the shower provided more than a cleanse. It cooled me during summer and warmed me during winter. I don't know what I would've done without it. The toothbrush and paste allowed for pleasant conversation with others each day. The sudsy soap and loofah, which lathered my body, made me approachable. The cotton towels dried me, allowing me to dress. Across the way, the refrigerator, containing all the food, provided more than just a place to store perishable items. It kept me alive and increased my strength with assistance from the stove beside it. Bread, water, and wine, the list of subsisting items endless, which I had ignored my entire life. I thanked them for their service and sustenance as I washed the coffee mug like a cherished heirloom.

I tidied the interior and phoned Nacca's Deli, advising

them I wouldn't be coming into work for the next few days. They obliged since they knew I'd been to hospital and sick, perhaps realizing the graveness of my situation more than I.

I exited the home, and as I reached the last step, I patted my pockets, realizing I'd forgotten the pills. Turning to reenter, a lone crow swooped onto the iron railing leading to my door. I said hello and it sat silent, studying me. Just as birds have an intrinsic migration plan, which include precise locations thousands of miles away each year, they may be intuitive to an impending human death. I must have saddened it. Inside, I grabbed the pill bottles and tucked them into my pocket. From the fridge, I retrieved two pieces of bread and broke them apart, placing them upon the steps. The crow still perched upon the railing tilted its head, winked, and cawed. I said you're welcome and asked it to wish me luck. It cawed again. I thanked it for its vote of confidence. A quarter of the way along Audubon Street, I glanced over my shoulder and noticed it eating the morsels. Seconds later, a few friends flocked to join the caloric buffet. I doubt the crow noticed my appreciative smile.

CH 8

I stopped at Alessio's, several blocks from my next destination, and like my prior visit, no one answered the door. I had a better chance meeting Lou Gramm, our local rock star from the band Foreigner, than having my only son greet me with open arms. I trudged twenty blocks down Monroe Avenue, then to South Goodman Street and turned onto East Avenue. At the curb, I clenched my jaw, staring straight ahead at an eclectic high-rise condominium association known as The Hermitage. The woman who lived in one of those units thought she had inherited the throne to England or Spain. Lidia, my Ma.

She purchased it, with the help of a divorce settlement from my father, before gentrification morphed the area into upper-middle-class. The association did their best to vacate her from the premises, even offering thirty percent above assessment. She argued and threw tantrums, standing her ground and refusing to leave. At one point, rebutting their proposal by asking them to haul her decaying body onto the street next to the garbage. They backed away. Thanks to her strength and pride she became the sole remaining person from her era in the building whom everyone despised.

I studied the glass turnstile trimmed in gold and revolving like a helicopter blade, waiting for the proper revolution to allow me through. One misstep and I'd be certain to die twisted like a croissant on the floor. My chance arrived. A man half my age, dressed in a tuxedo, polished shoes, and dark aviators, propelled through the entrance. I slid in, drafting him like a racer in NASCAR and made it to other side unharmed.

The next obstacle, the doorman. I approached the oak desk adorned with mosaics along its fascia. He knew me from past visits and never made it easy for me to enter the swanky compound, always creating an invisible wall to keep me out. Probably retribution for my mom and all her misgivings.

"Hello, Mr. Martin," I said, offering a brilliant smile. He didn't respond. His oversized, balding head gleamed like a well-oiled bowling ball while his bulging eyes perused a gossip magazine. With rigid fingers, I drummed the wood grain, attempting to gain his attention. "Excuse me." He didn't engage. I knew he saw me on the cameras. I cleared my throat. "I'm here to see my Ma. Can you let me in?"

He didn't respond, digging his fat hand into a small bag of potato chips, crinkling and crunching, then stuffing his mouth, licking each fingertip clean of crumbs.

"Hey. Martin. How about some service? I don't have much time." I knocked on the countertop.

"One second," he mumbled, flipping a page and cramming another handful into his mouth, the oily remnants dropping onto the cluttered desk like yellow hail.

"Come on, man."

He slammed the periodical shut, creasing his brow and huffed. "All you visitors are the same. Fine! Let me phone her to confirm."

"But, I'm here to see my *Ma* and you know me. Can't you just let me in?"

"Rules are rules and your *Lidia* wants everyone screened." He dialed on speakerphone, pausing between each number.

"I'm her—for chrissake. Funts and cuckers. *Testa di cazzo*."

Ignoring me, he cricked his neck, staring at the ceiling, the phone on constant loop to voicemail. "One last time, buddy. If she doesn't answer, you'll have to leave."

On the final ring, she squawked into the phone. "Whadda you want, Martino?" she yelled, riotous feedback shaking the speaker.

"Your *son* is here. He wants to enter and visit with you."

"Whadda you do? *Che fai* Nico?"

"Ma, can I come up?"

"I dunno know. Can you?"

"Come on, Ma."

"How are you, Nico?"

"Ma, please."

"How è Martino?"

"I'm fine, Lidia. Thank you for asking."

"See, Nico. Why can't you be nice like Martino? You always, how do I say… so stand—of—fish."

"I am not, Ma." The chip engulfing moron raised his chest with pompous panache and smirked. "Can we get this over with? I can't be at the counter all night. Let me in," I implored.

"Martino. Whadda you tink? We let him in *o* no?"

"It's your call, Lidia. I don't want to get involved. I know we can't keep him in the waiting area. Shall we send him away or…?"

"This is ridiculous, Ma. I don't have time for this crap now."

"Okay. Okay. Yes. It's okay for him to come in, Martino." The receiver clacked, shuddering us as we stood over the headset.

"Your lucky day, Nico."

"Anyway, I told you, Martin. We didn't have to go through all this hassle."

"I presume you're correct, but *rules* are *rules*. Break them for one, then we must break them for all."

"Whatever."

He buzzed me through a secondary gate, leading to a pair of gold elevators. I rode one of the boxes to the seventh floor, humming along to "Ring of Fire" by Johnny Cash. At apartment 718, I turned the handle, which happened to be locked, purposely on my account I assumed, leaving me no option but to rap the door. After the tenth knock, a door creaked down the hallway. Fearing a confrontation with a nosey neighbor, I banged harder.

"I'm coming," she screeched. The locks jangled and she appeared. "Whadda take you so long?"

I grunted. "Me? We literally just called you a few minutes ago." Dismayed, I lowered my head. "Why couldn't you open the door for me?"

"I did now," she said through a devilish grin. "Next time you justa come. No ask no questions. Come right away."

"I couldn't. Martin said you want everyone screened. Are you forgetting things these days?"

"I no need everyone to screen." She sighed, shaking her head, waving me through the entrance. "Oh… I am not too sure whadda wrong with everyone down here, *e* no, *signore*, my memory is justa perfect. Justa like when I wassa ten.

You probably forget the things. Next time justa give him the password."

"Ma!" I flailed my hands. "You don't have a password."

"*Si. Si.* I do."

"He didn't ask me for one." I followed her towards the kitchen, raising my voice with each step. "And why have you never given it to me?"

"I dunno know. I musta forget. I give you later. Make-a sure you no lose. Very, very *importante*. Be-cause if you do, I no give to you again. *Ascoltami.*"

"Whatever, Ma."

"Don't talk to me like that. I not a doggie," she sniped.

"What do you mean?" I jeered.

"You know exactly whadda I mean. Don't push me."

"Okay... Can I get the password now, even though it doesn't matter?"

"Sure. No *problemo*. The password is... Nicola. You need me to spell for you?"

"No."

"Good, *perche* I don't wanna spell."

"Funts and cuckers. And, you used my name? Amazing. Why in the hell couldn't you have told me that before? By phone, by mail, email. Even texts work, although my phone isn't so good."

She waggled her hand and winked. "It's okay. If it make-a you feel better, the idea cross the mind many, many times. I never remember it. Always so busy. So busy. I'm so tired."

"You're retired and have been for years."

"Other things take the time. The world is not you, Nico."

"I'm sure they do. Well... how have you been?"

She flipped her mood with a blink of an eye. "Do you wanna coffee, tea, beer, *o* maybe strong stuff?" Her smirk suggested she'd already dipped into the stash.

"I guess you've been fine. I'm well, too. Thanks for answering." I paused for a response and none arrived. "How about some water and a beer?" Drinking this early made no difference anymore.

"How about it? Give me *un secondo* and I fetch for you like dog." She patted her shoulder, then crossed her arms. "You can get yourself. Always lazy, you kids."

"You should learn to be nicer, Ma. Especially to me."

"I better than all you stupid girlfriends and that ex-wife. At least, I'm honest. Which remind me…" She tapped her temple. "You shouldda stay with the wonderful girl Beatrice. Too late to go back with that one, Nico? *O,* how about when you had our money and jewelry stolen?"

"Come on. It wasn't my fault."

She placed the drinks upon the table beside a small platter of cookies, then returned to the counter and filled a cup with espresso and Sambuca. Her daily ritual, which hadn't changed since I was a child. She sat across from me stirring and sipping the spiked coffee. With her inhibitions further reduced, she placed her hand upon mine.

"Imma so sorry, Nico. Too much time pass since we see each other. Too much time away bring bad feelings and memories."

She lied as she'd always done, searching for sympathy at my expense, only after having a drink, or two, or three. Without the elixir, she charged through fits of rage like a rabid dog with bloody fangs, coupling them with vocal jabs from a razor tongue. Other weapons of choice she used on me as a child included clogs and various shoes, oversized wooden spoons, and leather belts. Each of those items, at one time or another, contacted some part of my body. I retaliated as much as I could, but gathering the courage to battle Ma always fell short. Most of the time, I caved, locking myself inside the bathroom, whimpering and waiting for her to tire. Once she fell asleep upon the couch, I'd escape the house to safety.

"Alright, Ma. I accept your fantastical apology."

"Thank you my son." She crinkled her brow. "Imma not going to beat the bush or whatever they call those things. Our Beatrice call lasta night. I concern. Very concern."

I sipped the beer. It trickled into my lungs like lava. Coughing and wheezing, I massaged my throat and chest as if my hands had the power to cure my fit and ailment, but they didn't, falling short of any expected divine intervention.

"Drink some *acqua*, Nico," she implored.

I followed her advice, pointing and waving at the napkins on the counter. Her forte, instructing rather than helping. Once the attack subsided, I popped two pills and dabbed my eyes with the single napkin she provided.

"And…" I struggled to clear my throat. "What did she tell you?" I said, croaking each word.

"Some news, news about you, but I do not want to get involved."

"What did she say," I said, winded.

"That you are sick, Nico," she whispered, circling her hand towards me. "Is true?"

"Yes." I nodded with a frown. I never discussed my health with her because I didn't know how she'd react.

"You gonna be okay?" she said, pouring another shot of Sambuca into the empty espresso cup.

"I suppose."

"So sad. So bad. So horrible. When you arrive I try to hide what I know. Now, it's all open. Anything I can do?"

"No, Ma."

"*Poverino.* You are my only child. There must be something I can do," she said, bewildered with a bit of flamboyance, adding a new pour of Sambuca.

"There isn't, Ma."

"How long—you have?"

"What's it matter? I'm sure Beatrice told you."

"I promise she did not. We sit on phone crying, then silence, then cry again. She no wanna make-a me more upset. It's okay. I get it out. If no, I be crazy today in front of you."

"I'm sure and I don't know. I'd rather not think about it. It'll be fine whenever it comes."

Best not to give her specifics. She excused herself to the bathroom. Whimpering carried beyond its door to the kitchen for twenty minutes. She returned to the table with a box of tissues and a tumbler for the Sambuca.

"I understand if you no wanna tell me." She situated herself upon the chair, pale-faced and dabbing her swollen eyes. "You go see Papa yet?"

"Not yet, but soon."

"Good. Good. He look forward to your beautiful face."

"Oh… stop. Maybe handsome or cute but certainly never beautiful. Those days are long gone anyway."

Chagrined, we tittered in unison.

"I know. I justa try to be positive. Before you go away, I

wanna tell you something. It bother me for many, many years." She paused, scanning the ceiling and walls.

"What is it, Ma?"

"No. No. Forget I mention. I cannot say." Her face somber. "Best Papa tell you."

"Come on. You can't just say something, then take it back. Is it important?"

"Forget it. We focus on you. Throw away the other stuff."

"Okay, but you can tell me anything. It's now or never."

"I no wanna upset. Leave it. Papa will tell you. Maybe yes, maybe no. Who know? He is better with these things."

"Alright, whatever," I said, shrinking into the seat.

"But this I wanna say now." She held a breath, then sighed. "*Ti amo bello. Figlio mio.* I will love you until the sun expire and moon fall from heaven."

With welling eyes she rose from her chair and walked towards me with a slight sway, wrapping her hands around my face, planting a plethora of kisses across my forehead. We exchanged adorations, our lips quivering, then we embraced into a cocoon. She much shorter than I, like a child within my arms, as I was within hers many years ago. I didn't want to let go, and neither did she based on her grip, but my shoulders tired, weighted as if a yoke lay atop them. Reluctant, I stepped away from her. We returned to our seats and mused. Our history embroiled, and for most of my life, I thought she hated me, and in turn, I despised her. On more than one occasion, she had wished I had never been born or died at birth. Until today, and for that brief moment, all the pent up negativity receded into nothingness. Our finitudes equal because, for being human, that is the law. I hoped she wouldn't suffer when the time arrived for her, and someone would hug and kiss her as she did for me.

Hand in hand we walked to the door, our gazes aligned. "Remember, Nico, I love you no matter what. *Bello figlio mio*. I raise you the best I can with no tools, no support. My parents no help either. Not everything your fault. I sometimes say things in the moment I do not mean. Imma sorry for being wrong to you. I know it affect you. *Perdonami*. Your father and me never meet in the middle, but not be-cause of you. You have a good heart, even if it hurt right now. *Ti amo*."

"Thank you, Ma. I was skeptical to visit, but I'm glad I did. I would've regretted our lives during my last breath. *Ti amo*. I wish life wasn't so short and I wish some things could be different, but here I am and there I must go."

We hugged one last time and kissed each other upon the cheek. I rode the elevator to the ground floor with "Somebody to Love" by Queen keeping me company, wondering what she wanted to tell me. My father not the most eloquent speaker to deliver news or intimate talks. Hopefully, it wasn't about his or her health and more about something meaningless. I'd know soon enough. The doorman sneered as I walked past. I retorted with a devilish stare and mumbled *cretino*. He looked away, returning to harass another visitor. For a brief moment, I wanted to give him a piece of my mind, but the decision dwindled. Returning to this establishment improbable and using any additional energy served no value.

CH 9

Ma judged others from atop a pedestal, pointing and wagging her finger like a sword while lambasting everything and everyone in sight. Even positives couldn't escape the ridicule. This created a toxic environment for those around her, but to her credit, truth existed in a small percentage of her statements, especially about my ex-wife. Jolene Robinson, a former Hawaiian Tropic model during her late teens, strutted her long legs and red, Australian locks into a failed acting expedition. She possessed more than just beauty. Somewhere along the way she learned the art of manipulation, and when combined with carnal eroticism, she gained anything she wanted, except her face on *Italian Vogue*, or for that matter, on the local magazine covers. Commoners, such as myself, never questioned her demands nor rejected them.

We met inside Victoria's Secret at The Marketplace Mall. I, purchasing a nightgown for my girlfriend from the time, and she, strutting from the fitting room in a pink bra with matching see-through panties. I tried not gawking, but I think she noticed. At the cash register, we exchanged small talk, coy smiles, and our phone numbers. She rushed away, explaining her tardiness for a late-night modelling gig. I should've pressed about her rendezvous, but I didn't, later finding out it had more to do with videos than photos. A week or two later I called, then met her for a night on the town. The girl I'd been dating had dumped me, so I figured a date with someone new a no-brainer.

Our first two dates included coffee and drinks. The third consummated our relationship. We kissed and pawed each other during the drive to my place. Parking on the street, our passion fogged the windows. We straggled the walkway, fingers picking and plucking buttons from the other's attire. Once inside, we rushed to the kitchen, smacking the plates and napkins from the table, hoping our weight didn't snap its wobbling legs as we mounted it. We ended the evening atop the bed with our bodies intertwined. That infatuation continued for over a year, and because it didn't disappear, we decided to walk down the aisle. Well, to be honest, we married at city hall without telling anyone. When my parents found out they requested, more so demanded, we wed in a formal ceremony because per Ma, that's what good Italians must do, otherwise the vows are invalid. She castigated me as she had done when I was a child, demeaning me into submission. I didn't bother arguing and accepted her request as a law that could not be broken.

Fast forward. Returning home for lunch one afternoon, after two years of a happy marriage, the bliss ended with an abrupt bang, and not the good kind for me. I entered the bedroom calling her name with open arms, and to my horror, found her in bed with our neighbor's son who had just turned eighteen. I never contemplated such an abhorrent act could occur to me, but after breaking several dishes and punching a hole in the wall, I grasped the reality of the situation. We finalized the divorce several months later. No kids and no money allowed a seamless judicial process, although she kept the house. I had paid the mortgage, but because I couldn't secure a loan with horrible credit, we titled it in her name. The lawyer advised I had no legal angle, leaving me no option but to fold my hand.

73 Seager Street had changed quite a bit since I last visited in much the same way I had. My once vibrant smile and fervor that welcomed Jolene now crumbling like the walkway, the paint peeling from the olive ranch alongside fading blue shutters, the sagging gutters no longer catching rain. We fell out of love, but I still cared for her. No one could take away the special moments we shared together. One last time to be by her side, walk together in our home once more, graze her velvet hand, engulf those emerald eyes, breathe her breath.

I doddered up the shoddy steps, slightly winded, and tapped the crooked, screen door. A minute passed and no one answered. On my tiptoes, I peered through the oculus and spotted movement. My taps changed into determined knocks, rattling the wood frame as I called her name, disturbing the well-mannered and tranquil neighbors of this one-way street for several minutes.

A strawberry-blonde boy opened the door, gazing at me dumbfounded. "Hello, friend," I said with a timid, yet playful voice. "Is your mommy home? Miss Jolene?"

"I'm not allowed to talk to strangers, sir," he said, monotone with eyes reflecting the age of innocence.

"It's alright. I'm not a stranger. Can you please get your mommy? I need to speak to her." I paused and smiled. "Please…"

"Okay… but I have to close the door because I can't talk to strangers."

"That's fine. I'll wait here. Tell your mommy it's

important. Thank you."

"Okay. Be right back." His nonchalance didn't bode well for me.

He failed to close the door and pitter-pattered towards the bedroom I and Jolene once shared. I suppose I could've knocked on that pane where we spent numerous nights sleeping nude under the covers, but I didn't want to alarm her. The police arriving for a Peeping Tom isn't something I could handle with my medical issues. Then, they'd haul me off to jail for resisting arrest and trespassing. Prison time as a terminal patient not on any of my bucket lists. From the view I garnered, the inside of the home hadn't changed much, other than a weathering area rug. The furniture, the same as when we had purchased it years ago. The once ivory walls now blotted brown and yellow.

The little boy reappeared, startling me from the jaded reminiscence. "Mommy will be right out. She says to wait."

"Thank you. May I have your name?"

"I don't know. You're a stranger."

"It's fine. Your mommy knows me. I'm a friend of hers."

He crossed his arms and squinted, one bare foot overlapping the other.

"I promise mommy won't mind," I said, egging him with a pleasant smile.

"Fine!" He slapped his arms against his thighs, fists curled downwards. "My name is Declan," he said with a childish stutter.

"Cool name. Nice to meet you, Declan. Mine's Nico."

"Okay. I'm going to go now. Wait here. Bye."

"Bye, Declan. It was a pleas—"

My attempt to continue our conversation failed. He slammed the door with such force he knocked me backwards, then it recoiled open. My mind demanded entering, but my gut insisted otherwise. I sided with the latter, hoping Jolene showed. Ten minutes turned into twenty. I stepped inside, then retreated, my patience thinning. Thirty minutes passed. I debated to leave, rubbing my moist hands atop my shirt. Finally, after another fifteen, a thin shadow appeared from the hallway. Pink slippers with bouncing frills led the way. Her body wrapped in a similar colored robe with a large *J* stitched on the upper left. The bright, red hair from our youth now copper, twisted into a bun with several strands draping over a tired visage, which still held beauty from the last time we met.

"Hi." She paused, then sighed. "Nico..."

Her blasé attitude opposite mine, but I couldn't divulge the excitement, hiding it within the miniscule space of my stomach where butterflies sometimes fluttered, blooming my cheeks in the process as the one unfortunate side effect.

"Hey, Jolene. Great to see you. How—"

"What do you want?"

I inched backwards. "To say hello."

"How long has it been, Nico?"

"I think five years, give or take."

"I think more than that. So... is it the full moon of the fifth year that's brought you to stalk me and say hello?"

"No." I rolled my eyes. "How have you been?"

"You're just not going to stop. Fine. I've been good. I look like you. A little hungover." She laughed and blew the hair dangling across her cheeks.

I countered with bitterness. "I'm tired, not drunk."

"I'm sure, Nico. That was always your go-to excuse. People don't change." She groaned, gritting her teeth. "Did you wash your clothes in moonshine again?"

We had nights filled with drunken debauchery as did every couple I knew. It never rose to fisticuffs and usually ended with unbridled sexual adventures. Our drinking escalated to an everyday ritual when our relationship burned both ends of the candlestick. At that point, alcohol became the only way to numb the pain and escape the impending turmoil, since our game of chase and catch included lit sticks of dynamite that always exploded.

"No! You got one thing right, Jolene. People *never* change. Good we cleared that up and put it out of the way. Can we be nice to each other for a minute? I came here to talk. Maybe visit for a while." I paused. "If you'll let me."

"I don't think that's a good idea. Not today. I'm busy with the kid and recouping from last night." She looked over her shoulder. "Declan! Stop eavesdropping. Go to your room and play." She returned her attention to me, piercing the remnants of my soul with her green eyes. "Damn kids," she mumbled.

"But it's important to me. Let's sit down and talk. Have a cup of coffee or something. I promise to never bother you again. Ever."

"Oh, come on, Nico." She shook her head. "You're always *so* dramatic. I've heard it all before. It's not like you're dying and never going to see me again. You'll be here eventually, one, two, or three years down the road, knocking on the door disturbing me and my kid. Lucky for you, my boyfriend's not here. He would've smashed the door in your face or maybe even his fist."

She retreated, grabbed the door handle, and motioned to slam it. I flinched and she smirked, opting to stretch and arch her body along the rotting, wood jamb. She goaded me with that pose on purpose, knowing it would arouse memories of our intimacies. I did my best to ignore and pressed onward.

"Come on, Jolene. Don't be this way. We've had our differences. Let's put it all behind us. Look, I'm sorry for things not going perfect, but it wasn't just me. There are two players in our game."

"Nico… I don't have time today. The kid needs to eat and the boyfriend will be home soon. Come back during the week or something. Call ahead."

"You won't do me this *one* favor. Just one. I won't ever bother you again."

"Not today and not even if you were dying." She chuckled as if she wished my death upon her doorstep. "I'm just not in the mood for you right now. By the way, you scared my son. He doesn't like strangers, especially those that look sick like yourself."

"Fine, Jolene." I sighed. "I don't need your negativity. Sorry to have bothered you. Have a great life. I promise to never disturb you again. Hope one of your boyfriends raises your son with a proper upbringing." I contemplated her physique for several moments, ending at her eyes. "Goodbye. Forever. There was a time I loved you more than anything in the world."

"Stop being so dramatic, Nico. Grow up. Anyway, the phone's ringing. Have to go. Bye." She slammed the door and bolted away.

"*Mi sei distrutto. Cuoro rotto, spaccato,*" I murmured, fists clenched.

I lumbered the steps, wishing I could sprint. As my heart increased pace, I placed a pill under my tongue and begged it to dissolve on contact. At the end of the walkway, she returned to the door and yelled she didn't need anyone but herself and slammed it, shuddering my sternum. I turned for one last glance and waved. The motion futile since she probably wasn't watching. At that moment, I realized what was could never be, and perhaps I had lied to myself all this time hoping for a chance.

Wheezing, I trekked onward. Once out of sight from her home, I bent over and caught my breath. I had no desire to wipe the tears streaming my cheeks, or to deal with the ballooning pain in my chest. A certain reality set in as I thought back to Ma. Her earlier statements confirmed my failures, including my exes. She disappointed me more with her righteousness than the visit with Jolene.

CH 10

I moped to Liberty Pole Way. An unoccupied bench welcomed me for repose. I latched onto the handrail and slid upon the seat. Above me, galvanized cables created a massive web encircling a two-hundred-foot obelisk, depicting the freedom to protest war.

Several feet away, a menagerie of people awaited the B Line to transport them to the main terminal on Saint Paul Street. From there, they could travel to any destination within the city by bus, or anywhere in the country via train. I used it a handful of times as an excuse for the occasional reminiscent walk by Jolene's and for transfers, of course. Loose gravel and broken pavement surrounded the battered, plexiglass enclosure large enough for fifty people and a few pets.

It substituted for a pigeon hangout as well. A woman, much older than I, held a large bag of popcorn as high as her thigh, and every couple minutes hurled morsels at the frolicking birds. With each handful, they jumped and waltzed about the asphalt, pecking at kernels, then flying to their nests. Intrigued by her actions and wide smile, I approached, excusing myself between the hordes of people cramming the plastic cell.

"Excuse me, miss. Can I try?" I whispered, bending towards her ear. She didn't respond. "Miss... Can I feed the birds with you? Please."

She perused me, then glanced at my hands. Confused, I flipped them palm to palm. She nodded with intense eyes, then mimed a cup. I followed her lead, placing their pads together to form a bowl. She grinned, dropping several kernels into them. One by one, I dispersed them onto the pathway, and one by one, the pigeons pecked and flew away. She flung another handful for those I couldn't feed. In the time I turned to thank her, they had all disappeared. She attempted to mask her grin, but I noticed.

"Miss… do you do this every day?"

Silence filled the small space as I and the bus riders anticipated her response.

She scrunched her wrinkled cheeks and blinked. "Yes, of course," she said with a careful, Indian accent infused with years of wisdom. "If they are hungry you must feed them. A day will come when they are no longer hungry, or I am no longer here. We must do our best to take care of those around us, including the innocent birds."

She espied every person at the stop, including myself. With our eyes upon her, we all smiled in unison. Some returned to their conversations while others exclaimed buying popcorn to feed the birds when they returned.

I stepped away for a moment. Beside me, a stout man wearing a rainbow outfit with a headband to match whispered to me. "Some of those that are aged have acumen and innocence. Talk to her some more." His long, marigold beard rose with the breeze. "She's filled with more knowledge and spirit than all of us combined."

"Thank you for the advice. I shall."

I smiled and excused myself, inching towards the wise woman, and at one point, hovering. Her peculiar glance suggested I do something other than stand like an off-kilter statue. I pondered a dozen phrases for a proper reintroduction, settling for permission to sit beside her. She didn't utter a word, patting the plastic, blue bench. I obliged, extending my hand.

"My name is Nicola. People call me Nico. It's a pleasure to meet you."

She withdrew her hand from the popcorn bag. Icy, frail fingers wrapped in dark, weathered skin met mine with care. "It's good to meet new people," she said with a crackling voice. "My name is Fatimah. I've never seen you here before. Are you new to the area?"

"No, Ma'am. I usually walk the other avenues. I made a special trip to meet someone today and it didn't end well, so I found myself a place to sit nearby."

"Please call me Fatimah. Madams or Mrs. don't exist here. We are just who we are."

"Not a problem."

"Good. With that out of the way, let's focus on you." She paused, tapping her finger to her chin. "I presume a woman caused your discomfort?" Her chapped lips parted, exposing porcelain teeth fitted between those yellowing from age.

"It *was* a woman. How did you know?" I slapped my forehead, mouth agape.

"The sadness is chiseled onto your eyes. I knew the moment you looked at me. Your hazel eyes cry more than just for her. The pain is hurting your heart as well." She dipped into the bag and chucked a handful of popcorn onto the pavement.

"My heart aches for other reasons more serious." I sighed and slouched.

"We all have our burdens to carry. That is why our backs

are sore." She pointed to everyone at the bus stop, stopping with her finger atop my heart. "We must make the most of what is handed to us."

"It's not that easy, Fatimah." I caught a glimpse of her black eyes and my mind tumbled into hypnosis for several moments, awoken by a horn from a passing car. "My life is coming to an end soon. I wanted to do so much more."

"I'm much older than you, Nico. Mine has reached its course as well," she said, throwing another handful of corn delicacy. "Look at the pigeons." She pointed at the nibbling flock. "Each one of them has no idea what tomorrow will bring. They hope I will be here to feed them, so they can feed their families. When I'm gone, they'll have no options but to fly elsewhere and hope to find food. If they don't find anything, they'll die. Do you understand, Nico?"

"That we all die?" I said, stupefied.

"Yes, we do, but that's not the whole story." She adjusted the loose scarf upon her head, tucking grey strands under its sides.

"I don't understand. What is it about the pigeons?" I said, shrugging with a quirky smile.

She paused. The onlookers and I held our breaths, awaiting her response. "The pigeons are plump because of me. Tomorrow, they may shrivel without food, but they do not know for certain. They can only hope the morsels will be here and cannot prepare for what the future brings. You are lucky, Nico, because you don't have to hope. You know when your time will come and can adjust your life accordingly. Live the remaining moments to their fullest and all will be well."

"I don't want to. I want to live. I want more time."

"I don't have the power to provide that request, but I can show you something." She held my hand. "Place it into the bag and feed the pigeons."

I scooped a handful and lobbed them into the air, then followed with another, and another like a manic child shoveling sand on the beach. The pigeons swarmed like bees, filled their beaks, then flew to the neighboring trees. Amused, I turned to Fatimah. She reciprocated with an assuring nod.

"Slower next time, Nico."

"I'm sorry."

"It's okay, but do you understand now, Nico?"

"I think so. Let me know if I have it correct. They'll live for another day, but when it ends, it'll be okay because I, like them, have done all that I can?"

"Yes, but that's only part of it. Each bird you've fed now has your spirit within them. With each nibble, you've given them hope for another day. That's why I sit here and feed them. And, I, like them, hope when I'm gone someone else will fill my seat on this bench and give them an opportunity to survive." She glanced at those listening, returning to me. "Your spirit will live on, whether you want it to or not, with everyone you've touched in life."

"In all my years upon this earth, I've never thought about it that way."

"At times our lives consume us, not giving an individual any opportunity to think. One needs an extended stay in solitude to figure out the true meanings of life."

"Thank you, Fatimah. I wish I would've met you many years ago."

"Don't fret or live with regret. Today is as good as any

other. My spirit will carry with you until the end."

"I'm thankful for that as well." I closed my eyes, picturing the pigeons flying and cooing towards the blue sky. "May I ask you for additional advice?"

"Of course, Nico, but I cannot make any promises for the proper answer."

"Any is better than none. This topic is sensitive. It's about my... son.

"I will do my best for you," she said, stroking my hand.

"Well, I have a son whom I never met. He's an adult now. His name is Alessio. I'm not even sure he knows about me. I've been to his home, but he never answers the door. Will he accept me or will I die without ever hugging him, Fatimah?"

"Oh, my. This *is* a serious problem. When did you find about Alessio?"

"Yesterday, when I visited my first love. I hadn't seen her in years. She dropped the bombshell after I explained my fatal situation."

"Well, there's at least one positive, Nico."

"I don't see it. Please tell me?"

"She didn't have to tell you. If that had been the case, you would know no different."

"True, but it's more like a curse than a blessing, especially with my limited window."

"I don't think I'll live much longer either, so I understand. Let me think for a moment. I've never had a question like this posed to me. And, I certainly have the years to prove it." She threw a handful to the circling birds and closed her eyes. After a few minutes, she tapped my thigh. "The answer is in all of us as well as the pigeons. You are alive, which means you have hope to find him. Until the time expires, there's always a chance to reconcile. Don't forget your spirit has touched many and will propel you further. Don't doubt its power. It will all work out, and if it doesn't, you can take delight in the fact you tried with every ounce of your being."

"Makes sense, Fatimah. I'm grateful beyond words. Is there any way I can repay you?" I searched my pockets.

"No. No. Money defers, and at times even destroys self-actualization. Just be yourself, stay strong, and continue forward. Our souls have touched, even for this brief moment, and your spirit has repaid me." I remained silent, nodding with wide eyes, hoping she understood my gratitude. I clasped her hands within mine, then bid her farewell with a gentle hug, her petite frame collapsing into my chest.

I sidestepped the crowd gathering around Fatimah. Several strangers clapped my back, offering positive vibes for my quest, and some reassured me not to worry about the future because everything would be fine. The man donned in the rainbow attire wished me peace and invited me to return if I needed further support. With acceptance, we shook hands. I advised if I didn't run out of time, I'd bring a bag of popcorn for all to share with the pigeons. He nodded, leading a homeless couple towards Fatimah. I ambled the street, looking over my shoulder several times to watch the morsels shoot from the enclosure and the pigeons pounce and peck.

As I approached the crosswalk at the end of the block, the positivity Fatimah instilled in me dissipated. Alone, with not a pedestrian in sight, I leaned against the beeping, traffic pole, my stomach trembling and mind racing with the sudden realization of my finality. I searched my pockets, rushing to snap the lids from the bottles, and tucked the pills against my cheek. Their effectiveness was weak. Crouching with care, I eased atop the edge of the curb and below a sewer inlet. Through its gaps a swashing smorgasbord identical to my horrendous thoughts of the future. I closed my eyes, hoping to calm the rising bile.

The unfair universe had punished me. To argue with it as useless as hoping for a cure. Its responses certain to be vague, or worse, uncaring. I howled into my palms cupping my face, pondering other options to remove myself from this life, to beat the reaper at its own game, to take control and have power over the disease and death. The weight of those consequences like a thousand boulders crushing my shoulders into my legs. It was I, and I alone, left to deal with this disease and my demise. No one to hear me nor guide me through this dilemma. Perhaps my castigation derived because I wronged someone early in life, but even that unclear. Only one person came to mind, so I headed a few blocks to his home.

CH 11

Brooding along the avenue, I attempted to shake the loneliness, hoping someone would approach to console or convince me my new idea to end it all was flawed, but no one showed. As a child, the area bustled with cheer. Today, none existed with even the birds silent and not a yip from a dog. The sun from earlier steadfast behind ominous clouds, hinting to a thunderstorm or a quick downpour.

I stood on the sidewalk with my childhood home facing my back. Across the way, 26 Looceenah Drive, the place that altered my youth. There, I befriended Michael Pollock, a man several years older than I, who at times welcomed me, and at others, reduced me to the size of a pebble. After his parents passed, he inherited the mustard, split-level house. Today, on the lawn, two children in their early teens, presumably his, kicked a soccer ball. I crossed the street to approach them, then midway about-faced, and returned to my original spot on the sidewalk. Meeting him imperative; I couldn't be deterred by a mental block, remorse, or indecision. He could absolve my sins and organize my muddled mind. Perhaps the universe would listen as well and heal me with its understanding. Standing and staring wouldn't get that resolve.

I crossed the street once more, and this time continued with determination, but a few steps from the children, I froze, heaving at the familiar snapshots of Michael's domination circulating within my mind. A glass of water to soothe the nauseous churning impossible. I slid a pill into my mouth, hoping to quell the emotional tremors shaking my body. Steadying my back with a hand on hip, I straightened my shoulders and did my best to ignore the torment.

"Hello, guys," I said, clearing bile from my throat.

The black-haired boy held the soccer ball below his foot while the blonde boy propped his arms at his waist and offered a skeptical yet devilish glare.

"You look like you're dying," said the blonde boy with the fiendish face.

"I'm not."

"Are you sure, old man?"

"I'm not dying yet, dammit. Let's reset. I'm sorry to interrupt your game. Can I speak to your dad?"

"Can't you see we're not playing a game? Just kicking the ball around."

"Right. My bad, boys. Can you go get him?"

"No. He's inside. You can go get 'em yourself," sniped the black-haired boy.

The boys glanced at each other and snickered.

I ignored their jesting. "Okay, but are you sure I can just walk in? He's not going to get mad?"

"It's fine. He doesn't do anything anyway, except play on the computer."

"Alright. You better not be lying to me."

He shook his head. "Why would I lie?"

"I'm not sure." I stepped forward and the blonde boy blocked my path.

"Hey, mister. Why are you sweating so much?"

"Must be the walking. Good the sun disappeared to cool me off."

"What are you talking about, prehistoric man?" They looked at each other stupefied and pointed to the sky. "The sun's out. That's why we're playing in the shade."

I glimpsed above. "Nope. Only dark clouds." The sun hadn't shone since leaving Fatimah. The kids trying to take advantage of an ailing man who's trying to resolve something with their dad. I was once young and understood these games.

"Anyway, where can I find your dad?"

"Inside somewhere. We don't keep track of him."

"Fair enough, boys. Thanks."

"Hey, mister. You don't look so good. You should see a doctor or something."

"Whatever...," I said, mumbling several obscenities, then telling them to hush, assuming they didn't hear me because of their vulgar laughter.

Remnants of a rusted railing and protruding nails from the wooden steps led the way to the entrance. Inching the cockeyed screen-door open, I slid inside, stepping onto the soiled, linoleum foyer as I'd done many times as a child. The interior the same as I remembered, yet different. The carpets filthier, the furniture newer, but the aroma of latex, liquor, and Vaseline unchanged.

"Michael... Michael... Anybody home? It's Nico. Nicola," I said, tapping the door jamb.

A rumble echoed from the basement with no response. I repeated the calls between each knock, creeping further inside, using the adjacent wall as a pounding board. Persistence paid off and he responded with a more aggressive tone than I expected.

"What do you want? Go away! I'm resting."

"Your kids said I can come in. It's Nico. Do you remember me?"

"Nico. Who—what's Nico?" A list of obscenities followed. "Go away."

"Nicola Romano. From childhood. Your former neighbor. We used to be friends."

"Nico?" His tone flipped on a dime. "Oh, yeah... the I-talian who couldn't speak English. How you been?"

"I guess okay. I'm hoping we can chat for a bit."

"Yeah, no problem. Going to take a leak. I'll be right up."

The home an echo chamber. I'm not certain if he knew or cared. He streamed into the toilet bowl like the roaring Niagara Falls while grunting and complaining about my arrival. The pipes clanged against the interior walls, then squeaking and wrenching after running the faucet. The door slammed. He clomped up the stairs and squared himself. Startled by his appearance, I lost my breath, which turned into a coughing tantrum. An extended belly stretched his tank top, exposing most of his lower stomach and belly button. The full head of hair from many moons ago replaced with a polished dome. A bloated face formed thick folds around his ears, funneling into a double chin that would soon graze his chest.

"Hey, Michael. How's it going?" I said, withdrawn, as if my juvenescence reappeared.

"It's going. Been like forty or more years, right?"

"Yeah, it could be, but it doesn't matter."

"What gives? Why are you here?" he said with contempt.

"I don't mean to bother, but something came up in my life and the need arose to talk to you."

"Did you find God or something?"

"No."

"Then, it must be serious after all this time. About?"

"Well… us. About things that happened a long time ago. I need to clear them up in my mind."

"Alright. Let's go out back. I don't want to talk around the kids."

He led the way through the attached single-car garage and across the backyard to the shed where one small window provided light. As I entered, the dimness shivered me. We spent a multitude of time as children in this secluded room for more bad reasons than good. Without him noticing, I slipped a pill into my mouth, hoping for serenity and safety.

"Are you okay, man?"

"Yes…" I stuttered, losing my train of thought for a moment. "Of course." I couldn't help but lie.

"Have a seat. It's a comfortable lawn chair," he rumbled.

"Okay." The fraying fabric sinking as I sat, its tin legs flexing, yearning to collapse.

"So, where do you want to start?"

"When we—I mean when I was younger, some things happened between us."

"Yeah, I remember. What about it?"

I drew in a breath, held it, and exhaled, then held it again. I hoped for a cough or anything to stifle the conversation so as not to continue, but it never arrived. The memories, more so nightmares, abhorrent. I had yet to become a teenager, yet it lasted into my early teens. It began with innocent invites to play board games. Of course, I accepted them, but as each day and week passed the invites were exchanged for summonses. He'd offer lemonade, which

I gladly drank, but it never quite resembled lemonade, except for the color, the liquid scorching a path along my throat and into my stomach. I'd swoon, he insisting moving closer to me, saying he couldn't see the board or its pieces. His hand would caress my knee, then slide up my shorts, undressing me and forcing me to perform unspeakable acts for a child. I exhaled, regaining composure, and firmed my shoulders.

"This is difficult for me," I whispered.

"Will you get on with it? I don't have all day. I'm a busy man."

"Fine. This is difficult for me," I belted. "You touched… rap—forced me to do things to you and myself that I wasn't comfortable with. You forced yourself upon me for years. These actions destroyed me emotionally. You physically hurt me. You took advantage of a little boy, me. For all these years I've been ashamed."

I expected a response of some sort, but he remained silent, instead opening the small fridge beside the worn recliner where he sat. He retrieved a beer, spinning the cap, which emitted a hiss. A bottle of vodka followed from the same location. He swigged the clear liquor, chasing it with a healthy gulp of the ale.

"I've blamed myself all this time," I said. The remorseful childlike voice had returned. With his beady eyes intent on mine, he slugged another mouthful of vodka. "You pressured me into believing it was my fault and I never disputed it, fearful of being wrong. Was I?"

He groaned, quaffing and belched, then swiped his spit-smeared mouth with the top of his large hand, leaving a sopping streak.

"You can believe whatever you want, Nico," he said, snickering and swaying in the recliner.

"Do me the favor and answer my question. Was it my fault? Please, tell me."

"No, dummy. You're so stupid," he exclaimed, slaver trickling onto his chin, his eyelids twitching between blinks. "I said it so you'd take the blame from me. You don't understand what it's like to live in my body. The thoughts that go through my mind. I can't stop them no matter how hard I try." He finished the beer and acquired another, then swigged the vodka.

"And what about my mind, my pain?"

"You... You've been able to live your life without those urges..." The liquor invoking the inevitable slur. "What the hell do you know about anything anyway? You weren't the sharpest knife in the drawer."

He stood and approached, swinging the vodka in one hand while his other stretched to grab my shoulder. I flinched, lifting my arms and kicking to block his advance. It worked. His hand missed, grazing my knee. Before keeling, I shoved him and he stumbled backwards, one haunch landing on the armrest, the other dangling.

"I've lived my life burdened with indignity. You—you... funt scumbag." I had other choice words but refrained in order to keep buying bonus points from the gods. "And now, I realize at your expense. I even went as far as justifying my terminal illness as retribution for what you did to me." My heart raced. I hid the pain needling across my chest and along my right arm as best as possible. He would not get that satisfaction. "My wounds, my depression would've died with me if I didn't visit today," I said, hoarse, each word struggling to escape. "You're the one who should die, not me."

"I'm already dead with this incurable disease. Do you see a ring on my finger?" He raised his left hand. "My wife left me because I couldn't control my urges. She found the videos and pictures on the computer. Luckily, she didn't call the cops because she feared embarrassment for the family. She's taking the kids too. All I have is drinking to numb the mind."

"Serves you well, Michael. I hope you didn't hurt your kids like you did me."

"Are you crazy?" He flailed his hands. "I'd never hurt them."

"By no means is that a silver lining, nor does it pardon you. Karma will eventually snag your tail and swallow you whole. Tell me, Michael, why did you pick me?"

"Simple. You were a cute little boy and just a stone's throw away." His haughty laughter sent chills along my scalp, twisting my stomach. "I needed to satisfy myself and knew you'd accept the fault since you didn't know any better. The older ones caught on too quickly."

"If I had the energy, I'd kill you myself." I goaded him with fists raised high.

"Who are you kidding, Nico? I'm twice your size and you can barely move." He opened another beer and chugged it. "Anyway, I'm smart enough to pick those that aren't bigger than me. I like 'em young and weak," he said with a smug smile.

"You disgust me." I wanted to do something to him, but knew I couldn't.

"I'm glad. I don't think much of myself either. I think it's time for you to leave. I have to get back on the computer and take care of my sons. Glad you stopped to say hello. Too bad it wasn't under different circumstances and we were younger. I can use a bit of satisfying."

"*Testa di cazzo. Ti odio. Spero che soffrirai con dolori insopportabile.* To hell with you. I hope when your time arrives you will suffer."

"Keep that other language crap to yourself. We're in America. Speak English."

I mustered enough energy to rise with determination and kicked the flimsy chair against the wall. He smirked, pointing towards the door while he tipped back the vodka. I scampered, as best I could, across the backyard, through the home, and finally the front door, losing breath with each step. The kids kicking the soccer ball made a few snide comments, which I ignored, hurrying to get as far away as possible to rid the dejection. As I turned the corner, with his home far behind, I glanced towards the boundless blue sky. The sun had returned.

My enjoyment short-lived, replaced by discomfort and a pair of chalky pills snug against the gums. At the crosswalk, I leaned against a lamppost, contemplating the reasons I laid blame upon myself rather than he. Those perplexing answers could take years to figure out, which I did not have. The all-knowing dealer had dealt strange cards, and with time running out, a reshuffle impossible. Memories of the repugnant Michael and the others disturbing. I had to ignore them, him, the situation. Full steam ahead, traversing the avenues, and finding peace within myself while saying goodbye to those who mattered most and least.

GIANNI FRANCO

CH 12

I forced the memories of Michael and the other offenders into the deep recesses of the mind, replacing them with thoughts of never-never land filled with clouds for beds and eternal life. With each intersection I traversed, they faded. Just beyond Atlantic Avenue, the rolling aromas of yeast and baked bread enticed me like a butterfly to a Penta flower. A strip of bakeries from almost every ethnicity in the world lined both sides of University Avenue, serving warm pastries and loaves of all sizes.

I slowed, peering through their windowpanes. Some shops arose from the ashes of century-old buildings while others had been rebuilt from those abandoned for decades. The area rejuvenated into a European village with cobblestone roads, stucco facades, and mural paintings. The talented masons and artists relinquishing a piece of their soul onto the cityscape for others to enjoy for decades. Midway the street, next to a pet store, a ten-story relic named University Tower. The City of Rochester had undertaken a mammoth rehabilitation for the hundred-year-old structure, sandblasting and painting the brick fascia to match the different flags draping the storefronts. My childhood friend, Felipe Messini, lived in one of its historical units.

The incline of the stairs and width of the steps leading to the main entrance as steep as an Egyptian Pyramid. I clambered, stopping every few steps to regain breath, then, with some ardent negotiating for the final slog, I latched onto the handrail, using it like a climbing rope.

A doorman didn't guard this building, rather an iron gate that stayed unlocked during the daytime hours held the fort. Behind it, a sturdy Victorian door ornamented with copper figurines greened by their time soaking the metallic air. I turned the sagging, bronze handle, which hadn't had a deadbolt since I could remember. Lilac and cedar filled the vestibule, compounded by a pile of damp newspapers stacked in a corner. On my right, a peeling, plaster wall layered with round buzzers and paper tags slotted behind a steel lattice, most of which had no name or just an initial. His showed none because he didn't want to be found. If it wasn't for memory, I'd be playing the ring-and-see game to get me through the final stage. After depressing the cracked button several times, he called through the speaker.

"What do you want? Why you ringing my door?" he said, annoyed.

"Hey… It's me. Nico. Can I come in?"

"Sure, man," he said, relieved. "Sorry, didn't know it was you. I don't like strangers ringing me. Can't trust those people."

One elevator navigated the building, and on some days I'd wait thirty minutes to ride it to his floor. Luckily, today, no one stood in my way. The accordion gate, flaking paint and rusting, needed several slams for it to engage and run. The Otis birdcage inched its way to the tenth floor, groaning and squealing, as if it wanted to end its life carrying transients to their resting places. I paused for a few moments at 51, debating if I should enter, debating if I should confront him with my terrible news. Just go with the flow I mumbled to myself, then knocked on the door.

"Who is it?" he bellowed.

"It's me. Nico. I just talked to you. Let me in."

"Oh, yeah. I forgot, plus you never know who's knocking. Come in, man."

I scanned the apartment and found him reclining on a leather chair at the corner of the living room. His brawn chiseled onto his scruffy jaw, below firm, tanned cheeks, and a pronounced forehead. An overgrown fade, sans the typical goop holding it in place, flopped over his ear. A full tumbler swished in his hand, filled with a caramel liquid, scotch I assumed, which made sense for the weekend. Beside him, a couch as long as a car, and straight ahead, on an enormous wall, a mounted flat screen emitting almost blinding light from a television show. The mirrored coffee table complemented the mammoth marble countertops that held every appliance imaginable, suitable for a top-tier chef, which he was not.

"Hey, Felipe. Place looks great. Buy anything new since the last time I was here?"

"Of course, Nico. I bought a fancy blender to make those green smoothies. I don't really drink them. Think I had one in the last month. Still getting used to their taste. Some of my dates drink two or three a day. When they're here I blend whatever they want. My job is to make them happy. You want anything to drink? I can make you a kale special."

Trying to make women happy, an understatement for Felipe. I don't believe he ever elated them. He'd been divorced four times and engaged five. I suppose I would've stopped after two or three but to each his own. The fifth marriage didn't have the opportunity to begin. She stood him up at the altar.

He ended up having a stag party for the reception, which spiraled into a liquor frenzy that gave way to an emotional rollercoaster. His, of course. Sitting on the floor of the banquet hall, with his back against the wall and legs splayed, the bottle dangling between them, he proclaimed, between sobbing and laughter, from that day forward to only date and never get tied down again. Time will tell the truth, but I won't survive long enough to verify.

"No, I'll pass on the green," I said, shuddering, pursing my lips. Perhaps if I would've started that healthy diet long ago I wouldn't be in this predicament. No way to prove that option now. "I'll have some water. I need to take a couple pills."

"You sure look tired." His patterned, silk robe flowed at his calves as he strutted to the kitchen. "Expensive sparkling or tap?" he echoed into the icebox.

"Anything. You know I'm not picky."

"Sparkling it is. You're not doing any better since your last sickness?"

He handed me the embroidered bottle. Its vibrant calligraphy showcased its extraction from a mountain in France. I would've loved to have visited any of the European streams, but I doubt they'd let me drink for free.

"Not really, but we can talk about that later. Let's just chat about nothing for now." I chuckled, then held my breath to deviate a throat tickle.

"Alright, man. Cool."

"Who's the new girl you're making smoothies for?" I raised the glass and chased the pills with a sip.

"Rosalind. She's from one of the suburbs about twenty minutes away. I think Webster, Penfield, or Greece. Who really knows? I like her. Been dating a couple weeks. Beautiful with the same type of upbringing as me. Her mom is from Puerto Rico and dad's Cuban. I'll have to introduce you one of these days."

Felipe came from a Latin background like myself. His dad left Barcelona to work the offshore oil rigs in Venezuela where he and his mom met and wed. They emigrated from Venezuela to America about the same time as my parents. Those days they allowed sponsorship and had flexible borders. Spain, as well as the other European countries, had been decimated by the bombings during World War II, so new beginnings were essential.

"You going to marry this one?" I said, winking.

"No way." He crossed his arms with determination and firmed his face. "No rings, no marriage. Nothing. I promised already. That last one really sent me into a dark place."

Some love to be in love. Others just want to be loved to pass time.

"I know. Just making sure you didn't change your mind."

"She's probably not going to like my refusal when the time arrives to talk about it. And as we know, the marriage question is inevitable in most relationships."

"Have you told her about the others?"

"Nope. Don't plan on it either. If she found out, she'd never see me again. I'm damaged goods."

"I suppose some skeletons are better left in the closet. Yours *is* full. You should build another one." I razzed with a hint of truth. "But you never know, she might be into the no-marriage thing. It'll work out either way."

"You promise, Nico?"

"Not a chance. I'm not putting money on this one."

"Fair enough. I wouldn't bet on it either," he said, tittering.

I turned to glimpse the television. A camera panned across a manicured beach with rolling waves. The overdramatic actors, trained in kindergarten, swooned each other, angling to become the premier dater, acquiring a rose for a marriage that never comes to fruition. If only Felipe was younger, he could audition, win a hot tub fling, and lose another engagement live on air.

"How do you watch that garbage?"

"I don't. It's just on to fill the silence." He swiped the remote and changed it to a soccer match. "Hope that's better. Anyway, how's Ravi?"

Ravi, Felipe, and I grew up in the same neighborhood. We went to the same grammar school and played on the same soccer teams. As we aged, Ravi and Felipe drifted apart, but for some strange reason they remained close to me. I'm not sure what happened between them and I'm certain I didn't want to know.

"He's good. I saw him yesterday. He gives you his regards." Which he didn't, but it's best to keep the peace rather than break it. After my death, they'll have to learn to communicate more frequently and perhaps even revisit a close friendship. I can only hope.

"Cool. Next time you see him say hello from me as well."

"Of course."

I slid upon a bar stool at the kitchen island and propped my chin with my hand, debating if should tell him about my situation.

"You want anything to eat? Get your energy up. I have some of that expensive prosciutto from Parma," he said as a matter-of-fact.

Felipe generated a great living as an architect, redesigning most of the Center City and High Falls Neighborhoods, adding three high-rises to the Rochester skyline. When we were younger he vowed to never leave the city where he grew up. I'm not certain how much of the promise was true. Although the salary funded his lavish lifestyle, he may have relocated if it weren't for the divorces siphoning a good portion of the cash flow.

"That kind of eating isn't good for my health, but who cares anymore. Serve it up. You only live once," I said with a forced smile.

"Live every day like it's your last. You never know when it's coming."

"Very true, Felipe." The moment arrived to tell him, then vanished. Saddening him hurt me more than the pain in my chest. "The not knowing part scares me just as much as knowing. If anything ever happens to me…" I paused and swallowed. "Just know you've meant more to me than anything. You stood up to those who bullied me. You always stood by me and raised my spirit from the floor, especially after I lost Beatrice. When I was in the hospital and couldn't talk or move you brought me food and flowers. I couldn't have asked for a better friend, and may I say, brother."

"Oh, come on, Nico. Don't go getting all weird on me today. Let's just let life take us where it may and not think about it. Thanks for all you said. You're like a brother too and you do just as much for me. Remember when I was so drunk

I got lost walking home and you came to find me and led me to my door?" I nodded and grinned. "Or the time I ran out of gas during the middle of the night in that rural town that resembled the one in the movie *Deliverance*. You came to help even though you had to be at work in a couple hours."

"Those were interesting, fun nights. I thought we were going to get shot on the side of that road."

"Me too. So crazy. And you were the best man at all my weddings. If I was you, I would've turned me down after the second one failed. I promise if anything happens to you, it'll be a celebration and not a termination."

"Thanks, Felipe. That's all I want. I've lived a meager life and don't want the end to be the same. It should be a new beginning, regardless if there is or isn't another side."

He dipped below the counter, beside the refrigerator, and pulled a bottle of red wine from a temperature-controlled cooler. The cursive writing blanketing the label and a cork sealing its flavor suggested an expensive brand. I'd been accustomed to wines that came with twist caps and crooked decals, so I welcomed a taste of aristocracy.

"Let's have a glass or two to celebrate whatever life brings us." The electric corkscrew opened the bottle within seconds. He whiffed the cork and nodded. "This is the best stuff I have. I'm not going to tell you the cost. You won't be disappointed. I assure you."

"What I'm used to costs less than ten dollars. I'm easy to please. Red wine's good for the heart, too. Pour away, Felipe."

He filled two, tall glasses halfway. The oversized cups balancing on stems as thin as toothpicks. We raised them with a light clang, then sipped, followed by two harmonic sighs.

He didn't hesitate pouring when our glasses emptied. After a quick swallow, he set his glass upon the counter and marched towards me with his arms spread. Shocked, I swigged the wine and rushed to set my glass atop the counter. I made it just in time before he latched onto me with a bear hug. He stepped away and gazed into my eyes with tears trickling his cheeks, taking a deep breath, then spoke.

"Nico... I know everything." He patted his face with the robe and bit his upper lip.

"What are you talking about, man?"

"I'm not mad, Nico. I know you wanted to keep it from me because... well—because you care about my feelings. I couldn't ask for anything more from a friend and brother." He held up his glass, filling it. "I wasn't going to say anything, but ignoring it was just as hard."

I had no response. My mind occupied with memories of our times together, intertwined with the finality of these impending days. A gaping mouth is all I could offer, then my head swayed and an inferno erupted within my gut that rose to my nose. Gagging, I turned and snuck a pill, attempting to extinguish the burning with a healthy gulp of wine.

"I'm sorry," I said, my vision sharpening and pain subsiding. "I couldn't te—"

"Don't worry. It's not about me. It's about you."

"I couldn't tell you. I've been trying to since I arrived. How did you find out?"

"Well... Beatrice and your Mom called."

"Secrets are only safe when you're dead," I said, shaking my head and raising a fist.

"Don't blame them. They care about you. And me. All of

us care about each other."

"I understand." I lowered my shoulders. "Nothing I can do about it, or them. The end is near. Such is life."

"How long, brother?"

"I don't know."

"Stay with me," he beseeched with welling eyes, scooping a tear upon a finger, then clasping his hands. "We can make the most of your remaining time together."

"I can't. I must see others. I promise if there's time, I'll return."

"You better, Nico. Come stay here and be with me until whenever. *Me preocupo por ti. Te amo, hermano. Mi casa es tu casa.*"

We embraced. "Thank you, Felipe. I appreciate you and everything you've done for me. My life would've been worse without you. The spirit you've instilled upon me and those around you is irreplaceable. My friend, my brother. I am forever grateful."

He didn't respond, nor did I, alternating between firm handshakes and hugs. We sat for several minutes finishing the wine and studying each other between snuffles, I unable to articulate. That's how the visit ended. The rickety elevator shuddered me to the ground floor, and once outside, I sat upon the steep steps. Before venturing to the next stop, I scanned the building one last time, catching his gaze upon me from a window. I waved with a despondent smile. He dabbed his eyes with a handful of tissues and reciprocated, then walked away.

CH 13

Rambling along the walkway, the storefront window to Love 'N' Pets captured my attention. Its reflection solidifying my grim prognosis. I had aged since last viewing the mirror just a few hours ago. Sagging shoulders arched my back, jutting the shoulder blades like shark fins. A drooping chin begged to rest against my caving chest. In due time, it would. Unsettled, I scuttled away, but a few steps beyond the building, I turned, determined not to ponder the future and focus on the present. Years had passed since I entered the store to visit the adorable beings tweeting, purring, and yelping, soon to be freed from their temporary prisons and be loved by a family in a home.

I've always adored animals, but as a youth I wasn't allowed to have them. Ma thought they existed to live in the wild and never belonged with humans. When I argued other Italians had them, she'd tell me to mind my business and not focus on the other crazy families who'd succumbed to Americanization. I'm certain she was wrong because someone must've owned pets in Italy, but arguing invoked warring, inviting a belt or shoe whooping.

As I entered the store, a cowbell collar jangled against the metal handle. Frenzied, I lunged to silence it atop my palm so as not to disturb those resting inside. Bird seed, dander, and a hint of zoo swarmed my face. Oddly enough, I didn't wheeze or cough.

"Hello, sir." A chipper female echoed from an aisle

towards the center of the store. "Welcome to Love 'N' Pets. If you have any questions, please let me know."

"Thank you," I said, traipsing towards her. She much younger than I. Dimples complemented a full face and pleasant smile highlighted by blushing cheeks and eyeshadow as bright as her blue eyes; her blonde hair interwoven with strands of purple and pink.

"Not a problem, sir. What can I help you with?"

"Where do you keep all the cats and dogs?"

"Follow me." She windmilled her arm, leading the way to the rear of the facility.

"Perfect. I should know these things but—"

"It's alright, sir. It's my job to help people. We used to have them upfront, but then we received complaints from the city. They're just through here." She pointed at a door with a plague, *Those Inside Will Love You*. As I entered, meows and barks filled the room. "We keep them separate to reduce their anxiety, but they always know when we're coming," she said, scrunching her button nose. "Which cuties do you want to see first?"

"The doggies. I'll save my favorite for last." I simpered like a child opening a birthday gift.

"I just love them all," she said.

"The dogs?"

"Yes. The dogs, cats, fish, birds, turtles… You name it, I love them. Even mice, rats, and ants."

"Cool. I'm like you. And, I don't know why some of the animals get a bad rep."

"Me, either." She sighed and grunted.

She latched onto my hand and led me into a room. Above

the cages, a sign, *Yipping Love You.* Some of the dogs old, some puppies, some barked while others whined, and a few paid no mind, licking themselves or staring at the wall pondering their escapes.

"Oh my... they're all so beautiful—" I glanced at her name tag. "—Miranda L."

"They sure are. And what might your name be?"

"Nico. Nico R." She ignored my banter for our abbreviated last names.

"A pleasure to meet you," she said, extending her hand. I obliged. "Mommy is here my lovely babies. Do you all want to eat?" She conducted roll call with a baby voice, reciting each name within a laminated badge affixed to the crate. The dogs yelped as she stuck her finger between the grates and rubbed their noses, then turned to me. "One second. I'll be right back with the food."

"Take your time. I'll be here."

I thumped my fingers across the grates, and once realizing I resembled a prison warden, I retreated ashamed. Their situation unnerving; if they weren't locked in cages, they'd be roaming the streets hungry, diseased, or even dead. A few of them lurched forward and nuzzled between the metal spaces, ignoring my contemplations and searching for a bit of affection. As I extended my hand, Miranda barged through the door carrying a large bag of dog food, startling all of us. They realized within seconds their dinner had arrived and wailed in unison as I stepped away.

"They love me the most now." She giggled, tearing open the pouch. "Other times, they just like me."

"I bet they do. I always regret not having a pet when I

was young," I said.

"How come you didn't have one?"

"My parents," I said with a disgruntled sigh. "They weren't the nice, understanding kind. If, you know what I mean?"

She furrowed her brow. "I do. That's just awful. Some people are weird. Forget about the past. Did you have a pet later on in life?"

"Yes. A cat. Bella. She passed away. Cancer. I remember her scampering throughout my apartment like it was yesterday. She was just like a dog and even played fetch."

"So cute… and I'm sorry for your loss." She frowned and paused for a moment. "Maybe nostalgia will have you pick one out today?" She perked up, her dimples cute enough to tempt me to adopt one.

"I wish I could, but my time's limited these days. It wouldn't be fair to them. Otherwise, I would because I think I'm in love." I pointed to one of the dogs scarfing food. "Misty is a beautiful golden lab."

"She sure is. Came to us a couple weeks ago. Her owner passed away in his sleep. They only found him because the neighbors heard her wailing. Dogs are so smart." She nodded and filled another bowl for her.

"Agreed. But, cats aren't so bad either. They're my favorite. " I winked and stepped aside so she could reach the other dogs.

"Cats are coy, always thinking, and dogs want to just do it, whatever that may be. I'm about done. Are you ready to visit the kitties?" She meowed, filling the remaining bowls, and stored the food within a cupboard. "This way," she said, pointing at the other door.

"I'm a little nervous. I might fall in love again."

"Oh, I know. There's always someone to love if you're willing to let them love you."

We entered the room and above these crates the placard, *PurBabies.* The cages smaller than the others and stacked in similar fashion, each one with a laminated nametag as well.

"I must tell you I love them all, Miranda."

"If you decide to take one home, let me know." She winked and tilted her head.

I longed to render the impossible possible, but longing is only hope that, in my case, is a futile thought. "If I had a handful of wishes that would be one of them."

"Which one do you like the best. I can have you hold one."

"Really? You'd do that for me?"

"Of course. It'll cheer you up."

"How about... Mico, the American Shorthair with the spirals and stripes." I pointed like a manic kid wanting the contents of a cookie jar.

"He's cute, but aren't they all." She smirked and unlatched the cage. "Here you go, sir. I'm going to get some food for them. Be right back."

He crawled along my cradled arms, then craned his head and nudged my chin with his damp nose, his purrs massaging my chest. I lowered my cheek and caressed him, then kissed his fluffy white stomach, a pelt like a bowl of cotton balls. Memories of Bella, who left me far too soon, returned with fervor. Her quick, perky pace across the interior of my place astounding. If only I had more time, I'd take Mico home to experience the same. I explained to him my end was near with no resolve and if he came with me, he'd be disappointed to return to the pet store after my death. He licked my face and meowed, confirming he understood.

I snapped out of my daze when Miranda returned, carrying several empty bowls and a case of Friskies. The cats erupted into frantic meows, breaking from their self-cleaning regimen to paw their confinements with excitement. Mico, once relaxed within my arms, jumped to the floor and nudged Miranda's leg, hoping for first dibs. She opened the lids, filling the air with tuna and chicken. Mico received his wish and ate first while the other cats salivated, devouring their portions like a last meal once she placed them in the cage. After watching them eat, she set the empty tins into a recycling bin and turned to me.

"So, do you want to take him home?"

"Trust me when I tell you I want to, but I can't."

"You can. I know you said you're short on time, but even a couple years with you will be better than being locked in a cage at the back of a pet store."

"If only I had that long."

"Oh no… How much?"

"It's all unclear. They ran a bunch of tests and used that stupid program, iLifeCheck. It's safe to say I won't last two years, let alone one. Could be a couple days or weeks."

"Oh my. I'm so sorry. I hate that program too. It was accurate for Dad."

"Well… My condolences. I'll hope for the best," I said, grimacing.

"Thank you for caring. And, yes, that's all we can do."

"Only advice I have is not to get sick."

"I'll do my best, sir. I also read somewhere that soon they'll be able to tell how long you have to live at any age, including when you're born."

"Is that even possible?" I said, startled by the revelation. "I guess that's a good and bad thing. Either way, I don't like it."

"I agree. I wouldn't want to know. Anyway, we'll let the cats eat. Follow me through the store. I can show you around."

I waved goodbye to the cats and blew Mico a kiss, followed by a smile and a blink, which is how cats communicate with each other and humans. If they blink back, which Mico did, then they accept you. I followed Miranda to the fish tanks where she pointed at the exotic species, all of which depicted a rainbow. Next, we entered the avian section with lovebirds, parrots, cockatoos, canaries, parakeets, and many more. Their whistles and chirps provided a glimmer of optimism within my hopeless mind. I imagined Fatimah sitting here every day feeding them seeds, watching their flapping wings and pecking beaks. We ventured to the lizards and turtles, the mice and gerbils, and those too possessed beauty not found in the other animals. Their spots, mannerisms, and eyes spoke volumes about life, death, and the in-between, now understanding what Fatimah meant about the embedded spirit, which I sensed from Miranda. If only luck could return me to Mico.

"I'm sorry you're not able to take anyone to a new home," she said as we approached the checkout counter.

"I am as well. Thank you for the tour. I loved it."

"You're welcome. And, my pleasure. It's a tough job." She giggled. "I know you're jealous. Is there anything else I can show you, Nico?"

"No. You've done plenty with all these beautiful beings. You've satisfied this part of my life, and I know, when the time arrives, this was worth it. I'm going to tell a friend of mine about this place. Her name is Fatimah and she loves pigeons. Feeds them all the time."

"So cute and cool. They deserve love too."

"I'm going to come back with her so she can experience all the beauty."

"Please do. I'll be waiting. I don't mean to cut this short, but I have to get back to work. Thank you for stopping and spending time. In the remote chance the predictions are wrong, come back for a purring beauty. Mico will be waiting to be cradled."

"I doubt it'll be wrong. Thanks for offering. You're very sweet. I wish you the best."

"Toodle-oo," she said with a cute, childish twang.

She lifted a cardboard box from the floor and walked to an aisle, stacking canned food on a shelf. I paused at the exit and took one last glance at the interior. Behind those doors, at the back of the store, resided happiness and belonging for well over a dozen families. They just didn't know it yet, but I did. The bell from the door clanged as the door shut behind me.

CH 14

Several steps along the block a realization arrived; if I was a pet, no one would want anything to do with me. To enjoy my old, ragged, dying company for a couple months or days would be more tedious than scrubbing the orange from the bricks lining the buildings beside me. I hoped those I encountered didn't perceive me as such within their minds, but wishing to negate perception equals reality in most circumstances.

I came upon Haags Alley, a shortcut taken once or twice in the past, and scooted into it. Occupied with thoughts of being an imperfect pet companion, I stumbled, knee first, into the shoulder of a homeless man sprawled on the pavement. At first glance, his unflinching body, perhaps corpse, provided a reflection into my future. I sidled the concrete wall abutting his back with my palms, bits of loose cement digging and snagging the skin. While I tried to convince my wobbling legs to find an upright stance, it spoke, petrifying me.

"What you doing? You trying to kill me, man? Get the hell away from me," he grumbled, craning his head from a pillow fluffed with plastic bags.

I scrambled to stand, ignoring any pain. "I'm sorry. I didn't mean to—"

"To want kill me?" He gurgled, spit, then cupped his hand atop his brow and squinted. A slight accent filtered through, but I couldn't place it. Tobacco, shaken and stirred with whiskey, gin, and body odor, knocked me back a step. "*You* people all alike. Not bad enough I have to live like this and all you people want to do is execute or harass me."

A gust of wind delivered rancid air. I regained my footing and swallowed the phlegm rising into my throat. "It's not like that at all. I'm sick and lost my balance. It wasn't on purpose. I promise."

"Promises for Peter Pan. If not intentional, then give me some money," he said, ironing his matted, salt-and-pepper beard that extended to his chest. He struggled from the fetal position and sat, leaning his back against the wall, extending one leg, and crossing the other underneath. His black boots stained and torn sans laces.

"There you go. All *you* people do is ask for money. I do my best to help, but it's never food or a job. Always money, money, money. Why is that?"

"What you expect," he said, pointing leeward.

A rat, with a ball of molded cheese in its mouth, skirted the grimy wheels of a dumpster and disappeared into a hole in the wall. I peeked above its ridged lid and metal edge. A cardboard hut, no taller than my thigh, sagged. Its three moistened sides pitched by misshapen twigs and branches. All his belongings unclear, stuffed into opaque valises made from plastic or paper, sitting atop a quilt washed with mud, tar, and animal droppings. Beside them, a military-style backpack and an unlabeled one-liter bottle of cheap scotch or whiskey, certainly not tea.

Turning towards him, I crossed my arms over my chest and said, "So, you like the drink. Is that why you're sleeping in the gutter and yelling at me for accidentally losing my step?"

"Again, what you expect?"

"I don't expect anything from you. Just don't be rude when someone apologizes for something they didn't mean to do."

"You could avoid me, but you choose to no see me cause people like me don't exist."

"Look, I care. I'm passing through and not looking for trouble. I don't need the extra stress today. I made a mistake, but maybe you shouldn't have been in this place either."

"Stress, mistakes?" he blurted. "You no have any idea what these words mean. You tink you ask me when I was baby where I be in future. No way I say alley. If I know, I kill myself that time. No wait for this." He brought his hands to his face, squeezed his cheeks, and shuddered. "I hate life, my life."

Unsettled by his statement, I crouched. "I get it, man." I couldn't maintain the position under cracking knees, so I rose. "But this isn't the way to go about it. You have to find a better option because this isn't working for you."

"Do not be smug with me. Our roads very different, very same." He cleared his straight, black, grimy hair from his cheeks, then goggled me. "My eyes, you eyes, equal same, *Liver*."

"Liver. What does that even mean? Please enlighten me," I said, skeptical that anything he spewed made any logical sense.

"You ignorant. That what we call the no-homeless. The people who walk streets free and clear from death. They drink hot coffee and eat fresh food. They bathrooms private with four walls and door. *Livers* think they have all figured out cause they can't, or too afraid to suffer like us. *Livers* live, we die. They ignore cause it easier than facing reality."

"Stop it," I said, gesturing with my hand. "I understand more than you think. Don't assume… homeless man."

"We *human* and *homeless*, not *human-less*. Damn *Livers*. If you ask and not be so dumb, you know I have name. My name Vithyea, which is human. You no even remember me. I know you. Damn *Livers*." He gurgled and spat a dark glob. "I see you around neighborhood."

Awed, I stood speechless for a moment. I had to fix our interaction. There had to be more to this than just a vitriolic jest. Ending on this note not harmonious for either of us.

"Let's start over," I said, splaying my arms. "I'm Nicola. To most, Nico. I'm not trying to upset your daily flow. I tried to take a shortcut and ended up in this situation."

"That better. What you last name?"

"Why is that any of your business?"

"We the same, man. Look at you, butter eyes, you no have much time like me. Me, you, nothing to lose. I make deal. My last name is Pham. People from streets call me VP cause they no can say my first or last name." He winked, then grinned, exposing several missing teeth.

"Fine, VP. Romano is my last name. I'm Italian and you?"

"Good. Good. I like Italians," he said, nodding. "They always be nice to me. Hope today no different. I'm Asian. Maybe you already know that cause way I look. Vietnamese. So, you tell me why you look so bad, more bad than me?"

I didn't want to divulge any of my information, but then again, I had nothing to lose speaking to a stranger. "I'm terminally ill. My end is arriving soon. I skated this alley hoping to save time and energy to visit family and friends."

"Do they know you sick?"

"Not everyone. I've been trying to keep it secret, but those are hard to tame."

"Good you reach out to them. They appreciate to see you."

"I suppose. So, you said you know me. From where exactly?"

"The deli where you work. You the guy who put food for cats and humans outside. I eat spaghetti and meatballs a few times at deli. My girlfriend, Sarah, hang out in that alley more than me. She love the Italian free food."

"You have a girlfriend? But you're homeless."

"Yes, I have one. We have no money, but not disease people. Well… some have disease, but they die very quick. We, no health insurance on streets. So far, so good for me. Maybe lucky. One night Sarah surprise me with candle she find in garbage can somewhere. We go to park with food and two used bottle of wine from you deli. We have candlelight dinner under stars and moon."

"I never thought your people got along like that," I said, bemused.

"Come on, man. What you mean *your people*? Remember, we the same, just different luck."

"Then, what fortune brought you to a curb, drunk in a park beside a row of candles."

"You no care, so I no want to really tell you. No reason to talk to wall that no want to listen."

"If I didn't care, I would've rushed off by now. Tell me what makes us so similar. Please."

He patted his thighs, straightening the soiled fatigues. His eyes widened, exposing two ebony darts. "Okay, but I warn you. Too much bad luck for me. Myself and the world around me painted black like Rolling Stones song. I no lose limbs, but drink a lot of napalm tea. I born in Vietnam and come to America very young, maybe like you, except different country. Then, Vietnam War started, and cause America is new home, I sign up to fight in war against my country. United States government tell me I get automatic citizenship when I come home. They lie. Never happen. Then, from that point, it get really bad. Do you want me keep going?"

"Yes… please. I'm intrigued. I hope it's not bad."

"Okay. Bad is good. This worse than bad." He retrieved a flask from his military jacket and chugged. "It pretty good. Cheap, but good. You want some?"

"Normally, I wouldn't hesitate, but I have a lot of walking to do today. Thanks for asking."

"No problem. You very welcome. I feel it working." He drew a breath and sighed. "Okay, I ready. Couple months after I return from two tours, they deport me to Vietnam. Vietnam no like me anymore. They call me traitor. They hit me, beat me, lash me, and put me in jail with no bathroom. I fight with embassies, US and Vietnam, for almost two year. One day, Vietnam decide to send me to US. The US said no and no count my time in army. They take my pay, give me dishonorable discharge, and green card. No citizen like they promise.

"I unite with my family again, but they change the way they look to me. Too much happen. My family, me, broken. We no see each other same anymore. We like broken glass. I no find any jobs. No money. No care for my sickness from bombs. No sleep, no think. Always crazy from pain in body and mind. The ambulance noise too much, too loud. Every sound too loud. I scared all the time. Then, I get in trouble with police. Nothing big. Small things to survive. So, today, I here. Tomorrow, I no know. Every day and night on concrete bed."

Angered, confused, and saddened, I paused to absorb the glimpse into his life. I responded with the first thing that came to mind. "Why a dishonorable discharge?"

"I know but I no know. I tink cause they deport me, then jail in Vietnam. I don't know military rule. I know they lie. Maybe they no like me and say we no give Vietnamese people nothing cause of war. They take everything from me."

"But you gave your life for the United States."

"I do, but they no see it that way. They say get out, bye-bye."

"Can't you fight this? Find a lawyer to help for free."

"Yeah… lawyer coming soon in limousine to pick me up and go court. Maybe buy home and apartment for me. Like magic. When they come I ask for Johnny Walker, a carton of Marlboros, and silk suit."

"I get your point. Sorry for not thinking. I'm just stunned."

"Yeah… me too," he said with a chuckle.

"You can't keep living in these conditions. It's not healthy. There must be something that can be done. It's America for *chrissake*."

"Nothing. No worth trying. I one of many in city too small for all of us."

I scratched my temple. "Is there anything I can do for you?"

"No. Thank you for offer. You no look like you have money anyway, so forget before when I ask you. I get this far, so I tink I be fine. Sarah help me too. You need help yourself. Remember, you fall on me, not me on you."

I couldn't argue his point so I opted not to respond. I had a twenty in my pocket and some loose coins but couldn't give him the bill in case an emergency arose, which I expected with my health predicament. We expressed good fortune towards each other for our journeys, although our sullen eyes suggested otherwise.

He thanked me for the small change and said, "*Thần tốc. Tôi hy vọng bạn tìm thấy những gì bạn đang tìm kiếm.*"

"Thank you, I guess."

"Stay strong, *Liver*," he said with a grin.

CH 15

On my way to Alessio's, my chest and calves constricted. I stumbled, catching the edge of a building to break my imminent crash onto the pavement, swallowing another set of pills to chase a new wave of pain. Within minutes, adrenaline penetrated every fiber of my body, allowing me to regain my stride, determined to meet him.

Must move forward. Must survive.

At his porch, I jammed the doorbell and pounded the door, depleting the energy I had gained, forcing me to rest with my back against the wall. He never answered. Defeated, I pawed the metal jamb and craned towards one of the adjacent windows, peeping through an opening from a misguided curtain, finding no motion inside. I shouted his name, which cascaded into a whimper. Strange, he's never home. I'd continue trying and hoping until all hope evanesced with my last breath.

Ariel Tousi, known to most as Ariel Turquoise, rents a two-bedroom, two-story loft at 777 Highland Avenue. She's my lover, soon to be former due to my unfixable situation. Originally from Iran, she moved to Israel, then to France, then hopscotched to Montreal and Toronto, settling in Rochester for the time being. She speaks four languages, even teaching me a bit of French. An amazing artist whose canvas varies from paper to buildings for her masterpieces.

We met outside the Venice Café a few years ago. She was chalking a rococo homage to Hemingway and Picasso.

The two artists sitting beside each other; Hemingway drawing a portrait and Picasso scribbling prose. Impressed by her amazing abilities, certainly worlds beyond mine, I, with a shrinking voice, offered her a drink. She accepted after a brief hesitation, probably wondering why an older man switching stares between her and the drawing spoke to her. She later told me she paused due to desire. I think she said that to comfort me. Not sure what a woman fifteen years younger than I could want from me, but then again, here I am today about to knock on her door, having disconnected her doorbell because it disrupted her chi.

She answered, wearing denim overalls splattered like a Jackson Pollock and no undergarments. Those too disrupted her process while showcasing her fit physique. I had no reason to question or complain. Wavy, chestnut tresses, cupping her chiseled, almond cheeks and pillow lips, rested just above a toned waist.

We exchanged a long kiss and light embrace. "I've missed you, Miss Tousi."

"Don't say that too loud or the neighbors will hear," she snarled with a hint of sarcasm, turning on her tiptoes, welcoming me to follow with a flick of her hair.

After our second date she told me not to use her real last name, advising most people called her Miss Turquoise. The outlandish choice made sense considering her eyes resembled the Caribbean Sea. At first glance, I thought she wore colored contacts, but she proved me wrong on more than one occasion, and not just about her eye color.

After arriving in America, she said people didn't even use her first name and just called her turquoise. She explained she wanted to officially change it, then decided best not to pursue the initiative due to cost, and the possibility of returning to Canada or across the pond. I fell in love with a nonconformist and couldn't have wished for anything more. Well, other than the obvious, to live.

"Yes, dear. I mean—Miss Turquoise," I said with a timid smile.

A few more steps into the loft, she stopped, forcing me to bump into her sculpted derriere. I slithered my hands around her hips, then up to her bare shoulders. She tittered as I brushed her neck with my lips, pulling away as my heart rate increased. From my pocket, another pill for relief, understanding I'd have to control myself around Turquoise, or I'd die in her arms. Although not a bad idea, I had other plans and more people to see before my expiration.

"That's better, love. Come closer and touch me. I've been yearning for you. It's been over two weeks since we've seen each other."

From the get-go we labelled our relationship laid back. She concentrated on her artistic adventures and I reset my energy levels during our breaks. It was the only way to keep up with her. Our longest time apart lasted several weeks while I was in hospital. I'd lied to her at the time, telling her I went to Italy to visit family. I presumed she knew the truth, but the debate never arose. We'd never cheat on each other and that's what mattered most.

"I'd love too, but I'm under the weather today. Maybe next time."

"You do seem tired and sallow. Your eyes are more drawn than usual. Oh, love. My baby. Are you going to be okay this time?"

"Of course. I won't let you down my beautiful *artista dell'amore.*"

"*Bon.* That's what I like to hear my Italian stallion. Would you like something to drink, love?"

I couldn't tell her the truth. If I had, then she'd be distraught. Her art could suffer. Even though some damaged artists produce the best work at their destructive expense, I didn't want to be blamed for her next masterpiece, or possibly lack thereof. Her livelihood more important than my life and its inconsequential consequences.

"Sure. Some water. To cool off from your heat."

She blushed and smirked. "Are you sure you don't want espresso or something stronger to deal with a *belle femme sexy* such as myself."

She lifted the strap of the overall, pointing to what lay beneath. I shook my head with wanting eyes. Glowering, she flung her hair, spinning and thumping to the refrigerator like a ballerina. She swung the door, shaking loose wine and beer bottles, and swiped an Evian.

"Here you go, Nico. I'm happy you stopped to see me even though you won't touch me." She sighed. "Hopefully, next time you'll be ready for some fun. *Du sexe sensuel.*" Her expressions teetered between aggravation and delectation.

"I'll make it up to you. I'm sorry to upset you. *Tu m'as manqué*, Ariel."

"I know. You've already told me. And, it's okay. You're so funny sometimes."

"I love you, dear."

"Oh... I *love* you as well, love. *Je vous aime*," she said with a posh voice, which every so often trickled into our conversations. She hinted at nobility in her lineage, but I refused to press any further, fearful it would divide us since my family were vassals in Italy.

"I'm glad we met. I love you. *Ti amo, bella. Je vous aime.* You've shown me a great life."

"Are you breaking up with me, Nico? Because if you are, this is the worst time to do it. I'm not ready to end this relationship. You better—"

"Relax, Miss Turquoise. *Se calmer.* I would never do that to you or us."

"So, what are you trying to tell me? Come on, Nico. You never say things like this." She headed to the cupboard, then to the freezer, filling a tumbler with ice and frigid vodka. "See." She held up the glass. "You're driving me to drink."

"Okay, fine. I want to—" For a moment the thought crossed my mind to tell her my life had run its course. "—to tell you everything's going to be fine. I can't wait until I'm better so we can spend all our time making love."

"That's my Nico. I've missed you so much I can tear your clothes off right now. In fact, I have inside my mind. We're going to devote a whole weekend locked in my bedroom, only stopping for naps and bathroom breaks, which will ensure your energy stays up."

With her glass in hand, she wrapped her arms around me and squeezed. I nestled my face into her thick mane, inhaling the soothing coconut and lavender. The pain disappeared in that moment, my body aloft in the heavens, then the storm arrived, proving I existed in a fool's paradise. Dizzied, without notice, I fell forward and hung over her shoulder, wheezing. She propped me up by the shoulders, leaning the limp, ravaged gimp, myself, who had carried her to the bedroom countless times, against the counter, and screamed.

"Love. Baby. Are you okay? Come on, Nico. Wake up, love. *Svegliati. Réveiller.*"

She stroked my hair and patted my forehead with a cold cloth, holding the Evian to my lips. With my vision refocusing and a weak hand, I tipped it far enough to sip several drops.

"It'll pass just like everything else does. *Sto bene,*" I said, croaking each word like a drowning frog.

"There you go again with the loaded statements. Come on, Nico. Love, will you be alright?"

"Yes, my dear. I will."

I wobbled to the dining area and guided myself onto a chair, gulping the water, then missing the table and dropping the bottle onto the floor. Not bothering with the spill, she crouched beside me and slid her hand atop mine.

"Love, I have a surprise for you. It'll make you feel better." Her wide eyes glistening like emeralds as they met mine. "Wait here. I'll be right back."

"I promise not to run away," I said, then mumbled, "as if I could."

She kissed my cheek and smacked my thighs. I smiled and watched her tramp up the steps into the studio. Several minutes passed and she bellowed to let me know she'd be down in a second. That second turned into minutes. Rumblings and thrashings echoed throughout the apartment, of what may have been paper and paint brushes falling onto the hardwoods and not hysteria.

She emerged from the atelier holding a large item draped in cloth. She swayed down the steps, balancing it between her arms and bosoms while shouldering the wall and banister. Across from where I sat, she angled the mystery against the table, then spun to my side, kissed my forehead, and told me to close my eyes. I did as requested, but she insisted covering them with my hands.

"3-2-1, *voilà*. Surprise!" She shuffled a few steps away. I peeked for a second and watched the cloth parachute to the floor. "Time to open them. Tell me if you like it. Hopefully, you'll love it. *Je suis vraiment enthousiaste.*"

Agog, I blinked several times. As clarity set in, I realized she held some sort of square. I gawked motionless and wordless, attempting to understand how and what she'd done. The arcs, lines, and points strewn across the canvas in perfect harmony. They depicted reality far more severe than I had contemplated just a few hours ago. I wanted to scream, but not at her, at myself, not able to clear the horror from my mind. She meant well.

"What do you think, love?"

I inhaled and composed myself, gazing, about to cry. "I think... it's beautiful. Amazing, actually. How did you do it? And why?"

"Why? Because I love you. How—well, I'm a *sexy artiste*." She giggled, then traced the edge of the painting. "Remember that day you brought a picture album to show me your family and time in Italy?"

"Yes," I said, rubbing my chin.

"I stole one of the photos and *voilà*, here it is. Actually, here you are. It's you, when you were younger, sitting on the ledge of the Trevi Fountain in Rome."

"Oh my g—How long did it take?" I wanted to look away, but it, he, kept drawing me in.

"A little over a month. I took my time with it. Probably could've finished in two weeks, but I wanted perfection. Just like you."

"I love you and I love the painting. *Tu es remarquable. Perfetto.*" My eyes welled and lips quivered. I snuck two pills into my mouth, settling them against my gums, hoping they'd control my emotions.

"Oh, love. Don't cry or I'll start," she said, stomping towards me with her arms wide. Embracing, I nuzzled the nape of her neck. "I'm flattered you like it."

"I don't like it." Her eyes narrowed, but before she could protest, I interrupted. "I love it!"

My heart raced once more, and unlike the other occurrences, I couldn't control it, my head flopping like a broken teddy bear.

"Love. Nico. Please, baby. Stay with me. *Bébé. Amour.*" Her voice muddled as I saw her thrash my chest and back.

Focus. Be calm. Breathe. All will pass.

And as the darkness overcame me, I awoke with water dripping from my chin. "What just happened?" I wailed.

"Oh, love." She whimpered with dampened eyes. "Are you okay, *mon amour*? I thought I lost you."

"I'm fine. I'm sorry. I didn't mean to scare you," I said, wheezing through the words.

"Is there something you're not telling me? Do you need to see a doctor?"

"Yes. I think I should go see him. I haven't been well for

the last couple weeks and put it off." Not a complete lie.

"Well, you better go now, love, and stop being so stubborn. I can you go with you."

"There's no need. I can handle it." I firmed my shoulders and pretended everything had passed, hiding pain like a boxer punched by Mike Tyson in the tenth round.

"Please, promise me, you'll go straight away. *J'ai besoin de toi mon amour*." she said, latching onto my hands like a vise, tears trickling.

"I promise."

She released her grip and cuddled me. As much as I wanted to stay within her comfort, I knew the time to depart had arrived. If not, we'd spend it sobbing.

"I think I should go before I get more emotional," I said, inching to my feet with her assistance.

"Are you sure you don't want me to go with you?"

"No, dear. It'll be fine."

"And you're going to see the doctor after you leave me?"

"Yes."

"You promise?"

"*Je vous promets*. And, it's best I go alone. We don't need two stressed people in his office."

"Fine. And as much as I don't like your response, I understand. Take the portrait with you. Drop it off at your place before you see the doctor. Hang it in the bedroom or living room, so you can remember me every day when you look at it."

"I promise, I will." Telling her I wouldn't take it would be a cardinal sin, especially with all the work she put into it.

"Good. I'm kicking you out now. Go to the doctor. Make

sure you stop by or call me after the appointment."

"Of course, I will. I miss you always and forever, plus a day. I love you with all my heart, Ariel."

"You're so sweet, love." Her smile and jade gaze worth more than any amount of money, picture, and in my case, more than life, chilled my being. "I love you, Nico. *Mi amour.*" She soothed and completed me, epitomizing all that was good with a sensual flair no one could emote, except Miss Turquoise.

We laid the linen over the portrait with care. I departed not long after with the frame in hand. On the steps, an idea popped into mind. Rather than hanging it on my wall, I'd gift to someone special. I hope they'd accept it when the proper time arrived.

CH 16

I propped the portrait against my thighs and leaned, shading my eyes with a hand, staring at the high-rise diagonal to Ariel's place. Heaven's Parlor, its official name, but to most, Cremation Row. The locale depreciated the rents and values of the homes nearby because people didn't want to live near the dead. She loved it, even deriving inspiration from their souls, or as she put it, their aura will flow through my art. I never expected to visit a death processing plant, but here I am with reality stating otherwise, about to discuss the options for my upcoming expulsion from Earth.

Kominsky Funeral Services, who owned Heaven's Parlor, had multiple locations across the country, soon to be global. The company flourished, addressing the lack of green space for burials. I entered the facility through an automatic, sliding door tinted like night. Behind glazed glass, an obscured desk attendant welcomed me with a robotic voice. They advised I sign in at the computer kiosk behind me and wait to be called. I shuffled to the corner, using the portrait like a cane, and entered all my information into the machine, including cause of death. I sat within the cavernous waiting room on the sole red sofa. Centered and hovering below the mosaic ceiling, a transparent clock with no hands to tell time. Sitting, I pondered how they constructed the intricate illusion, hoping an invisible thread existed. If not, I'd stepped into the Twilight Zone, and Heaven's Parlor, a black magic sanatorium.

After several minutes, a man burst through a concealed

door just to the right of the front desk. Startled, I kicked the portrait resting against my leg. He took two long strides forward, the fluorescent lights casting shadows against the white walls showcased his large stature, his suit jacket stretching its buttons. Slicked, ebony hair lathered with oil matched his pronounced goatee and dark aviators covering his eyes.

"Hello. Thank you for coming. My name Yuri Kominsky. What can I do for you?" His dispassionate Slavic accent like molasses on the consonants.

"Hi. I'd like to have a tour of the facility to weigh my options."

"Come with me," he said, nodding. "When is your time expiring?"

"At some point in the near future. May I leave the portrait in the lobby?"

"Yes."

"Is it safe? It's important to me."

"Yes. No one else arriving today and no one comes here to steal. They come here to die. Follow me."

A few steps ahead, he bulldozed through a set of white double-doors that opened into a short, dim hallway with three elevators, each labeled red, yellow, and blue. Red arrived first, grinding to a halt and we proceeded. Once inside, he scanned me top to bottom and grunted, then selected its only option, B for basement. We didn't utter a word to each other as the elevator thrummed and squealed to the catacombs. It shuddered open to a dark passage with damp, cement walls emitting a repugnant must, strangling me. I couldn't take another pill. Traipsing behind, I debated if I erred selecting this dreadful location to handle my remains. I sought an exit to somewhere, anywhere, worrying he wouldn't release me from this dungeon.

He interrupted my thoughts with a thunderous clap and bellow. "We are almost there. Much cleaner. I promise."

We came upon a metal door with locks like Fort Knox. He retrieved a large set of keys from his pocket and unlocked each one without fumbling a single slot. It clanged open and revealed a well-lit room as big as a small grocer, but no pasta or potato chips on sale here. Caskets filled every inch of the space, showcased like cars at a dealership. Awed, I stumbled, never contemplating so many in one place, not even in a horror movie.

"Lucky, you did not fall. If so, we bury you today." I didn't reciprocate his haughty laugh. "No humor from man? Anyway, these are your options," he said, fanning his jeweled hand towards the glistening boxes.

"There are so many. Where do we start?" I said, still stunned by the vast display.

"Anywhere you like, but let me give you advice." I nodded with anticipation. "Do not come to buy Ferrari, if you only have money for Volkswagen."

"I understand." Although disheartened by his statement, I had no alternative but to continue. "Alright. It's now or never. Let's browse." We commenced down the aisles, he leading. "How much is the silver one?"

"Not silver," he said with condescension. "Platinum. Six figures."

"Oh, well, how about the bright blue one?"

"That one is made from airplane aluminum." He

removed his shades, exposing beady eyes with intimidating black pupils that quivered. "These part of new production line. Mid to high, five figures. You will be in casket. You will float like air. A lot of people like this model. Like flying big Cadillac."

"But, I'll be buried and dead. How will I be able to enjoy the aeronautical bliss?"

"You will enjoy it. Trust me. I do not lie. Everyone like it. Let's go. Keep walking."

"Okay." I shrugged and followed.

"We need find you something to fit *your* lifestyle."

"What's that supposed to mean?"

"I am sorry. Let me clarify." He pointed at my pocket. "Something to fit in your wallet."

"I don't carry one."

"Well, that could be problem, sir. Also prove point."

He led me down another aisle where the coffins dulled. "How about the brown and tan ones?"

"Better. Those are less expensive. Perhaps more with your reach. Brown is wood, low five figures. Tan is composite wood, a bit lower price, four figures. All come with variety of colors. We have some on floor and others we special order for you with catalog."

I approached the least expensive model and looked into the head panel, then prodded its soft interior and fluffed the pillow. To my amazement, its plushness exceeded any bed in which I had ever slept. He wasn't kidding. A nap in any of these models must be like sleeping on a cloud.

"What do they use to line these coffins?"

"The most expensive cashmere, then velvet. Cheaper model, suede or velour. They are stuffed with Eider Down, foam, cotton, wool, or horsehair."

"Impressive. I should've bought one for my bedroom twenty, thirty years ago. On that note, maybe you can explain something to me, so I can understand. Do you mind?"

"No. Go ahead. Ask away." He smiled, dabbing his fingers atop several strands of hair escaping from the over-applied pomade.

"I purchase a coffin and—"

"Casket, sir. Please."

"Okay…," I said, befuddled. "A *casket*, and, then you put me in the most comfortable interior I've ever experienced for thousands of dollars?"

"Yes, sir."

"And, I can't enjoy it, or use it, because I'll be dead. What's the point of selling these things, or, for that matter, you being in business at all?"

"You enjoy it. I promise. We sell thousands a year. Millions of people buried everyday across world. Trust me." He picked up a pillow and brushed it, then curled his fingers to his lips and blew a kiss.

"But, I literally will be dead. No pulse. No brain. Dead. And to top it all off, you suck all the blood out of me and replace it with embalming fluid. How can I enjoy the luxury of this… casket?"

"You will love comfort inside. Beautiful place to rest until second coming. Or, maybe third coming, if you are lucky."

"Okay, so if there's a second or third coming, how will I survive with no organs and embalming fluid for blood?"

"The master will take care of all." He pointed towards the ceiling. "Like magic."

"For *chrissake*. You're worse than a snake oil salesman. At least if I buy from them I can use it. What are my other options?"

"Sir, do not be rude. You have to die, must die. We all die."

My chest tightened and shoulders flared. Grimacing, I spun and inserted two pills into my mouth without him noticing.

"Sir, you will be okay?" he said, patting my back.

Damnit, he noticed. "Yes." The pain lessened a tad, allowing me to continue. "Options, please."

"We cremate you for couple thousand and place you in urn for few more dollars. We have several floors dedicated to them. Let us go. I show you. It is new, how do you say... rave."

I coughed. "Really? I pay you to burn me, then pay you to store my powder?"

"It is more than that. You will see soon."

We returned to the main elevators and rode the yellow to the eleventh floor. A much smoother ride than the red to the basement. We didn't exchange a word, instead dubious glances. The door opened to an expansive hallway. The walls and floors covered in white marble splotched with black veins. Rays of light refracted through the windows, bouncing from the polished stone, forming a plethora of rainbows edging the ceiling.

"Do you like? Me, I love," he said with pride.

"It's nice. It'd be beautiful if everyone wasn't dead." I snorted, which he didn't find amusing.

"Let us walk. All urns on each of the floors are encased in glass. We then place on bronze pedestal." He craned his head at one of the burn victims. "Very beautiful. The sun warm them almost every day."

"I don't think they need more sun. They're pretty charred already."

"Tone, sir. Respect the dead."

"Fine. Yes. It's a nice place. The music is pretty cool."

"We put on shuffle for you. You pick selection to play before you die."

"I find that more impressive than the urns. Well, if I were to sign up, how does this all work?"

"We cremate you, of course, place you in urn you pick, then you rest in beautiful, climate-controlled, private booth forever."

"Cost, please?"

"We charge monthly maintenance fee based on size of urn. Average two hundred per month. You have option to rent or purchase enclosure. The former also two hundred per month. Our special, today, just for you on purchase, save you boatload of dollars. I mean... casket-full. If you pay cash upfront, forty-eight thousand. If you take urn home, then free, other than charges for cremation and urn, plus few miscellaneous processing fees."

"I can't take it home. I'll be burnt into ash."

"You will have to find someone to take home unless you decide one of options we discuss. They *are* really beautiful enclosures. Glass and Plexiglas with window view overlooking city. And, don't forget music and dusting service included."

"You're still trying to sell me something I won't be able to enjoy. Hence, the whole death thing. Do I have any other options?"

"Unfortunately, no. Burial or burning at residence is

illegal, so whomever does deed will be prosecuted. Maybe someone can throw you in river, but I do not recommend."

"Oh, for *chrissake*. Even when you're dead you're not free."

"At least you can rest."

"Just stop. Let's go do the paperwork for a burn and rental with the option to take home."

"No problem. We skip blue elevator. That area more expensive because it involves casket storage in luxurious mausoleums. Follow me to office."

As we shambled the hallway I continued to prod. "And what happens if the dead me defaults on the rental?"

"Great question. We contact your family for payment. They have choice to keep paying, go into default, and have credit tarnished, or they can terminate your stay."

"What happens to the dead me?"

"Your family take you or we dispose you. We place you in river or ground if you have not defaulted. If you end stay in default, then we send remains to garbage dump. Both options incur minimal charge equal to one month's rent. It is like renting apartment. First month, last month, plus charge for cleanup. As bonus for you today, I will ignore credit check. You can send me music selection by email."

"Okay. Ariel will take me, if I don't pay. We'll figure it out. Let's finish this."

"Good. *Dobre. Yy robysh chudovyy vybir. Do skoroyi zustrichi.*"

Life summed up by the rules of a funeral home. Speechless, I followed him into his mammoth office. The mauve walls blanketed with paintings probably valued in the thousands, juxtaposed by lavish Art Deco furniture. He plopped into a leather chair behind an oak desk thicker than a wall and glossed like a new car, retrieving a contract from the rearward metal cabinet labelled "low-end" and slid it between us. I flipped through well over fifty pages, which included more disclaimers than a divorce. I listed Ariel as the guarantor and hoped she'd pay for my remains when the funds expired. He wished me a good day. I didn't respond, storming from his office with my strongest stride. I snagged the portrait and crashed into the automatic glass doors, almost shattering my shoulder. I'm sure if the glass had broken, he would've charged me triple for the damage.

GIANNI FRANCO

CH 17

Lugging the portrait a feat at this stage of the journey. Twenty blocks and two shortcuts brought me to 420 Claybourne Road, the picture frame straining the arms like a sixty-pound dumbbell. I'd made it to visit with *Zio* Agostino on my father's side. The shoddy, small home vexed the human spirit. Swaying upon his rocking chair on the porch with a drink in hand, the rotting slats below teetered with him in unison, somehow refusing to buckle after years of pressure. The stoop fit two chairs, his included, and an oversized bucket for a table, which held two ashtrays, his lighter, and an unmarked bottle of clear liquid. I navigated the steps with care, hoping not to chisel another concrete chunk loose, adding to the exposed layers of rusted rebar and metal mesh.

"Nico. Nico. My nephew, Nico," he warbled with a strong Italian accent, accentuating each vowel. The hooch, he always referred to as the water from the gods, had given him the power to sing today, although out of operatic tune.

I leaned the portrait against the adjacent wall and sat on a padded, vintage, folding chair. Adjusting the seat, one of the legs slipped between the planks, gouging a piece of the damp, unpainted wood, almost sending me to the muck beneath. I realigned and steadied myself.

"How's the water, *Zio* Agostino?"

"Good. Very good. Do you want a sip, *o* two, *o* three?" His laughter carefree and resonant. He twirled the red, plastic cup in the air, then zipped it to his lips for a sip.

"Oh, *Zio*. Is it vodka or grappa today?"

"Come, have a taste. *Un poco. Non ti fa male.*"

He stretched his arm towards me. A hint of wine confirmed grappa. He tilted it, allowing me just enough of a sip to fill my bottom lip. It scorched a path to my stomach, then rose like an atomic bomb, clearing my sinuses and eardrums. Perhaps a ruse, but my heart even seemed to reset itself. I wondered if my predicament could've been prevented had I consumed this elixir instead of the others during my lifetime.

His wizened face formed a curious smile while his bloodshot eyes met mine. "I have weaker stuff. There... next the ice bucket." He pointed at the floor behind him.

"Maybe in a bit," I said, fanning my face and wincing, hoping for the burning to stop. "Water might be a better option for now."

"Be my guest. Inside. Go. Go. *Bello nipoto*. You are so welcome." He swung his arm towards the door with cup in hand.

"Thanks. In a second. So how are you, *Zio*?"

"I'm good. What'd I tell you? Don't call me uncle. We too old for that. Agostino or Augie as the Americans say. I told you many times when we reach a certain age no need for fancy titles."

"Okay. I'm just so used to it."

"Oh, Nico. It's not good. Don't do that." He paused, then brushed his stubble as white as chalk. "Just like me. I change from grappa to vodka and vodka to grappa, sometime whiskey and wine too. Everything need change. For better *o* for worse."

"I've always loved your outlooks on life."

He nodded. "*Compa*. Look my beautiful garden." The

dedicated section filled most of the front yard with an array of vegetables and flowers, abutting a tall fence curling with vines. "Those plants, they change all the time. They produce, then die, then produce, then do it over and over. Without them and change, we all be dead."

"You should've been my papa."

My father, the stricter version of his brother. He handled most things with caution and rarely took any risks. Life's a journey and not a race he'd say. I wonder how he's going to handle knowing I've reached the finish line before him. I should've rushed to try everything in the short amount of time I had on this planet.

"He was like me. Sometime even more adventures than me." He gazed at sky.

"What happened, Agostino?"

"World War happened. *La guerra.* We were young. He a little older than me. Maybe ten when the war start and fifteen when it end. One day we kick the soccer ball in the street, next day, the bombs fall from the sky. The town erase. Destroy everything. The asphalt field we play broke in many pieces. The games we no play no more. Instead, we shovel pavement to clean road. Pile on pile, tall like houses. If we no clean, we no can walk for food and water.

"One particular depressing day, the sirens blare from morning to night. So many bombs and missiles big like cars fall from the sky. A piece of bomb hit the home of friend who kick the ball with us all the time. He die. Burn the whole family alive. *Peccato.* They never find the bodies, but I know it was him because we never play again. We explore the home many months later when the fire finally extinguish. I find little skull with some hair still sticking. I start to shake, then cold all over my body like when you see ghost. I didn't know what to—" He shuddered, his rosy cheeks paled, sipping from the cup with a trembling hand. "Anyway… me and your father run so fast our feet could not catch our bodies. We slip and fall several times on our way home, locking ourselves inside bedroom, hoping and praying for no more missiles. No more death. Unfortunately, the bombs no stop for another five year. I never forget Rocco, and neither will your dad." He wiped his eyes with the back of his hand and gulped the liquor. "Your dad wants each day to last. He very careful and try to make the most because he no know when they end. I am opposite. Reckless, maybe little crazy. I want everything possible before everything end. Rocco Caruso change the way we look at life forever. Who knows?" He shrugged with a chuckle. "If war never happen, maybe I be like your father and he like me."

"Papa never told me that story."

"He doesn't like to speak about the past. Italians are like that. We very complicated people. I learned be different when I come to America. Several girlfriends and a couple ex-wifes teach me how to open up. To talk."

"That's what Papa needed. More experiences. Instead, he settled."

"Well, he take safe road, Nico. He have experience, just different one. You no blame him for doing what he did."

"Look where it got him. It's just pointless. I like the way you did it."

"Sometimes the safe way is not always best, and sometimes it is the best. Either one, does not mean they wrong." He raised the cup. "*Cincin* to your papa and me. We still end up in the same place like everyone else, getting old and waiting for the end to come. Well, enough about us. You never show up for no reason. *Che ti porto qua* today?"

"It's complicated. I'd rather talk about you and Papa for now."

"What else you want to know?"

"For starters, pour me a smidge of that clear gasoline. I still haven't figured out how you drink it like water."

I flinched at the thought of his full, plastic chalice. From a sleeve stacked beside the cooler at his feet, he flipped one onto the bucket and dropped in two ice cubes.

"Lots of practice to numb my tongue. Tell me when to stop."

I waved for him to stop before he even tipped the bottle. "Too much. *Basta*," I barked. He ignored my instructions, filling it to the rim.

"Don't worry. I finish what you can't," he said, laughing, then drank. "What else you want to know? Ask me anything, but not too much. The grape juice start catching me. And, I don't want to write book with you."

"Did you ever have kids?"

"Come on, Nico. You know I no have any."

"I mean ones you might not know about," I said, chortling.

"I don't think my ex-girlfriends or wifes would do that to me."

"What if they were trying to protect you?"

"Protect me from my kids? Why would they do that to me?"

"I don't know. Just wondering."

"Nico," he said with a steeled face. "I never been violent or do anything bad enough to have them hide baby from me."

"I didn't mean to insinuate or presume."

"Then, what, why the questions? Come on, Nico. *Ti amo.* Tell me anything."

"Don't tell Ma or Papa. Well, I've been told, I, we, had a kid. Have a kid. She didn't want to tell me back then. He's obviously an adult now."

He coughed up the grappa, the contents from the swaying cup dribbling onto his hand.

"Amazing. *Olé.* You must be so excited. You're a papa and we added someone new to the family. Your dad going to be so happy. Did you tell him?"

"Not yet. I don't know if I should."

"Of course you have to. He wants to know, especially since he is old. Hell, we all getting old and time for new things is almost gone."

"There's more to the story. I don't think I should tell you that part."

I looked at the cup upon the bucket, debating if a sip would loosen me up to tell him or choke me into fainting.

"You need to tell me. I'm your *zio*, but I treat you like son because you no have brother or sister. You have to tell me because I respect you. You need to respect me. Who save you all the times when you get in trouble and too afraid to call your papa?" His prior cheerfulness replaced with a demanding gaze and scrunching brow.

"You did."

"You wake me all the time crying on phone because you lose a girl. *O*, when you too drunk to make sense, I sit and listen. Who always there to give advice at any hour of the night?"

"You, Agostino."

"*Coretto*. Then, I deserve to know everything."

"You're not going to like any of it."

"My job is to listen, not judge, just like before." He refilled his glass and waved to continue. "*Provami*. Try me, Nico."

"Fine, you've been warned." I paused, then trickled some grappa onto my tongue. Much to my surprise, a cough didn't arise. I straightened my shoulders and firmed myself upon the chair. "Well, do you remember Beatrice?"

"Yeah. Your first girlfriend. You come to my house crazy the same night you lose your virgin with her. Day of innocence. *I giorni dell'innocenza svaniscono come stelle*," he said, shaking his head with yearning eyes.

"I remember. Let's not talk about that part," I said with a bashful smirk. "So… on one of the non-virgin nights I got her pregnant. She never told me and ended our relationship. I went to visit her yesterday. She explained we have a child."

"What the heck… Did you do something to her? Are you joking? What happen?" he said, befuddled.

"No way. We had our arguments but we never got physical. Once, I think she shoved me and I tried to shove her but missed because I was drunk. She was drunk too."

"I told you about that kind of stuff. Don't ever raise your hands to hurt someone or you will be in trouble."

"But Dad—I mean Agostino. I didn't do anything. I cared more for her than anyone else in the world. She was supposed to be my soulmate and here I am. She lied about our kid." I lowered my head and lifted the glass, lapping the rim for a hint of liquor. Anything more might kill me.

"Maybe the shove *o* maybe something else. You have to understand a few things in life, Nico. You always look at the way the other person see it?"

"Okay. I understand."

"You never know what it can be that make someone mad. You always look at someone perspective. *La prospettiva.* But what is in the past has passed, so we must move forward. We can always improve our lives until we are dead. Have you met him? Did she give you contact information?"

"She gave me his address. I've been a few times, but no one answered. He's probably busy with life and not worrying about someone he doesn't know. I'll keep trying until I can longer try. That's the story."

"What's his name?"

"Alessio Nicola Russo." I smiled like a father in the birthing wing of a hospital. "I was thinking, with all due respect, if she hated me that much, she wouldn't have given him my name."

"Only middle name." He sighed, then puckered his lips. "But… I agree with you. She give you that much. Maybe whatever happened was not that bad. Just the twists and turns of life. You need meet him very soon no matter what. You have mission."

"I promise that's what I'm doing. There will come a time when I can't chase him anymore. I hope I can find him before that happens."

"He probably busy, but I know you meet him and everything will be *perfetto.* He will hug and love you. You will see. You be there for each other like nothing be missed."

"I think that's easier said than done. Time is always against me, us. I'll do my best."

"I know you been sick before, but you okay now. You not… dy—"

"No. It'll be okay. I just hope I have time because you never know what the future holds."

Good thing Ma didn't get along with him or she would've called him to gossip about my sickness. I lacked the courage to tell him, not wanting to hurt or stress him at his age. My demise certain to create a whirlwind of negativity within his heart and mind. He invested more in my life than my parents had. The late-night calls the tip of the iceberg. He filled the void when my friends weren't around, providing reprieve during family arguments. At one point, handing me a set of keys to his home and setting up a spare room complete with a bed and television.

"It better be okay because I no want to know what I do if something happen to you."

"Don't worry. All is well." I found a lull to situate my escape or he'd continue to prod and I wouldn't be able to keep lying. "I don't mean to cut this short, but I need to get moving. I have a couple more stops to make. Hopefully, Alessio will be one of them."

I rose from the chair and latched onto the portrait's frame.

"I want to ask before. What is under the cloth? Are you going to tell me *o* do I beg?"

"It's a painting. Ariel, my girlfriend, gave it to me today."

"That's so nice of her. She a great woman. What's it about?"

"Me," I said with a timorous voice.

"Show me, Nico."

"I'm not so sure. It's personal."

"Come on. You have to show now that you tell."

"Alright." He deserved to see it. I leaned it against the wall and pinched the linen at the edges, revealing the portrait. "Hope you like it."

He perused the painting in silence for over a minute, nerving me. "It's beautiful. *Bello*. She show *le anima di te*. How she do it?"

"Thank you. Her artistic talent is beyond me. She painted me from a picture she stole from one of my photo albums and surprised me today. I haven't decided what to do with it, but I have an idea or two."

"Well, you can always give it to me. I will honor it, and you, until my last breath."

"I'll keep you in mind. I promise."

"Good enough for me, Nico. I know another person who want it and I don't think he say no."

"Papa?"

"Yes, of course. One hundred percent he hang on his wall. Maybe ride around in his car." He roared with laughter, then followed with a hacking cough.

Covering the portrait, I nodded and slid the grappa towards him. He raised a thumb and poured most of it into his cup. I staggered the crumbling steps and crossed the yard, admiring the radiant colors from the azaleas, tomatoes, zucchini, tulips, marigolds, peppers, and many more. From the sidewalk, I turned and waved. He lifted his drink and returned the motion with his empty hand, smiling with firm lips, cheeks struggling to rise.

CH 18

Lackadaisical with lethargic limbs, I wandered a few blocks debating on who or what to visit next. An idea dawned, not my best, but nonetheless, one which needed tending. Connor Doyle, known to most in the neighborhood as the crimson bandit, needed to be confronted. Other names were thrown around as well, but those were filled with vulgarities. Some suggested he was given the nickname because he was always caught red-handed. They were wrong. It had all to do with his tapered goatee that stretched to his collarbone. He may have dyed it because it didn't match his blonde locks, which he wore like a military man minus the experience. As a child, he boasted about his German and Scottish descent, and one day, out of the blue, claimed neither of those existed, and replaced them with Austrian. I think the sudden change had more to do with his enthrallment for evil leaders from world wars than anything else. We were classmates during grammar school, then acquaintances. Ravi and Felipe loathed him, but I pitied him.

He loved drinking and drugging, which inevitably drove him down a dark path with a rap sheet as long as a roll of toilet paper. A few weeks ago at Nacca's Deli, I overheard one of his many enemies talking about his release from prison and new mandatory home. He'd served three years out of six for grand larceny and assault. Today, I hoped to resolve an issue that occurred decades ago, uncertain if he'd be interested or even sober enough to listen or remember.

A wrought iron fence, ornamented with piercing spades, some missing and some new, surrounded the property. An unmanned gate sagged on its hinges, leaving a valley of mud and pebbles at its base from all the swings it had endured. I leaned against its rough edge, gazing at the elms and maples sprawling the courtyard. Beyond their blooming branches, a dilapidated four-story mansion, once known as The Palisades, a popular rental destination. The City converted the home on Elmwood Avenue and renamed it the Thompson Halfway House, a communal rehab for those in need. I staggered atop the checkerboard walkway, balancing the portrait between my hands, avoiding the deep craters created by missing stones.

I tugged at the handle, but it didn't budge. Peering through the window, two, armed guards stood erect, one at each side of the front desk. The tallest, resembling a modern-day Frankenstein, pointed at me, then the adjoining wall. I raised my hands and shrugged. He retorted with disgust chiseled onto his face and both fists in the air. Then, just above my right shoulder, a squeal and crackle. I flinched.

"Are you checking in?" said a hollow, mechanical voice. I attempted miming, hoping he'd understand. "Please... push the yellow button and speak into the panel. We don't do hand signals here."

I did as told. "No. I'm visiting someone."

"Do you have an appointment?"

"No. But—" I began to state my case, only to be interrupted.

"I can't let you in. Call and make an appointment."

"But, sir. I'm sick. Look at me. I know you can see. I know you can't be that dumb. I'm not here to cause any trouble. I just want to make amends or be amended."

"I can't. I'm sorry."

"Sir. I don't have much time to live. Please." He dipped behind the front desk as I continued. I couldn't just walk away. This needed to be done today. "Sir, I'm dying. I've walked all this way for resolve. Please, let me in," I said, dispirited.

He reappeared, the monotone voice screeching through the speaker. "Okay. You can come in."

The door buzzed and the lock clacked. I lurched forward, pulling the handle, but it snagged. Stepping back, I glimpsed the guards laughing and signaling. I charged the door and banged the window. The buzzing arrived once more, then ceased, then restarted as if playing an inharmonic song. Scowling at them, I whacked the glass with a fist and tried again. This time it opened. I sighed and stammered up the steps leading to the foyer, balancing my body against the handrail. Neither guard motioned forward, their hands steady on holstered guns. Approaching the front desk, I surrendered with one hand while the other secured the picture. A stout incarnation of Igor stood to the left, and his pal Frankenstein, who approved my advance, spied from the opposite side with a devious grin. A young woman, entering data and flipping through loose pages upon her desk, squinted. I acknowledged with an innocuous smile. She tilted her head towards the clipboard at the corner and blinked.

"Who are you here to see?" she demanded with a New York City twang.

"Connor—Connor Doyle," I said with hesitation.

She looked me over, then exhaled. "Sign in," she said, flipping her ironed, dark hair from her full face and striking nose. "If you have any doubts, then you shouldn't be here."

"I have to be here," I said, quivering while printing and signing my name on the form. I eyed her tiny nametag. "Maryanne."

"Good, then you should understand the process. Barry, go get Connor. Third floor. Room 301. If you have any problems, radio down to Gary," she demanded. He acknowledged with a wave and tromped up the stairs. Maryanne returned to her files, smacking her lips on a fresh piece of gum as Gary sized me up.

Connor, who I didn't recognize and assumed to be him, walked ahead of Barry, guided by a firm shoulder grip on his slouching shoulders. Disheveled reddish hair replaced the youthful blonde cropping a swollen face etched with scars. An untamed goatee brushed the collar of a torn t-shirt, two sizes too small, stretching around a bulging waist. An array of tattoos, bright and blackened, covered his arms and chest with a blue teardrop under his left eye.

"Here he is," the guard groused, nudging Connor against the edge of the front desk.

Maryanne jotted onto paper, then looked up. "Did he give you any problems?"

"If he would've, he wouldn't be here." He tapped the butt of the holstered gun.

"If the two of you want privacy, you can go into the next room," she said, directing us towards a short hallway.

"Thanks. Can I leave the portrait at your desk for a few minutes?"

"Yeah. Sure. I don't think any of us want what you're hiding under there anyway."

I extended my hand towards Connor. "How's it going, man?"

He didn't reciprocate, trudging towards the room like he wore cement soles. I followed. We sat across from each other on pink, plastic chairs with a matching table, splotched with frayed bumper stickers.

"Why are you here? We're not friends," he said with intense eyes.

"Yeah. That's true. It's been many years. Something's happened and I want to clarify a few things with you."

"Really, man? I don't need any of this crap right now, you damn dago. I just got paroled. Isn't that good enough for you?" He furrowed his brow, then centered his fists upon the table.

"Look, I'm not here to brawl and no need for name calling. As you can see I don't look well."

"Whatever, wop." He proceeded to crack each knuckle on both hands, then ran his fingers through his hair. "Fine. Go ahead. But I don't have all day. I'm tired." The dark circles under his eyes confirming the admission.

"One day, when we were younger, you came to my parent's house. My Ma made lasagna. After eating, we went to my room. My eyes were heavy from all the food. As I fell asleep, I watched you creep into the hallway."

"So what? I probably went to the bathroom. You came all this way for nothing, dummy dago."

"No," I exclaimed. "You stole over a thousand dollars and a gold chain with a diamond-encrusted cross from my parent's bedroom. You avoided me for months after that day. In fact, you disappeared."

"Big deal. I don't even know what you're talking about."

"It is because I was blamed. The necklace was an heirloom, handmade over five generations ago." I dug into my pocket and cupped two pills into my mouth. "You hurt me, my family. Why did you steal after all my parents did for you?"

"Get out of here." He motioned for me to leave. "I didn't do it. Anyway, you can't prove a damn thing," he said with a knavish grin.

"I'm not going anywhere. You know as well as I that's not true. No one else was in the house. You stole from me, from us. I even received beatings for your actions. They lasted weeks. My Ma still hasn't forgiven me."

"Fine. You caught me, dago Nico." He sniggered and raised his hands. "It probably was smelted or went to the pawn shop. What's it matter now? No one cares. Things are made to be taken in my world. If I didn't steal it, someone else would have."

"Dammit. For all these years it's bothered me. I need to know why." I growled, slamming my palms against the table, gasping for breath while my heart hammered the skin.

He sat still for a moment, then heaved a deep sigh towards the ceiling. "What did you expect from me? You didn't have my life. You wouldn't understand."

"Try me, Connor. Do me this one favor and repent for at least one of your wrongs."

He searched the room, then kicked the table. I winced. He lowered his head and mumbled, "Will you get the hell out of here, if I tell you?"

"Yes," I said, relieved, assuming he was going to strike me with a left hook to the jaw.

"Fine," he exclaimed. "My home wasn't perfect like

yours. My Mom and Dad were drunks, then there was the abuse. I was on my own since I can remember. I needed the money and the jewelry was a bonus. They paid me well in hock. Are you satisfied?"

"You could've stole from someone else."

"You were an easy target."

"No, we were not. I want to know why you needed the money, my money."

"To feed myself. To score some dope. To escape the hell within my house. I've stolen from many people, so don't take it personal. It's what happens when you get the raw end of the deal. Lying is better than facing the truth most times. Now, are you satisfied?"

I pondered his response that lacked an apology, yet I couldn't fault him, but he did have the power of choice. "Yes, and you still have time to change."

"I don't want to change. Besides, you just don't wake up one day and it's all different. Have you noticed where I live? No jobs, girlfriends, or successes come from a halfway house, let alone a criminal record. Wish I'd never been born. My life was over before it began."

"Excuses don't excuse you for being a piece of human crap."

"Of course they do. Anyway... speaking about life being over." He surveyed me and puckered his lips. "Considering your paleness, you probably don't have too much longer either."

"Is doctor part of your resume as well?" I said with sarcasm.

"No, but you learn plenty in the joint. Watched people die from AIDS to cancer and everything between. You, my friend, don't have too long."

"Whatever. Let's end this. I've had enough." I offered a handshake, which he pushed away. "Suit yourself. Since you aren't dying, you should give going straight a shot."

"Look, man. I didn't ask you to come here. I don't want anything from you. I hope you find whatever it is you're looking for before you die. I'm not it. When you walk out that door, I'm not going to think about you. In fact, I've never thought about you. I have my life and you have yours. Our paths crossed only for a few blips in the universe of life. Now, be on your way dago. You've stressed me out. I need to get some rest."

He bolted from the chair and rushed out of the room. Disconcerted, I sat like a statue, contemplating our encounter. Logic existed in his statements, but the condemnation he thrust upon me undeserving. I capitulated and shambled to the front desk. The guards standing stern observed my every move, oblivious to the yells and grunts coming from Connor as he stomped up the stairs.

"Things didn't go as you planned?" Maryanne scoffed.

"When do they ever?" I wanted to tell her to shut up and mind her business, but those guards, itching for a fight, would crush me.

"Seems like never in your case."

"Whatever. Sometimes comments are best kept to oneself," I said, dismayed, then nodded.

"Hey, Nico. If it's any consolation, some criminals like to stay in the misery lane. It's not your fault."

"Thanks. How did you..." She pointed to the form I signed, confirming where she got my name.

"Your portrait's all safe. Have a great rest of your day."

"You as well." I shuffled through the exit. "And you two goons need to relax," I mumbled. They didn't hear me because they didn't give chase.

CH 19

As I crossed the avenue my legs filled with heat, melting my feet into my boots. Shuffling, a rolling wave like stabs from hot pokers rose and fell along my shins. Raising my slacks to the knee revealed purple balloons stippled red on each leg. Stunned like I'd been punched in the gut, I seesawed between my heels and tiptoes, then gravity showcased its strength, forcing me forward. If not for luck and a bit of quick-thinking, I would've fallen flat on my face. The sturdy, oak frame of the portrait had saved me, wedging itself across my collarbone. Its pain less than the others vacationing throughout my body. The realization about my health, which I had ignored for years, roared into my mind like a freight train. I should've heeded the doctor and not skipped all the appointments, but then again, sulking at home or in a hospital room would be worse. Trudging to the remaining destinations an impossible feat in this condition. Pouting, I finessed the portrait onto my palms, then inched my way down for a seat upon the curb, hoping a few minutes rest could provide rejuvenation. The wish short-lived as the aches and burning returned. I swallowed another set of pills, but they had minimal effect. I lowered my head between my knees and sobbed. So much to accomplish with a body who no longer cared about my goals.

A rumbling engine shuddered my sternum as it parked a few feet away. Someone must've called a fire truck or ambulance to pick up the decaying slab of meat taking up space on the street. I cleared my eyes with a sleeve to gather a better view. A black and white checkerboard on a yellow backdrop came into focus, All Day Taxi.

A man shouted something unintelligible from the passenger window. I nodded with indifference, too tired to provide anything additional, but I don't think he noticed. Before my next thought could process, he stood beside me, tapping my back.

"Buddy, you don't look well." His accent comforting but unrecognizable to my fatigued mind. "Are you going be okay?"

"To be honest." I dried the remaining drops from my cheeks with the back of my hand. "I don't think so." My chest stiffened. "One second." Infuriated with my condition, I collected another set of pills and threw them into my mouth, crunching them with one bite.

"Come on, buddy. Don't say that. You be fine. I help you. Give me hand," he said, surveying me.

I struggled extending it. "Ready?" I said with more doubt than certainty. His hands, soft and cool, slid around my wrists and heaved me upwards. I staggered to find footing, using my weight against his arms. "Thank you, sir. I'm not going to be okay, but I appreciate the help. My body no longer wants me."

"That very funny, buddy. We must do the best we can," he looked up to the sky, "with the will from above."

"I suppose, but it's bad for me. Anyway, my name is Nicola Romano. Most people call me Nico."

"Pleasure to meet you. I am Abdi Amir. Are you Italian?"

"Yes, from Celano in the Abruzzi region. And you?"

"Somalia. Italian one of our languages during war and after. I like to think Somalians and Italians are almost same. We go back many centuries."

"Really? I guess you learn something new every day as long as you're alive."

"What happening to you, buddy? Maybe I help."

He glared at the road. The passing cars honked, some screeching their tires, one almost slamming the rear bumper and sideswiping the driver door. He gestured several vulgarities. A few drivers and even passengers bellowed out the windows to move the car. He ignored all requests, more concerned with my situation.

"There's nothing you can do for me, my friend. I'm dying. Go. Go on with your life. I don't have much time. I've been visiting people around the neighborhood before it's all over. I just met with someone at the halfway house who wronged me and my family." I pointed to the shelter. "And, when I exited my body quit. I don't know how I'm going to finish seeing the rest of the people."

"Is that why you were crying?"

"Yes. Not only has my body become my enemy, but so has time."

"I help you."

"No. You have to work. Don't worry about me. It'll be fine. I'll figure something out."

I moved a few steps, hoping to acquire a stride to show off my good health, instead my knees buckled. He lunged towards me and forked my armpits with his hands, lifting and stabilizing me with his small but herculean frame.

"I will help. From Somalia to Italia, we are same. Human to human. Better to help someone who has less time than me. Work will be here tomorrow and day after. You okay to stand by yourself for few moments?"

"Yes."

"You certain?" he said with a quizzical face.

"I promise I'll do my best. I should be fine."

"You better be. Move body against frame of picture. Just couple minutes. I need call dispatch office. Tell them I cannot work."

"They'll fire you. Don't do it," I implored.

"It be okay. No worry. I'm best employee in Rochester."

"But, Abdi… I don't have any money."

He shooed me away without a response, dashing to the driver's side, and slamming the door shut. Balancing on my heels, hands crawling along the rear bumper, I searched for stability. From the open window, I overheard him speaking with the dispatcher. He explained a family emergency had arisen and wouldn't be able to make it in today and possibly tomorrow.

"We all set," he said, skirting the taillight and leaping towards me.

"I hope you're sure."

"Everything perfect. Now, come with me. Put your hand on my shoulder." He led me around the vehicle like a maimed cow. "Put body against fender. I open door."

"Okay, but I hope it opens wide enough for me to fit," I whispered.

"It is fine. See." He motioned with a satisfied smile. "I help you into backseat. Not a limousine, but better than rickshaw," he said with a chuckle.

"I bet the rickshaw holds more excitement."

"Yes. Yes. It does, but this one have air conditioning. It work perfect. Very smooth for the ride."

I slid onto the leather seat. It hugged my thighs and supported my back. The luxuries of owning a modern-day carriage.

"What kind of model is this car? Is it Ford?"

"Yes. Ford Crown Victoria. Comfortable. Plenty of room. You can sleep in backseat. So big."

"I like it. Good choice for a taxi."

"Yes. Yes. I put picture in trunk. And no worry, it is safe. I wrap with big blanket." Before hauling off, he lifted the cloth, and peeked. "Very beautiful art. Is it you?"

"Yes. A younger me who had many years to live." I reminisced with a sigh.

He shrugged. "Only thing we cannot control is age. Every day we older." He grabbed the frame and rushed to the trunk, situating it for a few minutes, then returned to his seat. "What you do with it?" he said, his gentle brown eyes meeting mine in the rearview.

"I've been weighing two options. I want to give it to my father, but now I'm thinking to bequeath it to my son."

"You have son, too?"

"Yes. I just found out. I'll meet him for the first time in my life, if I ever find him. I'm a little nervous. Do you have any children?"

"Yes. Yes," he said with excitement. "Two boys, Aaden, Erasto, one girl, Uba."

"Cool. I can see you love them."

"Yes. And, no matter what happen he love you too. You his father. You share special bond no one else does. Well, except the mother, her bond stronger, since she carry him for nine months and nurture him. Mothers always more important."

"We shall see, Abdi. I will do my best to meet him. With your help, it'll be easier. I've walked so many miles in the last two days that my body has given up. I keep taking pills the doctor gave me, but I think they're hurting me more than anything."

"I do whatever you need. If doctor say they are good for you, then you listen to him."

"I suppose you're right."

"Where do you want to go first?"

"To visit my grandparents. They live in a nursing home and are close to one hundred years old."

"That's amazing. Every year we live longer and longer. Someday we live two hundred years."

"I wish that was today," I said with a hint of futility.

"I understand, buddy." His eyes sank below the rearview.

"I promise I don't have many people remaining to visit."

"Whatever you want, buddy. I be here with you until the end if you need me."

"Thank you, Abdi."

"No, problem, Nico."

"You know, I'm somewhat spiritual but don't believe in any of that religious stuff. I do have to say it's pretty weird we found each other today. I still need to see people, especially my son, and without you, it'd be impossible. Very odd. Don't you think?"

"Easier to think it is odd, than realize it is not. Everything happen for reasons. Always. Something or someone control all." He glanced at the headliner, brushed it with a fingertip, then brought it to his lips.

"It's never been proven. How do you know?"

"Growing up in war teach me many lessons as child. Many people from my city, Kismayo, die, from disease or murder, every day around me, yet I survive. I should die a thousand times, but only injured three." He pointed to his chest and abdomen. "Metal from al-Shabaab bomb when I was ten, and the other from American bomb on thirteenth birthday. And today, with guidance from above, I live in America with family I could only dream about, giving them life with no war. I hope my children never suffer like me. The fact I survive and move forward with strength of a thousand men prove life is not under my control."

"What about those that died in your city?"

"What do you mean?"

"Did they mean any less because they died and you survived?"

"Quite the opposite. The plan from Allah already set for them. They accomplish things I could not before they depart this world. I must trust everything that come from above is good. If I doubt, I would not be here, today, helping you."

"I suppose you have a valid point. In either case, I'm glad I met you," I said, smiling with gratitude.

"Me as well. Enough about religion. You speak English very good," he said with amazement.

"Thank you. I studied many years, reading books and dictionaries. English is a difficult language. You speak well, too."

"I try best I can. I am still learning. Maybe one day I talk like you."

"As long as you have time, you can do anything, Abdi. Let's go visit my grandparents."

"Yes. Yes. What is the address?"

"1600 North Clinton Avenue. Living Hope. It's a new facility. The other closed due to more health violations than a rat commune."

Elysian Fields, at 2100 Saint Paul Street, should have been called Dante's Inferno for its deplorable conditions. Plastic sheathing, sopping with mold and precipitation from each of the four seasons, enclosed the outdoor walkway leading to the recreational area lined with disintegrating turf. They had occupied one of the dilapidated, ranch homes for more than a decade and vacated the premises less than a year ago because the City shut it down. My grandparents sought comfort in making a house a home, yet wallowed in a sty none of their own. Glad they moved, albeit by force.

"Shame, shame how they treat elders in America. In Kismayo, the children tend to the needs of the older people." He glowered in the rearview, shaking his head. "I hope mine will do same for me." I agreed with a subtle nod and wink, uncertain if he noticed my appreciation.

CH 20

We didn't exchange a word for the rest of the short ride, which would've taken over thirty minutes to walk. He alternated the faint music between compact disc and radio. The former, I assumed, a ditty from Somalia; the latter, the opening chords of "Patience" by Guns 'N' Roses. If only I could conjure that virtue. By the time the song ended, he pulled into a metered space in front of the tall building. He ignored the "No Standing" sign and turned on the hazard lights.

"Very nice place, Nico."

"Yes, much better than the other one."

"Will you wait for me?"

"Of course, buddy."

"How long?" I scooted forward and hung my arm over the passenger seat. "I don't want to take up all your time."

"I wait until you are done visiting your grandparents. Then, I take you to next stop. You let me know when you are finished."

"What about your family, your kids?"

"Do not worry. I call my wife and explain. She nice woman. She understand my new friend sick and need support. It be fine. I promise," he said with a boisterous voice and broad smile.

Relief replaced distress, and for once during the last day or so, I didn't need to place a pill between my cheek and gum. Jovial, I clapped his shoulder.

"Thank you, Abdi. I don't know how to repay you."

"No money, buddy. Repay me by being satisfied with the aspects of your life. Allah will take care of everything for us."

"Okay. Will the portrait be safe in your trunk?"

"Yes, yes. Don't worry. Go see family. Give them my regards."

Daunted by swollen limbs, I exited the taxi with care, slogging the paved path under gold and silver arches as tall as two stories. Blight nonexistent at this senior-living community with lavender, vanilla, and lilac soothing the airways. Mosaic floors with intricate circles, spirals, and various depictions of local landmarks guided the way to the counter. A sign reading "Welcome to Living Hope" was attached to the wall behind it in massive multicolored letters.

A guard, wearing a pressed suit and badge, scanned the area like an owl. Inside an elaborate oval kiosk, the concierges discussed the upcoming agendas while glancing at several large monitors, neither bothering to notice me, then the man abruptly broke from the conversation, stunning me. "How can I help you?"

"I'm here to visit my grandparents. Paola and Peter Porto."

"Did you schedule an appointment for your arrival?"

"No. Is this something new? Check your system. I'm on the approved list." Granted, I couldn't recall the last time I visited.

"In a moment I'll do that for you, sir. Your name first, please?" He adjusted his tie, then the keyboard ahead of him.

"Nicola Romano. Some call me Nico."

"I'm not interested in nicknames but thank you," he

said, his tone placing me in an interrogation room like those on television. "One moment while I scan the system."

I grunted and leaned against the desk, attempting to alleviate some of the stress upon my bloated and weakened legs. He didn't care much for my issues.

"Sir, please step away from the desk. You're shaking the cameras."

"How could this colossal construction even move?" Brooding, I narrowed my eyes towards his gold placard etched in calligraphy. I couldn't read the intricate design. It could've been his first, or last name, or maybe he just had one. I had no interest in asking, doubting he'd tell me anyway. "Mr. B—"

"The name is Braun, sir. And, I don't need an attitude today."

"I'm sorry... Braun."

He smirked, then continued. "Look, I'd let you in, but if I do it for you, I'll have to do it for everyone. I'm just following the rules, plus *they* watch me." He angled his head, twisting it towards the glass balls hanging from the ceiling. He switched from wannabe cop to conspiracy theorist with a blink of an eye. "*They* run this place tight. *They* don't want it shut down like the other places." He hushed me, then whispered, "*Big Brother* is on everyone's ass about these types of residences. You're welcomed to sit in the waiting area. We have comfortable leather chairs. Some recline."

"Every security guard must go to the same damn school in this city because you all have the same responses. Please, I don't have all day. I'm short on time. Can you do me a favor and just speed it up. Buzz me in. I've been here before. Shouldn't be too complicated."

"One moment, sir."

"Look at me, man." I attempted a lunge over the counter, but failed. "Do I look like someone coming in here to rob the place?"

"You do not, sir, but rules are rules. If we didn't have rules, then we wouldn't have that word."

I had no immediate response to his rambling. Even with not being born in this country, I knew he spewed gibberish. "Come on, man... Braun. I'm dying. I came to bid them farewell. Final goodbyes. Please, don't act this way towards me." Damn communities are almost as bad jail. Can't visit without permission and can't enter or leave without a pass.

He stroked his full beard and peeped the camera for a few moments. "Fine. If you're that sick, then go on ahead. Hope you feel better." He bowed his head and grinned, then called to the security guard. "Mitch—he's good to go." As I walked away he whispered, "I'm just following the rules. *They...*"

"Jerk. How am I going to feel better, if it's terminal?" His daftness deserved more ridicule, but I didn't have the time.

I hobbled to a set of four elevators, calling a car to take me to the third floor; the polished, gold doors distorting my already repulsive figure for worse. In the distance, an older woman, wearing pink pants and a flowered blouse spanning Ariel's paint spectrum, grinded her walker against the tiled floor, the tennis balls encasing the rear wheels shredded, each scrape echoing the hallway as she inched closer. I should've asked to borrow one from Doctor Gordon to help me trod all these miles. I turned away for a split second, and as I spun back, she stood beside me. She rounded her back and leaned forward, locking the front, rubber pegs into place, gripping the duct-tape handles tight. After my front desk experience, I wasn't in the mood to chat. She squashed my hope for silence.

"Well, hello… sweetie. What's your name?" She flicked her head, clearing the silver bangs from her eyes.

I rolled my neck, staring at the ceiling, hoping she'd stop.

"Sweetie… what's your name?" she said a few times, the redolent gin stronger with each request.

I surrendered to her pestering with a soft voice. "Nico."

"Did you say Johnny?" she squawked, then hissed. "My name is Susanna."

"Nico, *not* Johnny. Pleasure to meet you." I faked a smile, resting my shoulder against the floral wallpaper beside the elevator door.

"Johnny is such a nice name. What brings a young chap like yourself to this waiting-to-die facility?"

Correcting her served no purpose. "Well—" I processed her sobering statement for a moment and couldn't dispute it. "—I'm visiting grandparents on Ma's side of the family. The Portos."

"Oh, how nice. I'm certain they know me and I must know them. I'm sure they'll be happy to see you. And it's great you still have them around." The elevator dinged and the doors burred open. "Can you guide me in, Johnny?" She extended her hand.

"Yes, no problem."

"Thank you, sweetie."

We walked into the cab holding hands, her fingers frail and frigid. I selected the third floor. She stretched with an arching fingertip and pressed the twentieth.

"As I was saying… Good they're alive. Most of the

younglings coming through here are wearing black, tending to last rites, and setting funeral times."

I deflected, opting not to tell her about my ailment or what lay ahead. "You must have a great view from the top floor?"

"Oh, yes. I own one of the penthouse suites. I decided long ago not to give my family any money when I die, so I spent it all on myself. Screw them," she said with puckish laughter that ended in a smile of the same nature. The elevator stopped at the third floor and the doors opened. "Have a great day, Johnny. Say hello to your family. I hope I can see you later. I think me and you can have some... fun, if you know what I mean," she said, then followed with a crackling purr.

I waved and stepped into the lavish hallway, carpeted like an upscale hotel and not a senior living facility. Susanna's penthouse probably as extravagant as a home in Beverly Hills. In hindsight, I should've asked for her hand in marriage. Midway the corridor, I arrived at unit 315 and rapped the door while humming. I waited several minutes, scanning for other tenants, and eyeing the one-way peephole. The locks clacked and the door swung open. A rush of mothballs, tomato sauce, and stale coffee swarmed my face. Paola stood, beaming porcelain dentures and teetering on a cane, which she used more for an accessory than a medical need. A faded coloring exposed grey streaks through a loose ponytail.

"Hello, Nico." Her once welcoming blue eyes had clouded. "So nice to see you again. Come in. Don't stand out in the cold."

"Mrs. Porto. So glad to see you as well. I'm sorry for showing up without notice. I just had to see you and Mr. Porto."

"What do I always tell you?" she said, waving me inside.

"I can come any time?"

"And…?"

"To call you Paola, and Mr. Porto, Peter," I said, hanging my head with embarrassment.

"Correct. Let's sit in the living room where Peter's resting. Or, to reiterate, where he's staring into space."

Morose, she picked up her pace to the couch, dragging the cane. She heaved the clear plastic from its corners, folding and crinkling the unyielding material like aluminum foil. She hauled the oversized blob, half of it jabbing the floor, the other chirring against her skin, and stuffed it into the closet. She swiped a set of pillows that had scattered onto the floor, fluffed them, and placed one at each armrest.

"I'm sorry it's so messy in here."

From my position, the interior of the home spotless. I eased myself onto the firm cushion, the chocolate suede as new as it had been years ago. The plush carpet like tall blades from a summer lawn, begging bare feet to slither between their soft bristles. I refrained from the temptation.

"What brings you to visit, Nico? It's been over a year, maybe two or more," she said, hanging the cane over the armrest, and perching her hands atop her lap.

"Wow, it's been that long? I was just thinking about both of you and wanted to say hello."

"Well, hello, Nico. Was there anything else?"

"I meant I wanted to chat for a bit."

Well, that was part of the whole truth. I thought about divulging more, but after glancing at Peter sitting stolid in the recliner diagonal from me, I withdrew the option. He stared straight ahead into nowhere, or possibly somewhere. His sharp, judicial mind from years ago nowhere to be found. Hair as white as flour and parted to the right without a strand out of place. Bifocals, with oversized pads taped at various spots along the frame, rested atop the bridge of his nose. I couldn't give them my news, but trying to outfox Paola, who had multiple, advanced degrees, could prove difficult.

"How's he doing," I said, nodding my head towards Peter.

"Some days are great, others I wish he were at peace. He probably doesn't even know you're here. He just watches... nothing." She sighed and with a delicate finger wiped her eye.

"Can I try calling out to him? If that's okay with you?"

"Sure. Go ahead. I do it every day. It's like fishing in a vast lake with millions of fish who aren't hungry."

"Mr. Porto— Peter. Can you hear me?" I paused, then repeated, amplifying my voice each time. "Peter... Peter." As I turned to Paola, shrugging and raising my hands, he replied. A brilliant smile scrunched his cheeks against glistening eyes.

"Little Nico. How have you been?"

"Great." Flabbergasted, I stumbled through words. "Are... you... okay, Peter? How do you feel?"

"I'm doing well. Life's a bowl of cherries without the pits. How's my little girl, Lidia? She better be treating you well."

"She's okay," I said, addled.

"She's my favorite only child." He giggled like he'd been tickled.

"I bet she is. She misses you and is going to visit soon," I said. Awestruck, I glanced at Paola, then refocused on Peter.

"Good. I can't wait to see her, Luigi. Take care of her. I love her more than words can express. When are you two walking down the aisle?"

I played along not knowing what to say. "Well… soon." A glimpse into his mind better than none. "You'll be handing her off to me. Are you ready for the big day?"

"Oh, yes. She told me she loves you like the stars in the sky," he said, tracing the air above him. "They're so bright and beautiful. Hey, I have a secret for you. Do you want to know?"

"Yes, please."

"Don't tell her I told you or she'll get mad, but I saw the wedding dress. It's fit for a princess, my little princess. She reminds me of Paola on our special day. I miss them. Give them my love. I'll see you soon."

At that very instant, his face returned to a torpid state. The chill tingling my scalp spread to my spine, then iced my body. I peeked at Paola and noticed a quivering lip. I whipped my head away from her view, not wanting to cry, not wanting to shock my heart with more pain. I snuck an aspirin into my mouth, grinding it to chalk between my teeth. She heaved a breath and cleared her throat, grabbing my attention.

"That's what happens, Nico. One moment, the man I know and love, and the next, a living corpse. It's horrible. I know this is bad, but I'll repeat it; I wish every day for him to be at peace."

"It's okay to think that way. I completely understand. I assume the doctors can't help?"

"There's no cure. iLifeCheck predicted this a couple years ago. I think we were one of their first test subjects. I was too embarrassed to tell anyone about it. Eventually, he'll even forget to breathe and eat. His organs will forget to function. Sometimes, when he doesn't come around, I have to attach a feeding bag to him. I can only hope he doesn't realize what's happening to him because I just couldn't…" She bit her lip and sniffled, gripping the pillow and pressing it against her chest.

"I'm sorry. I wish I could help." I winced. The throbbing in my legs had returned from sitting too long.

"Don't be sorry. Never apologize for things that aren't your fault. Life is complicated, but watching someone die is the most difficult. Luckily, you don't have to worry about that just yet."

"Yeah, but you never know." I chose vagueness because my emotional conviction wouldn't allow me to disclose the severity of my matters. Adding to her plate of misery wouldn't be fair nor pensive. She'd grieve for me when the proper moment allowed. I hoped no one would tell her about my death and spare her any additional hurt, but I doubted my family could keep secrets.

"Don't talk negative, Nico. You'll be fine. You're much younger than Peter and I. For chrissake, we've almost reached our centennial. I know you've had your health issues, but you have plenty of time ahead of you. You reach a certain point when it's just not fun anymore, when everything just stops. I call it the transition. The one piece of advice I can give you is not to get as old as us," she tittered, then sobered her tone.

"How come? I thought living long is the bee's knees. All the magazines and television shows talk about it."

"I'll tell you why." She slapped the pillow. "Those people are fools and never interview us. Go to the community room downstairs and you'll see a remake of George Romero's *Night of the Living Dead.* Our generation is wearing diapers like children, swallowing twenty pills a day, most of which are missed doses because there are too many to track, and watching all our friends die. That *isn't* a walk in the park nor does it make my future any easier to digest. Don't misunderstand me either. I like the sun, the flowers, the birds, but there are opportunity costs to everything. Just look." She pointed to Peter. "That's not living. That's hoping every single day for death to stop the mental madness. Anyway, let's talk about something else. I'm fed up with this crap."

"Agreed. Can I have some water?"

"Sure, but wouldn't you rather have coffee? It's what you drink all the time."

She rose and hobbled to the kitchen where the effects of Peter's plight and her age became evident. Dust devils danced as she walked past the sink overflowing with crusted dishes. The marble countertops clear of any appliances, except for the stained, coffee carafe sitting upon its burner. Beside it, remnants of Styrofoam and adhesive bestrewn atop the oven.

"The doctor says to take it easy on the caffeine. Blood pressure or something like that."

As the ice maker crunched and droned, she whistled a tune and turned towards me, then filled a tall glass. I glanced at the fancy refrigerator, opposite mine, which spurted an orange liquid, forcing me to fill empty bottles with tap water. The cube dispenser had rusted shut, so every two weeks I'd purchase a bag from the grocery store or gas station.

"Alright. If that's what he says, then listen to him. *Un po vino*? Maybe a few sips will get your blood pressure down. We have plenty. Peter certainly doesn't drink anymore and I try to be good." She winked with a smirk.

"Okay, but just a smidge in a tiny glass. You're not wrong

in what you said. Life is a crapshoot. The older we get, the less the doctors let us play."

"Yeah. It only took me a hundred years to learn. Oh well, what can you do?"

We both chuckled as she handed me the drinks and sat upon the couch.

"How's your mother doing?"

"As nice as always towards me."

"I don't know where we went wrong with her. Is she really coming to visit Peter?"

"Not sure. I just said it to make him smile."

"She hasn't been here in many years. I think she has a hard time dealing with what happened to Peter. You'd think at her age she'd be able to deal with it. She's an uptight shrew."

"If I see her, I'll relay the message to visit you."

"You can tell her to call me. She doesn't have to visit."

"I will."

I wasn't surprised she didn't want to see Ma, but it was a positive for me. That statement confirmed Ma didn't call to tell them about my bad news, clearing away some of my guilt for withholding the secret.

"So, how is your health, Nico?"

I wobbled my hand in the air. "Well, you remember I was in hospital." She nodded with disappointment, then bowed her head. "They did a few tests and told me to watch a few things so I don't get sick again." Not the whole truth, but not a lie.

"You look paler than usual today. I noticed when you sat down, but I didn't want to meddle."

"It must be the lighting. I'm a little tired, probably from walking."

"If you ever want to talk about your health or anything else you can trust me. I won't tell your mother."

"Thank you. I appreciate it. You've been a better mother to me than my own. Your love for me amazing and infinite. I wanted to tell you in person and hug you. I wish I could do the same with Peter, but he won't know."

"You can still hug him. Maybe he's awake somewhere inside."

We met at the center of the room, alternating our embrace multiple times, trying to find the proper position to say goodbye. I refrained from squeezing too hard so as not to break her bony shoulders and protruding ribs. My eyes dampened, but I clamped the inside of my cheek, holding any sentiments at bay, repeating to stay strong within my mind. She sniveled and cleared her throat. We exchanged our love and stepped away from each other, retaking our seats. It was easier with Peter because he, like a doll, lacked any response. We sat in silence glancing at Peter, then the ceiling, then straight ahead, then at each other.

"Oh, Nico… I never, in my wildest and craziest dreams, thought Peter and I would end up here, like this. Our journey has been long. Some days, I hope tomorrow never arrives. It'd be so much easier rather than being old and alone. On that note, do you want to hear a story I've never told anyone, including your mother?"

"Of course." Intrigued, I scooted forward on the couch.

"A little bit of history before you leave." She squared her shoulders and placed her hands atop her lap. "Well, this is before your mom, Lidia. Not sure if you knew, but she was born in Italy during one of our extended visits. Our families watched her for several years, so Peter and I could get situated in America, then brought her back with us when she was older. Perhaps, that's where we went wrong with her, but I digress."

"Really? I didn't know that. She never told me."

"Yes. There's more. Do you want me to continue?"

"Please," I said, scooting to the edge of the couch.

"Well, we arrived at Ellis Island aboard a ferry, transferred from a freighter carrying supplies and such because we didn't have money for a flight. Manure and urine mudded the floors of the hull. During the trip, which took weeks, we weren't allowed in the clean areas. The captain and shipmates checked on us every few hours to make certain we didn't leave our filthy quarters or die, yet some did. The first week we vomited, but by the second we became accustomed. The immigration people processed us like cattle. They told us many times we weren't welcomed on their soil, but had to accept us per their orders. They went as far as changing Peter's first and last name, Pietro to Peter and Portomaggio to Porto. We visited his family quite a bit, by plane of course, but they weren't happy with him because of the name change. They called him a traitor. They didn't understand he had no choice. I was fortunate because they overlooked me, so I kept my name, Paola Piccolo."

"Thank you for sharing. That's an amazing story, yet so horrible," I said, peeved, slapping the armrest.

"It sure was and now look at him. He accomplished so much in so little time with nothing to show for it, except sitting in a chair and forgetting to talk and eat. His family won't even visit. It's just us, or rather me, until the end arrives."

"Have you asked them why?"

"Once in a while we chat. They say our streets are too dangerous with guns, drugs, and politics. I can't say I blame them, but I think they won't let go of the grudge. That's an Italian for you."

"Such is life, right?"

"It is, Nico." She lowered her shoulders and yawned. "I'm getting tired. I don't mean to be rude, but I need a nap."

"It's not a problem. I have to leave anyway. I'm visiting someone else."

"Well, have fun and welcome to old age. Only way to get through the day is to nap like a child."

"Get your rest, Paola. Thank you for visiting with me and chatting."

"You are always welcome. I hope to see you soon. Try not to let so much time pass next time." She took a breath and paused. "By the way… something just came to mind."

"Sure. What is it?"

"You should go visit your other grandparents at, you know… the cemetery. Talking with them might provide some solace."

"Great idea. I'll go once I leave here."

"Okay, Nico. Stay strong."

I patted her shoulder as we kissed each other upon the cheek. I waved to Peter, who didn't flinch, then let myself out. I expected Susanna spilling champagne or gin from a flute while pushing the walker, but the hallway and elevator remained quiet. I skirted the guard and the rude receptionist, welcoming freedom at the exit.

Abdi sat within the cab, as he promised, talking on his cell phone and fiddling with the dashboard. I tapped the window with a knuckle, hoping not to disturb his privacy. Alarmed, he snapped his head towards me and narrowed his eyes. Once recognizing me, he smiled and waved to enter.

"Everything okay, Abdi?" I whispered, pointing at the phone.

"All good. Talking to wife. She always very nosy."

"Is she mad?" I said, concerned.

"No. No. She making food for kids. She asked how you are feeling. I told her you are doing well for now and that you are visiting family. She said you stay positive."

"I'll do my best. My legs are burning. Hopefully, it'll pass."

"How are they?" he said, pointing towards the building.

"Very old and sick. My grandfather has lost his mind with Alzheimer's and Dementia. My grandmother tries to help him and herself. Getting old isn't fun."

"Oh, I know, Nico. What she say about your situation?"

"I couldn't bring myself to tell her. I don't want to overstress. Her plate is full with Peter and his sicknesses, plus they're almost one hundred years old."

"Amazing to reach the age. You did right thing."

"Thank you for agreeing."

"No problem. Where next?"

"If you don't mind, let's go to the cemetery and visit with my grandparents on Papa's side of the family. I'll apologize in advance because it's a little out of the way."

"Oh, buddy, it no matter. We have car. You do not have to walk anymore."

"Good point, Abdi. You're a great man with a perfect heart."

"Nobody is perfect, but I try my best. Let's go," he said, nodding to me in the rearview as we sped off.

GIANNI FRANCO

CH 21

Holy Sepulchre Cemetery appeared against the faint backdrop of the roiling Lake Ontario in the Charlotte Neighborhood. Three-hundred-plus acres filled with thousands of embalmed corpses, all who had succumbed to the forces of nature, lay in their expensive, oblong homes. My grandparents died decades ago. At that time, Rochester had enough land allocated for its citizens to bury their dead underground and not in a high-rise like Heaven's Parlor. As devout Catholics, who considered cremation demonic, they bought their tombs well in advance, vowing not to be buried in a denominational graveyard. They had researched flying their caskets back to Italy and found the option too costly, so Holy Sepulchre became their permanent residence.

Abdi winded the car along the narrow, curving path for about a mile. A Saint Luke medallion encased in glass rose from the ground like a lollipop, marking the vicinity to their graves. I called for him to park at the edge of the manicured lawn where fresh cuttings whirled with the breeze.

From Saint Luke, I counted ten headstones straight ahead and three to the left, learning the route from the map they handed out during the funeral. On any given day, one could spot infrequent visitors because they'd roam the tombstone trails for hours. My grandparents' graves laid bare, unlike the others draped with flags and flowers, both synthetic and natural. I assumed no one had visited for a while. Then again, I couldn't blame them or myself because there's nothing to see and no one to talk to at a graveyard. I attempted to sit beside their low-lying headstones, but my legs wouldn't allow the bend. Leaning against a tall memorial behind me, I wondered what the dead could offer me. As instructed by my predecessors, I bowed my head and prayed:

Hail Mary, full of grace. The Lord is with thee.
Blessed art thou amongst women, and blessed is the fruit
of thy womb, Jesus. Holy Mary, Mother of God, pray for
us sinners, now and at the hour of our death, Amen.

"Hey... *Nonno* Ciro. How's it going?"

No response arrived, which I expected, asking several more times. As I rolled a stone under my boot, debating if I should leave, a familiar, hoarse voice floated towards me.

"*Buongirono. Come stai*, Nico?"

"Oh my... *ciao* Ciro. I guess I'm fine. Wow, your accent has disappeared."

"Yes, we don't have them in the afterlife. Are you really fine?"

"I suppose I could be better. *Stanco.*"

"What's wrong? Why?"

"*È un disastro.* Life's handed me a lemon and I can't make lemonade anymore," I said with a somber tone.

"Is it serious or are you just pulling my leg? You used to do that all the time. It was so funny and cute."

"It's bad. That's why I've come to visit, to reminisce, and maybe get some advice."

"What's bad? Are you getting another divorce? Did you lose your job?"

"None of those. The truth is I'm losing my life. The doctor hasn't give me much time. I wanted to pay my respects before I go."

"*Che bello*. Thanks for thinking of me, Nico."

His face came into focus, but not as I remembered when he passed from cancer one dreary day in a hospice. The drawn, sagging skin replaced by a smooth, tanned complexion. Mahogany hair, which had thinned and whitened like a wispy cloud during his final months, puffed around his ears, the bald spot centered atop the scalp replenished with curls and waves.

"You're welcome. You look great, Ciro."

"Yes, the afterlife treats our looks well," he said, beaming.

"It's too bad we didn't get to spend more time together. We lost each other so early."

"I wish we could've as well. Life is odd. We all know the end is coming, but we never know when. You get that one sickness you can't shake, then one day you awake, and realize it's for the last time."

"I don't know what to do about the end, Ciro."

"Nothing you can do. Don't worry about it and accept it when it arrives. Getting all riled or nervous isn't worth the extra stress. If you follow those emotions, you'll die sooner."

"I understand, but everything used to be so much easier."

"That's hogwash," he sneered, shaking his head. "*La vita è sempre bella e sempre scura*. Maybe it's easy for the first ten years. After that, it's all downhill. This is just another problem you didn't have before, but you've had problems your whole life. If it's not your job, it's your partner, or your car, or traffic, or your neighbor, or money. The list is endless."

"I want to return to those earlier times."

"We all do. Like when I used to bounce you upon my knee. Gabriella would be in the kitchen drinking wine while stirring the sauce, wafting garlic and oregano throughout the home. We'd join her and sing "Ti Amo" by Umberto Tozzi until it was time to eat. I never told you, but by the time we sat, Gabriella and I were tipsy. But... those days ended, as well as my life."

"How is *Nonna* Gabriella? I wish I could talk to her as well."

"She's well, gallivanting the afterlife, enjoying herself like she never did as a human. I don't see her as much as I'd like to. Less problems on this side of the Universe. Actually none, now that I think about it. Frees up one's time."

"I don't believe in any of that religious mumbo-jumbo. Hell, Heaven, and unicorns are all the same to me," I said, waving my hand.

"Of course, it's your choice. It's good to have hope in something, regardless if it does or doesn't exist. Even unicorns need companions," he said with a haughty laugh.

"Good point. It seems to be working for you and Gabriella."

"We are here, we are there, we are everywhere. It's all what you want to make of it. You may be wrong and you may be right, but I'm not here to tell you what to think. Just stay positive until the end arrives. Take it with stride. Fighting the outcome isn't a good idea."

"It's not that easy, Ciro. I'm frightened about everything. I don't want to miss the sun, flowers, family, and friends."

"As a positive, when you're dead, your mind won't be alive to miss anything on Earth."

"Another good point. I hope you're correct."

"I am. I've already been through it. You have to trust me, Nico. I promise it'll be okay. You just have to get over the hump of death. Surrender to it."

Pondering his statement was short-lived. Footsteps rustling a pile of crisp leaves captured my attention. I turned towards the pathway, thinking Abdi had decided to accompany me, but it wasn't him. A young woman wearing a black, pearl-embroidered gown walked hand-in-hand with a boy in a fitted suit of the same shade adorned in rhinestones. Dark hair poked through their white mantillas, cradling similar visages. They approached, espying me between whispers. I moved away from the headstone, hoping it wasn't one of their relatives. The woman continued onward, but the boy tugged her hand. They stopped.

"Sir, are you alright?"

"Yes," I said with a fainthearted voice.

With seraphic eyes steadfast on mine, he said, "I promise it'll be okay. Come on, Mommy. Let's go see Daddy."

"See, Nico. You don't have to take my word for it. Even the lad understands," Ciro said, staring at me with vindication etched onto his smug face.

With care, I regained my position against the tombstone and indulged him with sarcasm. "I guess a passing stranger knows more than me, or us."

"You, not me. Just know that everything that comes to pass has a resolution. There's no way to fight it or squash it. Everything is inevitable. You can't run from anything because it'll always catch and bite you, whether it's a shark or rabbit."

"Anyway, why are we here," I said, dejected.

"It's simple. You came to see me to give you closure. Do you realize I'm not real and just in your head?"

His laughter reverberated like a staccato drum. Any of my hopes for eternal resolution dashed. He, nor I, existed, or he lied, as he done many times in the past.

"Forget it, Ciro. I wanted an answer and all you gave me were what-ifs. You're wrong about everything."

"No, Nico. I'm here to help you, not hurt you. Like when I cradled you as a child and filled you with love and hope."

"That doesn't exist and never has existed," I said, slamming my hands against my thighs.

"Acting like a child will only get you so far. You have to face your realities, irrespective of their outcomes."

"I love you, Nonno, and Nonna, but we have to end our conversation. It doesn't do me any good. I hoped for resolve, and instead received demoralization."

He firmed his face. "You get what you ask for, you damn ingrate."

"Fine," I said, gritting my teeth. "I'm done with you as I was many years ago. Try to rest in peace, but I know it'll be difficult in the hell you've woven."

"Nico, don't act as you always have. Take this final opportunity to place your mind at ease."

"I can't relax. The tales my soul has spun are enshrouded with the tattered ends of what should've or could've been. You have nothing to offer me, except unicorns and false hopes. Our time is over. I can't deal with you anymore."

"Me? Look in the mirror. I—am—you."

"That's not true."

"It is, Nico. Listen to me… I—am—you."

"No matter. It's time to move forward. We played irregular games throughout our lives where I lost every match. You fail to understand the toll it took on our future. Let's end it, Ciro."

"Fine. Good luck to you. You haven't changed one bit since you were a child. You've always taken the simplistic approach to your life, our lives. I've never done anything wrong to you and expected respect, especially at my grave. *Disgraziato*."

"Respect begets respect and that rule should never falter. Your obscure explanations are nothing but useless conjecture."

"Our perceptions exist at opposite ends of the spectrum, yet they, we, are the same. How can this be, Nico? I've got everything to lose from you, and you have everything to gain from me. We'll end it as you demand. I just hope whenever your time arrives, you find peace, even if it's a sliver."

Disgusted by our interaction, I refused to respond, flailing clenched fists above my head. Before storming off to the car, I turned towards the graveyard path. The boy in the black suit whipped his head and espied me with a fiendish grin, then disappeared with his female counterpart. Not even they supported me any longer.

Abdi, a pleasing sight for a sore soul, met me at the door. "Who you talking to," he asked with a skeptical yet jovial tone.

"Long story. My intentions were good, but they didn't end up the way I expected, just like everything else in my life. Grandfather isn't very supportive."

"It be okay, buddy. All pass with time."

"Even the little boy with her mother didn't seem to like me."

"What boy?" he said, confused.

"She wore a black dress and he a suit, both with matching mantillas. They walked up to me and chatted for a moment."

"I no see no boy, no woman."

"Of course there was, Abdi. He told me everything will be fine."

"No, Nico. I am sorry, but no one there, buddy. I be watching you whole time."

"Come on. Are you sure?"

"Yes, my friend. I swear upon my mother life. Only you there. No one else in cemetery. I get out of car to check you, but decide leave you alone so you can talk with angels or whoever."

"I don't understand. They were there. I saw them. How? Why?"

"In my country, we learn, sometimes, when people approach the end, they want to see things to make them happy. Maybe, it was best to see boy."

"I suppose. I hope it gets better." I said, creeping into the backseat, discouraged with the possible outcomes.

"Me too, buddy."

"Let's head out."

"No problem, buddy. Relax a bit. It's okay."

CH 22

The car motored through moderate traffic, opposite of most gridlocked days. I angled the top of my forehead against the cool window while the sun warmed my hair. During my life in this city I never noticed how the buildings and homes cascaded like mountains along the avenues. Walking never provided the proper view, and on those few occasions I was a passenger I never looked, or was too inebriated to care. The landscape faded as we sped up, replaced by a park sprawling with evergreens, swings, sandboxes filled with children, and families celebrating with flaming barbecues. Just beyond, a familiar bus stop, where I'd met Fatimah.

With urgency, I trumpeted Abdi. "Stop."

"What is wrong, buddy," he said, twisting in the seat, searching all the windows.

"Please, stop. I must see someone. She's inside the bus enclosure."

"No problem," he said, gripping the steering wheel and motioning. "There, we park ahead."

He turned on the hazards and parallel parked the car into a curbside spot. Although the sign stated "No Long-Term Parking", he barked to ignore it. I slipped a set of pills below my tongue, wriggled from the rear set, and wobbled to the bus shelter.

The man in the rainbow outfit greeted me at the entrance. "I'm glad you returned," he said with a welcoming smile, chucking a handful of popcorn onto the pigeon landing, the cooing birds zipping about like manic hens.

"I was passing," I said, pointing at the cab, "and wanted to say hello to Fatimah."

"I figured she told you to come in her own special way."

"What do you mean?" I said, narrowing my eyes.

"So... you don't know?"

"No."

"We're celebrating. It's okay you forgot to bring popcorn." He passed me a small bag. "Feeding the birds is what she would want us to do," he said, extending his hand into mine and patting it.

"I still don't understand."

"A few hours after you left she..." His gaze turned somber. "She departed as well."

"When is she returning? I don't have much time. Abdi may not wait for me. I'm sick and need to see others," I said with panic. "When—"

"She's not, Nico. I was sitting next to her. While we were chatting, she heaved a sigh and collapsed onto her side. We called the ambulance. They arrived and tried to revive her for about twenty minutes. Her body didn't respond to treatment. That's when I realized she wouldn't be coming back." He sniffled. "The EMT glanced at her watch and pronounced Fatimah dead. I don't recall the exact time. They carried her away on the gurney with a sheet covering her face. No one inside this enclosure had a dry eye. Even the pigeons quieted. After we ran out of tears, we decided to celebrate her life with what she loved best, feeding the pigeons. And we've been doing it ever since."

Speechless, I spun, searching the bus stop and bystanders, then staring at the popcorn in my hand, wondering how this could've happened. She didn't show any signs of sickness. She was old but so are my grandparents.

"Are you sure?" I pleaded.

"Yes, unfortunately. She was at that very seat and now she's gone."

He pointed with an unsteady hand. The spot now occupied by several stuffed animals, birds to be exact, surrounded by varying popcorn bags, and a couple religious symbols. Adhered with fraying masking tape and centered on the Plexiglas, a black and white picture depicting a younger Fatimah.

"This is horrible and sad. Bloody hell. Funts and cuckers."

"Excuse me. What does that mean?"

"Nothing. It's just not fair, then again, what is?"

"I agree, Nico. Sometimes we never know when it's our turn to go."

"I wanted to ask earlier. How do you know my name?"

"Fatimah mentioned it several times during our conversation after you departed. She said you have a positive aura, which I can sense now. She doesn't say that about many people. Prior, we didn't have a proper chance to introduce ourselves since we were in passing. I'm Frederic Gustav. Most call me Fred or Gustav. I'm not too picky. Pleasure to meet you again. I wish it was under better circumstances."

He extended his hand once again and I reciprocated with a handshake. Then, he surprised me with a gentle hug, which lasted longer than anticipated. His embrace comforting, considering my destiny mirrored Fatimah's. The lavender and mint exuding from his clothing soothing to my lungs.

"Come, let's sit. Rest your legs for a bit," he continued, stepping away from me. "Here, next to Fatimah's seat. We'll feed the pigeons and chat."

"Perfect. I'd like that. Just one second."

I waved to Abdi standing beside his car and peeping my direction. With his attention upon me, I flipped my thumb. He nodded, pulled out his cellphone, and placed it to his ear, then returned inside the vehicle. Gustav led the way, excusing himself between a few standees crowding the space, his large stature parting them like the Red Sea. We slid upon the plastic bench, our legs almost rubbing in the cramped space.

"I meant to ask you last time and… I hope I'm not prying, but why is your outfit so colorful?"

"You're not, and it's a good question. I don't dress like this every day, just some days. I'm on the main float for the Pride Weekend Parade."

"Cool. I'd come watch, but considering my situation I can't."

"It's all good—well, not about you. Anyway, you know what I mean."

"I do. We're fine. So, where are you from? You speak perfect English, but I can't place the accent," I said.

He adjusted the stuffed animals with precision, making certain they didn't fall to the floor while attempting to give me more space.

"Yes, I studied the language for many years. Born in Sweden, then moved to Spain, then France, and finally America. My father, Swedish, and mother, French. Are you

Italian?"

"Yes, you guessed on the first try."

"I love Rome, Venice, the Adriatic, and the breathtaking Apennine Mountains. I hope to revisit all of them someday soon."

"I agree. Italy is amazing. I always wanted to visit Sweden, Spain, or France but never got the chance. Now, it's too late."

"There's always the possibility you may return as another being or your sickness may go away."

"I don't think that's possible."

"We have to hope. Remember everything Fatimah told you. Her knowledge extended beyond our simple minds. She could access the spirit, the soul of everyone who communicated with her."

"I don't doubt her intelligence. It's just—I don't believe."

"I understand. Sometimes the signs will make you a believer. Fatimah told me a story once that cleared any doubt in my mind. Would you like to hear it?" I nodded with eager eyes. He continued after clearing his throat. "Well, I'll do my best to paraphrase. As a child she ventured with her friends along the banks of the Ganges River. Its water as dark as night and filled with the ashes of millions who were cremated upon the floating pyres in Varanasi. On this particular overcast day, she decided to break free from her group and climb along the jutting rocks of the seawall, three times her height. A courageous child needing to explore.

"A few yards into the acrobatic feat, a section of the ledge crumbled below her tiny feet, sending her into freefall. She said the moist air had caused a mental lapse, which made her reckless. Out of nowhere, a branch, no wider or longer than a shoelace, popped from the wall. She latched onto it, and defying physics, it held her weight. At that moment, all went silent within her mind, and she gained the strength to climb to the top. Panting and wiping tears from her eyes, she noticed silhouettes of her friends creeping closer but well out of reach, their howls and screams muffled. At one point, she thought she'd succumbed to the watery abyss. It wasn't possible she drowned because she was conscious. As her breaths returned to a normal pace, a pigeon landed at her feet, pecked her ankle, and flew off cooing. Her friends huddled around, picked her up, and carried her home. That same night the pigeon appeared in her dream and brought with her the goddess Ganga. She showed Fatimah her future life and assured her not to worry when the time arrived to venture into another being."

His gaze invited immediate feedback, but due to my wonderment a few minutes passed before I responded. "That's an awesome story, but with all due respect, my experience with religion has been awful. I'll soon find out what does or doesn't happen. We'll chalk up her scenario to coincidence or luck."

"Trust me. There's something or someone out there who watches over us. She mentored me, teaching me how to be who I am today without any fear or judgement from anyone. Without her intuition, I'd probably be dead," he said with conviction.

"I'm not trying to offend nor pry, but what happened to you, Gustav?"

"You're not. I like telling people. There's always something to learn from someone no matter who they are." He threw a handful of popcorn at the huddling pigeons, watched them peck the food, then returned to me. "I'd been living in America for less than a year, drinking and drugging, and one day, out of the blue, I decided to take the bus. Fatimah was in the same place where you met her. She called me to sit by her and told me she saw the darkness in my soul through my eyes. We talked for hours, then days, then weeks, all the while counseling me to find the root of my problems. We did, and today, I'm proud to be who I am," he said with a hoarse voice and welling eyes. "I wear my colors with pride and no one questions me. People even ask me for advice and I do my best to help them. You never know if that one interaction can change someone's whole life as Fatimah did for me."

I wanted to respond, but the words never made it to my lips and not because I didn't care, rather the plethora of emotions spinning in my mind concerning Alessio, Ariel, Beatrice, my grandparents, life and death. I'd be leaving everyone behind, not able to help them during their tribulations.

"I understand and agree," I said, unmoved, throwing popcorn to the pigeons, hoping the diversion would reset my thoughts, ridding the anxiety.

"Thank you. Some don't. They write me off as a kook. Enough about me. Fatimah hinted you had some issues as well. I can take her place, if you want to talk. I know you don't have much time, but it's better to clear your conscience when you still have the chance."

"I appreciate your offer. I meant to say more than just *understanding* what you went through. The words, I can't find them."

"It's okay. Just talk to me. It'll alleviate your mind."

"I'm not so sure."

I scanned the crowd from all walks of life standing and sitting, as well as those interacting with the pigeons. They didn't need to know about my problems.

"Don't worry about them. Look, if Fatimah was still here, would you talk to her?"

He made another perfect point. "Yes, of course."

"Then, it's a no-brainer. Gustav is your *new* Fatimah. I promise it'll help. It did me."

"Alright," I said, skeptical.

"It's fine. Just think about the pigeons." He scattered a quarter bag across the sidewalk. "They won't bother us for a while." He patted my thigh. "To be blunt, death is around your corner. Air all your grievances about whomever or whatever. Don't hold back. Everything is fair game."

"Great point. Well… I have a son whom I've never met. Been trying to meet him and every time I go to his place, he's not home. I'm starting to think he's possibly avoiding me. Please don't sugarcoat your response."

"I promise I won't. He might be hiding from you or he's always out with his friends. I have a kid, a girl, and we're close, but I only see her once every two weeks. Always busy dating or partying with friends. One weekend a festival, and the next, hiking the Adirondack Mountains. I can't keep up."

"You have a child?"

"Oh, yes. My ex-wife, Angelina, gave birth to her when I was locked in the iron closet. Paradise, my daughter, is cool with everything and understands my life wasn't easy, as well as Angelina."

"You have a great ex and kid. Unlike mine, if he's hiding from me. That bothers me the most and I don't know what to do about it."

"You said no sugarcoating." His face firmed. "Look, you've never met him. You can't expect him to be waiting for you. If he is hiding from you, then it's probably for good reason. He may be afraid to meet a father who's dying soon. Wouldn't that defeat the purpose for him to have a father for a few days, weeks, or months?"

"Yes, but blood is supposed to keep a family bonded. Isn't it? That's what I was taught."

"Blood is sometimes thinner than water when you add improper ingredients. You can hate your mom, dad, uncle, or whomever. They're just people like everyone else. You're doing all you can to meet him, so if that's all you get out of it, then it'll be fine. At least you tried. There'd be a problem if you didn't."

"Yeah, I suppose you're right."

"No point blaming anyone, including yourself. Time is everything and you're out of it, plus it takes too much energy, and you can't afford to lose any more of that either. A dying pigeon no longer swoops for food, or in our case, popcorn. They rest."

"You make a good replacement for Fatimah."

"Thank you, but she'll never be replaced. I'm just a good copycat who knows how to listen and understand. You mentioned you weren't a fan of religion. What happened in your life to cause that?"

"I don't know." I waved him off, flicking a few morsels to a solitary pigeon loitering at the edge of the enclosure. "Let's talk about something else. Religion and politics should never be discussed."

"I understand but in this case, your case, it's best to discuss it. If you get it off your mind, you'll have space for something else."

Getting into this discussion wasn't on my top ten list, let alone a top twenty. The opinion I shared on this topic with a select few sometimes caused others anguish. Although, after speaking with Michael, I realized fault may not always reside with the victim. Gustav continued to prod and I could no longer put up a wall.

"Fine. You're not going to like what you hear."

"Try me. Fatimah will be proud of you for dealing with your religious beliefs. Just take a deep breath, Nico."

"When I was young, I used to be an altar boy. I served during normal church hours, after school, funerals, holidays, and even taught other altar boys. Several times Father Dunnkirk called me to his rectory office. He'd give me a glass of grape juice and some candy. Then, I'd wake hours later lying on his sleeper sofa, holding a pillow and a teddy bear. I'd ride home on my bicycle or he'd drive me home in his Cadillac. I felt dirty every time. The nightmares started soon after. As I grew older, I realized what had occurred was not normal and may have happened to other altar boys. That realization convinced me if a man from God could be that evil, then religion could not exist. I'm content believing that until my last breath. It'll never change so don't try to convince me otherwise. That's the story sparing the details, which neither of us need."

A tear dribbled down his cheek, halting atop his thick beard. He slouched and lowered his head, staring at the bag of popcorn within his large hands. As each second passed, he tightened his grip, wringing the paper into a knot, crumbling all its contents into powder. We sat in silence for several minutes. The bag fell to the floor and he raised a sleeve to his eyes, taking a deep breath, and engaging me with a sullen face.

"I'm not sure what Fatimah would say. I can only wish those atrocities never occurred to you. I won't convince you to change your mind about religion. If I was in your position, I would probably think the same about it. Can I offer you a hug?"

Without responding, we embraced, he squeezing the breath from me, only letting go when I began to wheeze and cough. I slipped a pill into my mouth and chewed, the fragments burning my stomach.

"It's best I head to my next destination. The clock keeps moving forward and I have no way to stop it," I said with a short sigh.

"I understand. May I give you one last bit of advice before you leave? I think Fatimah would agree with it." I nodded. "This might not sound good right now, but think about it before your time arrives. For peace within your soul, you should visit this priest and address his evils. You'll walk away with one less burden. I know it's easier said than done. I only ask you to think about it."

"I'll take into consideration. It's not a bad idea. Keep feeding those pigeons for all of us who no longer will be here. Thank you for talking with me. You would've been a good friend. If only we would've met earlier in life. I'm sure you get that all the time from all the people you meet."

"Thank you as well and not *all* people like me. Remember, I'm the guy wearing rainbows, but I know what you're saying. I'll honor you in the short time I've known you,

and yes, we'll feed the pigeons until they're as big as chickens."
We both laughed. "I'm proud to call you a friend," he said,
tapping my shoulder. "Perhaps, you'll get well and visit us
again. No one really knows the future," he said with a smile
that puffed his cheeks like baseballs. We shook hands and bid
each other farewell.

CH 23

I plodded to the taxi, stopping for a brief moment to empty the remaining kernels from the popcorn bag, spreading them along the sidewalk. The pigeons waddled and pecked as if it was their last day on earth. I attempted petting two, but they circumvented my hand like winged mice. Abdi must've been watching because he met me at the rear of the vehicle and opened the door.

"How it go, Nico? Did you meet her?"

"Unfortunately, no. Per Gustav, she passed away."

"So horrible. Come. Sit." He directed me into the car and onto the bench seat, steadying my body with his arm under mine. "We talk where it cooler. Too hot outside today." He edged the door, watching for my legs, and closed it. "Very weird... I drive by here every day and never notice her. What happen?" he said, situating himself upon the front seat, then glancing at the rearview.

"One day she's here and the next day she's gone. A wonderful and knowledgeable woman who traveled thousands of miles and touched the lives of many. The people at the bus stop are honoring her and her best friends, the pigeons."

"Is why everybody feed popcorn?"

"Yes, she did it almost every day. She loved them and gave them hope. I learned an important lesson from her."

"What she tell you?" he asked, raising his brow.

"She said everyone we encounter throughout our lives is

affected by our actions, good or bad, and the recipients never stop to recognize the magnitude from the interactions. We ignore perspective even though it's easy to perceive."

"Very interesting. I never thought like that way. I need be more careful with people near me."

"Yes, you should. Also, when we meet proper people with good intentions early in life, then everything can progress easier. Although I don't have any proof, considering the way I turned out. I ended up speaking to one of her friends, Gustav. A cordial man with a heart and soul as large as the Universe. Anyway, my apologies for taking so long."

"No problem, buddy. You have me until you decide you don't need me. Do—not—worry. Where next?" he asked with a chipper voice, tapping the steering wheel.

"It's time to see Papa. About five to ten minutes from here. 609 Sonora Parkway."

"Okay, but may take little longer because traffic. You rest, I drive. I keep radio low."

"Thank you, Abdi."

I heeded his advice, reclining against the headrest and closing my eyes. "The Cat's in the Cradle" by Harry Chapin in rhythm with the dancing springs above the wheels mollifying me into a doze. A snickering child appeared, his body swaddled with a blue blanket. Beatrice rocked in a chair holding him in her arms and whispering, "Hush little Alessio, don't say word, Mama's gonna find you a father soon." I called to her. She stopped singing, ogled me, and smirked. I asked her why she didn't tell me about him. She bowed her head and returned to Alessio, humming and conversing in baby talk. A younger version of myself stepped towards her with outstretched hands. He had no voice, miming the words love, both, and you. She didn't care, continuing to focus on Alessio. He inched closer and caressed her cheek.

"What happened?" I shouted, jolting from the seat.

"I have no choice, buddy. I can't miss it. Pothole too big. Lucky, no have flat tire."

"Oh, Abdi." I puckered my dry lips and kneaded my eyes. "It was a dream, or nightmare, neither which I could bear. Good I was stirred."

"What it about?"

"Alessio, my son, and his mother, Beatrice."

"Something bad happen?" he said in a dispirited tone.

"I'm not certain. A bit, I suppose. I don't think I wanted to see what came next."

"I have visions like that too. Some scare me almost to die and other are different where I sit on beach of beautiful island."

"Perhaps it was a sign from another world. I have a request since it occurred."

"Of course, what I do to help you?"

"Please, take me to my son's place. I want to see if he's home. If not, we'll return to my father. Is that okay? I'm sorry for the short notice… But the dream."

"Yes, buddy. Yes, I understand. What the address?"

"313 Hemingway Drive."

"Not far at all. We be there five minutes. I step on it."

He didn't exaggerate, squealing the tires, pumping the brakes, and roaring the engine. We must've beaten his estimate by half, taking shortcuts through alleys, and running two red lights.

"We here, buddy."

"Thank you. Can you open the trunk?"

He pressed the button inside the glovebox and the lid opened.

"All set. Do you want help?"

"I think I'll be okay. If not, I'll wave or tap the car."

I grabbed the portrait, which considering his driving, sat centered and unscathed, folded into a multicolored quilt. Holding the frame tight, I guided my body along the car to his open window.

"I wanted to check-in and let you know I'll be back soon. Please wait for me."

"Will do. Take time, buddy."

A gust hit me as I turned the corner at the front of the vehicle. Its force weakened my legs, sending me sideways and towards the broiling hood. I couldn't drop the frame. I wouldn't. My jutting knee caught the bumper, saving a crash to the pavement and a mangled canvas. I cringed with scorching legs, attempting to find balance. Wobbling on my heels, the frame snagged a piece of sharp plastic protruding from the headlight. With my body in freefall, I suddenly stopped midair.

"It is okay. I am here to save you," Abdi said, holding my shoulders and straightening my back.

Comprehending his calculation to catch me boggled the mind. I thanked him once again and hoped my overwhelming gratification hadn't lost its virtue on him. I marched forward to Alessio's door, step by excruciating step, resting the portrait just under the doorbell against the wall, then hammered the button like a skilled telegraphist translating a novel. No response. Miffed, I pounded the door with the pad of my fist, stopping between barrages to recuperate breath and dab the beads of sweat dripping from my brow. For a second time, no response. I grabbed the painting and turned towards the walkway. As I stepped forward, a bang emanated from the front window. He couldn't hide forever. I had caught him. Struggling to garner a view between a set of bunched blinds, I peeped a cat. It had jumped from the couch, knocking over a lamp, and nestling within the conical shade. Discouraged, I returned to the taxi and tapped the trunk. Abdi waved and the trunk opened. With care, I rewrapped the portrait within the quilt and closed the lid.

"Nobody home?"

I plopped onto the backseat. "Nope. I keep trying and nothing. Bad luck, just like the rest of my life."

"I understand, Nico, but you no give up. Give another chance. I believe it happen. Allah bring him to you. Trust the power around you. They provide."

"I'll try my best."

"Good, all we can do. Where to?"

"Back to Papa. He'll answer the door."

"No problem, buddy. We arrive soon. Do one favor?"

"What's that?" I said, massaging the rippling pricks along my legs.

"Keep hope alive until you no longer can."

"Okay, Abdi, but I don't think my body wants to continue any longer."

"It will. It will. Are you show picture to your father?"

Blaring the horn, he alarmed me, then screamed out the window at a car that almost clipped the front fender. The tires howled, followed by a hint of burnt rubber through the air vents.

"Watch it." I did my best to yell, but it came out jumbled, shocked by the possibility of dying in a car. It should've happened since bad luck was the only luck I had. "Damn crazy drivers. Now you know why I don't own a car." Another set of pills swallowed, hoping to assuage the carking nausea.

"Don't worry, buddy. Happen all the time." He shrugged, tapped the headliner, then kissed his fingers. "What about your father?

"What about him?"

"Will he see picture?"

"That's going to be a firm no. I don't think he earned that option. Maybe he will after I'm dead."

"We have arrived." He braked, bouncing me from the seat, then slammed the shifter into park, and turned towards me, his elbows upon the center console and head snug between the seats. "I understand. Good he have another way to remember you. For now, enjoy time with him."

My otiose torso ignored the command to move, ending the attempts with a series of grunts. He bolted from his seat, and snapped my door open, asking me to lean against his body. I followed the instructions, latching onto his arm with a weak grip, and lumbering to my feet like a baby taking its first stand. As my heels dug into the pavement, my mind spun like a wingless dove spiraling from the heavens, the blurring earth below unveiling the impending doom.

Breathe. Breathe. It will pass, Nico.

Conviction prevailed while Abdi balanced me against the closed door. He asked if I was well enough to visit my father and I reassured him everything's fine. I lied, but had good intention. Scuffing the walkway bought enough time to align my vision. I pressed the buzzer for three, long intervals. As I stretched for the fourth, the locks clacked and the door creaked open. His walker squealed forward, abut to the soiled screen separating us.

"Nico... *figlio mio*. Been very long," he said with longing eyes and a quasi-smile, which I couldn't decipher to be positive or negative.

"It has, Papa. How are you?"

We hadn't spoken in quite some time due to a heated argument about Ma. I decided to spend Thanksgiving and Christmas with her one year because she was lonely. Rather than consoling herself within the depths of a bottle and hearing about it through a phone tirade, I made a solid effort to deliver organic happiness in person. She ended up drinking anyway. I followed her lead, and then she cussed me out, locking herself in the bedroom while I watched television until the early morning hours. I explained the scenario to him, but he didn't care, even though holidays weren't his cup of tea. Luigi, just as stubborn as Ma, and at times less forgiving.

"Good for my age, I think. Where you been, Nico?"

"Dealing with *things*. Busy. Do you want to invite me in or shall we talk between the tattered mesh?" I leaned against the wall, trying to alleviate the pain from my weighty legs.

"Sure, of course, of course. Come in."

He spun his rickety walker. Susanna from Living Hope must've had the luxury model. I followed at slow speed, which I didn't mind, giving me a chance to further recuperate. Any fast paced jaunts well in my rearview. Perhaps he had an extra one of those walkers to lend me for a few hours. If I remembered, I'd ask.

His home opposite Ma's. Flimsy paneling and stained, floral prints covered the walls. The appliances and Formica countertops over twenty years old. We sat across from each other at the kitchen table, adjusting our chairs closer to its edge, their worn legs carving the linoleum floor in unison.

"I visited Nonno and Nonna at the cemetery." I tried my best to hide the scowl.

"How it go, Nico?" he said, folding his hands atop the vinyl tablecloth, imprinted with grapes, bottles, and carafes.

"Not what I expected. It didn't end well. Ended up arguing."

"Yes, he is a hard man. I remember, he always very difficult. Remind me of you."

"Like you're a bowl of strawberries," I retorted.

"Well then, I guess everyone have issues."

"Whatever. Talk to Ma?" I said with a hint of sarcasm, which he bit into and spat back at me.

"Why I talk to that b—," he paused, glanced at the tablecloth, then snapped his head upward with contemptuous eyes, "—bad woman. Better I no call her any names today. My blood sugar rise again, then I get dizzy like this morning. Can you believe someone called two times and hang up? I say hello and nobody answer. Damn jokers. I start yelling at them to stop. I bet Lidia trying to kill me from the phone."

"Do you always have to be so rousing?"

"Yes. If she could, she kill me ten times over, plus one more for good measure."

"I'm sure it wasn't all her fault."

He shrugged, then straightened the cuffs on his blue shirt, blotched yellow around the collar and across the chest pockets. "You no look so good. What gives, Nico?"

"Why do you care? It's not like you ever call or visit me."

"Do not act this way. You still my son. I deserve to know."

"*Deserve*? That word is like wet spaghetti flying through the air. It only sticks when it finds a wall. Am I supposed to be the wall today?"

"Come on, Nico. Tell me. You cannot discount the time we spend together. I raise you. With Lidia, of course."

"I'll make a deal with you father. You tell me things about you and I'll divulge everything about me." I smirked with a hint of victory in my eyes and a thought of an impending checkmate.

"Let me get drink. I think about it."

"Whatever you want," I sneered.

He balanced himself upon the walker handles, leaving it behind, and shambled to the kitchen counter, avoiding the stained cotton balls strewn across the floor. He threw the cupboards open, bouncing them from the hinges, done more for show than an actual malfunction, since he retrieved only one glass. The freezer door suffered the same abuse. He retrieved a butter knife from one of the inside shelves and chiseled through a plateau of ice rising from a plastic tray. The cubes clanged like metal dice into a tall tumbler. A healthy pour of bourbon filled it halfway, followed by a splash of cognac. I don't believe the drink had a name, other than alcoholic.

He lifted his glass with a crooked smile, then sipped, and shivered. "You want some?"

"I don't think so. How do you drink those liquors mixed?"

"You are one to talk. They keep me sane, and today, it allow me to deal with you."

"Aren't you sick? You shouldn't be drinking the hard stuff."

"Sick, schmick. A stick here, a poke there and all get fixed. It don't matter in the end, *specialmente* when it near."

"Are you talking about me or you?"

"Me, of course. We have no talk about you yet, because of ultimatum."

He plunked onto the chair, his forearms smacking the table, nudging its edge against my chest. Oddly enough, his drink didn't spill or dribble a drop. He leaned back, folding one arm over his belly, the other raising the glass.

"We ready to talk?" he said with a slight slur.

"*Non so perché mi tratti in questo modo, Papa.* I suppose, but for now it's you who has to do all the talking."

"Go ahead with the question. Imma warning you. Don't make this take all day."

"*Questions* and I promise not to. Although, if I had the time, I would. Where were you all those nights when Ma sat home drinking and pacing the hallways of our home?"

"Come on, Nico. Forget it. Imma no answer that one. Give me something normal to talk about. That stuff too deep. Too complicated. *È personale.*"

"Personal? I'm your son. She would take out all her aggressions toward you on me when you didn't come home. You disappeared for days, even if you were home. Tell me what happened. I need to know. I've waited my whole life for the answers."

He tipped a large gulp, setting it down, and clasping his

hands as if praying away my interrogation. My stern gaze told him otherwise.

"Fine," he said, heaving a sigh, followed by a grunt. "You not going to like this, but you ask for it." He wiped his brow with the back of his hand, nibbled his lip, then pressed his fists together straight ahead of him. I shrugged with indifference. Like it mattered at this juncture of my life. "There more to it than what Imma about to tell you. If you decide to know that too, then we talk about." I nodded. "Lidia and me reach point in our relationship where me and her don't want to be together. I more than she. Our love and lust fade into a black hole. We fight, sometimes loud and violent, like you experience. I reach a point where I could not fight anymore. In the beginning, I left the house for walk around the neighborhood. Then, that escalate to bars and cafes. I befriend a woman and we explore each other mentally and physically." He locked his eyes onto the corner of the ceiling with a gaping smile. "She open my mind. I find myself again. I meet other woman, then another. It snowball and I become very happy. Like I a teenager again. I hope you understand, Nico."

"I don't believe you would put me and Ma through all of this for selfish reasons, all revolving around one thing, sex. How could you? Why didn't you just end the marriage?"

"Eventually, we do. And, you are correct, by the time it end we hate each other so much. It affect you too. I'm so sorry. *Mi dispiace*. We stay together for you and didn't know it was you we hurt the most. I realize much later in life that negative emotions are not easy to hide. They spread like fire around everyone."

I swallowed the rising bile, scooting the chair, hoping

any movement would shake the pain. It proved futile. As he swigged, I dug into my pocket and retrieved a set of pills, slipping them into my mouth with a slight of hand. I chewed slowly so he wouldn't notice, tucking the unbroken remnants against my cheek.

"Take it easy with the pills. They are dangerous." I ignored him. "I see the pain in your face. I give up. I tell you rest of story. This will maybe hurt more than what I already say. I don't know how to word it for you in good way."

"Just tell me. I can handle it. I want to know everything." I rasped, regaining my breath.

"Okay... Here go nothing. Lidia and me get married young. And just like most couples do, we try to have children. Make a family. A year or two pass and nothing, so we went to our doctor. He send us to specialists and they send us to even more. So many tests, x-rays, exams. At first, they think the problem reside with her uterus, but in the end it was me who had issues. Sterile. *Un disastro. Non poso fare figli.* We even fly to Italy for experimental treatment, but they could not help us. The doctors say it happen because of childhood illness. She never forgive me. I no forgive myself, until I break free from her. We—"

I grimaced. "Are you about to say something I don't want to hear?"

"Look, Nico. We have no choice. We want a family," he said, stone-faced and sober. "We find an agency in Italy who advise us on the process and qualifications. They place us on waiting list, and after a couple years and lots of paperwork we receive you."

"I don't believe this! What the damn hell are you telling

me? You waited until my dying days to reveal something like this?"

"Dying days? *Cosa stai dicendo*? What that even mean?"

"Never mind that for now. You had decades to tell me and every year you forgot to tell me. You have to be the worst person living on this planet." Roiled, I pounded the table, shaking its legs. "Let me have a sip of your drink. Now, dammit."

He slid the glass towards me. I curled my fingers around its center and inched it to my mouth. A smidge dabbed my tongue and burned like acid. I closed my eyes and puffed a few quick breaths through my nose, hoping my heart didn't explode from the stress. Dying in my father's arms not on my bucket list.

"Did the liquor calm you, Nico?"

"No. Nothing will ever fix this. Who are my parents?"

"Mom and me." His wide smile exposed his aging teeth and pale gums.

"That's not true. My biological parents. Who are they? Can I contact them?"

"Unfortunately, no. They die in bad car crash in Italy. The agency would not release names to us. We know you survive because you were in back of car in baby seat. They tell us if you be anywhere else in car, you die. We very honored and thankful to be granted the opportunity to have you. You are blessing in the horrible circumstance."

"If you were anyone else, I'd reach across the table and strangle you."

"Calm down, Nico. You in no shape to do those kinds of things, plus you should not be mad at just me. For start, we give you opportunity to continue your life with a family, which is better than foster home for who know how long. Plus, you come young, so accent not bad like us. Second, Lidia, your mom, play a major role in not telling you. I bring up many times, but she insist to keep quiet and say no. She did not want to affect you whole life. Maybe you go in downward spiral because you already have habits." He mimicked lifting a glass to his lips and puffing a cigarette. Good he didn't find a way to ape my *other* vices.

"Maybe you caused my drinking and whatever else because you didn't tell me. Did you ever think of that?" I wet my tongue once more with the gasoline from the tumbler.

"We never know, but I find that very doubtful. I think Lidia was correct not to tell you. Certain skeletons better left buried in the ground and throw away the key. It's easier on soul and mind. I'm sorry it be this way. Now, tell me about this dying you mention."

"I don't want to tell you any longer," I said with a fierce face, cheeks aflame.

I tasted the drink one more time, then slammed it atop the table and slid it towards him. He swiped it with magnificent speed and gulped what remained. The alcohol must've given him power because he drilled me for information once again.

"Tell me. I don't want to get mad, Nico. We made deal. I keep my part. Now, your turn."

We sat silent. This is what Ma meant by telling me to ask Papa. She was too afraid to tell me. Her hands as soiled as his in this cover-up of conscience. I owed him my promise because all the blame didn't fall upon him. I couldn't die knowing I'd lied to him or anyone else. Some things are better to be known.

"Fine... I'm dying. It's my heart. I keep popping pills to get me along to the next hour, or day, or whenever to visit another person I need to see, but I know that won't last forever. That's the reason I'm here."

"What the heck. Come on, Nico. *Dio mio*. You are lying or exaggerating. It cannot possibly be true. No. No. Imma older than you. I certain to die first and alone. Just look at me walk. Imma cripple in the stupid, standing wheelchair. It barely hold my weight. I shoot myself with all the drugs and drink too much. No. No. *Dio mio*." He spun the rocks glass like a top. "I don't believe *you* now. *Non dire bugie*. Don't say stupid things." He waved me away. "I need another drink."

"I'm not lying. It's over. I didn't want to tell you, but I have to honor my word. Without that, we have nothing, contrary to what you and Ma did to me."

He pushed himself up using the edge of the walker and lumbered to the counter, refilling the glass with bourbon, foregoing the cognac. He sucked down a shot, refilled it, and returned with the bottle in hand. He labored the circumference of the table palm over palm, then stopping beside me, and as I turned to face him, he lunged his arms over my shoulders. The dead weight raked the chair backwards, almost tipping it. Good thing it didn't happen because I wouldn't be able to move him off me. They'd find our bodies weeks later atop each other and think it was a murder-suicide. He kissed me upon the cheek and forehead as he had done when I was a child. Papa, although not my biological father, provided guidance and experiences I would not have had in this life, especially if I never exited the foster system.

I expressed my love for him and for the first time during our lives together he reciprocated. With tremendous effort and my heart under control, we rose to our feet and gazed into each other's eyes, time suspended.

"I was wrong for snapping at you. Thank you for saving me from an orphanage, for raising me, for giving me a chance in life. I know you meant well hiding the truth from me, but it still wasn't nice. I do wish we had more time together. I wish I wasn't dying." I cleared my throat and sniffled, resisting the urge to sob. "There are many things I wish I could change, which had never crossed my mind prior to today."

"*Ti amo*, my beautiful Nico. *L'amore di un padre non è sostituibile. Dio mio.* I'm sorry for the wrongs I did to you. I never make enough time for you and now, *bello* Nico, you don't have any time remain for me. I hope you think to stay with me until the end arrive. *Ti amo*." He turned away and patted his eyes with a soiled napkin from the table.

"Thank you, but I can't. I have a few more visits, which are of utmost importance. It'll be okay. We've shared enough in our lives." As we embraced, an idea popped into my mind. "I have a question for you. If you can help, then I'll forgive some of your wrongs."

We stepped away from each other.

"Yes, Nico. Ask. Ask. I do anything I can."

"This may seem odd, but do you have an extra cane I can borrow?"

The question stopped his tears and he asserted himself with a second wind, scratching his temple and twisting his chin.

"I believe I do. One second. *Un momento, bello* Nico. *Dio mio.* I be right back."

He shuffled to the closet and rummaged through its contents. Boxes tumbled, coat hangers clinked, and various articles of clothing fell onto the floor. After a few more thumps and thuds, he turned towards me with splayed arms and a wooden cane in hand.

"*Questo qua.* This art handmade in Italy by carpenter Giancarlo, but the village call him Geppetto. It made from black Cherrywood and the horsehead handle is bronze. Better than this stupid walker. Maybe, I keep. Just joking." He maneuvered it under his hand like a batonist.

"*Un carpentiere stupende.* It's beautiful."

"Yes, it is, just like my son." He handed me the crafted stick.

"Thank you. I'm sorry to cut this short, but I must go now."

"I understand. Do what you must do."

At the door, we waved at each other. He told me to return at any hour, leaving it unlocked for me to enter. I accepted with a nod and exited, the cane clicking in rhythm with my steps.

Several feet from the taxi, I surrendered to the shock of what he had told me and my future. Abdi rushed from the driver's seat and greeted me with open arms, his eyes moist as well. I draped my head over his shoulder and he caressed my back, relieving some of the stress.

"Thank you for waiting," I said, breaking our silence with a scraping voice.

"It will be okay, buddy." We stepped away from each other. "Come, have seat." He led me to the rear door and opened it, guiding me inside.

"It's as good as it will be. Time keeps running and it's difficult to catch."

"It is, Nico. What a beautiful cane," he said, twirling it within his grip and inspecting its intricacies.

"A gift from Papa."

"And a very good one. It will help you."

He rested the cane upon my lap, closed the door, and took his seat, drumming the steering wheel. "Where we go next?"

"Great question… Let's go to church but not to pray."

"What do you mean?" he asked, scrunching his nose.

"I don't think it's appropriate to tell you just yet. Later, possibly. Gustav suggested I face the demon haunting my soul."

"Okay, buddy. No problem. Which church?"

"Saint Patrick's of the United Trinity."

"Oh, that is very beautiful place. The design, the architect is amazing. We have some in Somalia that look like that."

"Yes, gothic."

CH 24

W ith both hands clutching the cane, I craned to view the oxidized angels resembling gargoyles sitting atop two spires overlooking East Main Street. Beside me, a fatigued and disgruntled Atlas holding the world atop his shoulders. I understood his plight. Slit by a scalpel into the ashen-stone façade, opaque windows prevented any view into the interior. Intimidating, bronze doors, with saddened caricatures of priests and martyrs along the handle returned me to the days of an insignificant self. I snaked between them, wedging the cane against their heaviness.

A gust of incense and melted wax blew across my face, soothing my lungs and calming my heart. As an altar boy, I spent many hours assisting the clergy. Donning a twill alb, I rang the bells, served wine, prayed with the parishioners, and placed cubes of Frankincense, Myrrh and charcoal into the censer, its aromas comforting to those mourning.

Before the nave, a fountain, as large as a bath, recycled thousands of gallons of holy water through the mouths of four cherubs mounted on each of its corners. I soaked my hand, spritzing drops onto myself, wondering how the churchgoers could tell if the holy water had been blessed and sterilized.

Marching ahead, my boots and cane clacked against the glistening tiles in tandem. On either side of the polished benches, chiseled columns ascended to the domed ceiling blanketed with elaborate murals, illuminated by a rainbow beaming through the stained glass.

The monstrous altar, covered by a platinum canopy, oversaw empty pews today, but on Sundays they filled for those searching to be blessed or absolved of their sins by the master sinner demeaning them from the pulpit. I grazed its cold, gold edge, surveying the emptiness, wondering the reasons egregious acts occurred within these walls. Behind the tribune, and a floor below, a hallway led to the rectory where no guarantees for an answer existed.

Laboring, I followed the curved stairwell to the lower floor, tracing the cracks on the plastered wall with a finger as I descended. At the end of the spiral, I firmed my heels onto the plush shag and pivoted. That sudden movement twisted my spine, sending a shockwave to my calves. I ground another set of pills between my teeth.

Must keep moving. Persevere, Nico. Persevere.

Mildew filled the air as it had when I was a child. Centered in the large room, a small, metal desk accented with two folding chairs. Kitty-corner on the opposite wall, a brown leather couch. Above it, a portrait of the most recent Pope hung next to a blue-eyed Jesus, who must've been born in Germany and not Bethlehem. Beside it, the familiar orange door leading to the interior of Father Dunnkirk's office stood ajar, allowing me to glimpse the plaid sofa bed where I once lay. Everything had changed, nothing had changed.

"Hello, sir. How can I help you?" The nun, with an Eastern-European accent, smiled, lifting her flawless cheeks chiseled from stone while her cobalt eyes placated me.

"I'm here to speak with Father Dunnkirk. Excuse me—Father Jerry Dunnkirk."

"Sir, are you a parishioner?" She cleared several

strands of blonde hair protruding from the bandeau. "Only parishioners are allowed to speak with Father Dunnkirk," she said with a deadpan tone.

"Well… I have been—am an attending member." Lying my only option to meet with the unholiness. Honesty sending me out the door and to the curb, thwarting any possibility of potential closure.

"Good to know, sir. May I confirm with your name, so I may look you up in our system?"

"A name?" I said, stupefied.

"Yes, sir. We keep track of all the members within the congregation."

"Oh, you mean contributors not members." Her contemptuous glance suggested she didn't appreciate my veracious statement. "Yes, Romano is the name." If she actually searched for me, she wouldn't find it. I gave up on the church years ago. I thought leaving the brainwashing group a better option than getting kicked out of it.

"There we go. I found you. Luigi Romano."

"Yes, correct. That's me," I said with confidence. Close enough. He didn't give much, but it was good enough to get me in, plus he owed me for all the lies.

"We appreciate all you've given to us. Looking forward to seeing you on Sundays and we hope you can find it in your heart to give more. Every little bit helps our Church."

"Okay, I'll try. Can I meet with Father Dunnkirk now?"

As if Papa could spare any money these days. They should send him free medication in exchange for decades-long donations. The Church never missed an opportunity to request more contributions, wanting to fill their coffers behind the ruse of getting people through the fantastical pearly gates. The megastructure on the first floor worth well over fifty million could pay for thousands of families in need, but they always want more.

"You may. He's in the confessional. The center booth on the right side. Just enter if the curtain is open."

"Thank you. Can I peek into his office? I used to be an altar boy at this church."

"Sure, but only a peep. It's private. Do you need help walking?"

"No. I'm fine."

As fine as eating burnt toast without water.

I lurched to the door and with my cane nudged it open, inching a view around the jamb. A blast of sandalwood musk mixed with cinnamon and vodka, which I was told many years ago to be grape juice, brought back the nightmare with such force I lost my breath as if someone had hit me in the gut with a baseball bat. Behind the barren desk, a burly leather chair and a picture of he and a Pope shaking hands. Brown, rimmed glasses, with lenses like windows, surrounded his deceitful eyes, which had stolen more than the kingdom of heaven from many. Just below, a pointed nose arching like an eave over his thin lips. Dark hair, oiled and raked to the left like a tilled field. Pitted scars and valleys etched his face like a dried riverbed. A forced gum smile pulled the edge of his mouth downward, exposing bucked teeth and a recessed chin. I scowled, snapping away from the door, latching onto the handle, and slamming it shut.

"Are you okay, sir?" Her voice teetering between concern and spite. "Do you need assistance?"

"Yes… yes. I'll be on my way to see the *Father*. I don't have much time. Thank you for your help. I hope your god strikes him down," I mumbled as I turned to exit.

"What did you say, sir?"

"I said, I hope you have a good day."

I waved and hoofed the spiraling steps to the confessional, shaking the brief thought to kill him. Approaching it, whispers and whimpers floated towards me, then Father Dunnkirk demanded the confessor say twenty "Hail Marys" and fifteen "Our Fathers." If only repeating something makes the sins disappear, then life would be a bowl of cherries. I leaned against a pew, waiting for the tormented churchgoer to exit. The curtain opened and out walked a disheveled man, crying like a child. A sleeveless shirt showed track marks on his skeleton arms, the bones stretching the skin like saran wrap. He glowered at me, then lowered his head and ran away. Without anyone present in the church, my time arrived to speak with Father Dunnkirk. I hobbled into the booth, smaller than a coffin, and leaned the cane against the wall, sitting upon a wooden seat with a thin black mesh separating us.

"Bless you, child. God welcomes you," he said, monotone in the same voice as years prior. His silhouette completed the sign of the cross.

"Thanks. Good to know."

A long pause ensued.

"You're welcome, my son. Please continue."

"With what?" I didn't know the next steps in this process. Decades had passed.

"Not a problem, my son. I'll help. You can start with,

'Bless me Father for I have sinned', then tell me how long since your last confession."

"Alright… Bless me *Father* for I have *not* sinned. Hey, Father, do you ever confess?"

He paused and retreated from the lattice, then returned, angling his head against the frame, attempting to identify me.

"Excuse me. Is this some kind of joke? Blasphemy is not accepted in God's home," he said with vigor. "You must respect the Lord's house for it is holy."

"It's not a joke, *Father*. I'm sure you know blasphemy better than I in this grandiose home. Don't you?"

"If you are here to confess, please do so, otherwise, please be on your way."

His gall reprehensible.

"I will not leave. You'll deal with this now while I'm still alive. Tell me, churchman, what's considered blasphemous?"

"Fine, I'll indulge your game. You must be one of the poor souls who doubt the power of the Lord. Plenty of things are irreverent, swearing, adultery, lying, fighting, stealing, and murder. There are too many to list. In essence, anything to do with hurting others as well as yourself. Are you familiar with the Ten Commandments?"

"I suppose," I said with sarcasm, which he ignored.

"Any violation of those rules is considered a sin."

"Does molestation fall within those guidelines as well?"

"What?" A thud echoed inside the cubicle. "Of course, it does."

"Good. Now, with that out of the way, do you know who I am? Do you remember me?"

"No. How can I? I meet thousands of parishioners and

your face is blocked by the grille. Stop playing games. What is it you ask of me?"

"Your younger parishioners and altar boys might not have the logic to process your impiety yet. I used to be one of them, but now I'm older and know better. Do you think they know?"

"I'm certain because they respect this Church, unlike you, you fiend."

"Do you know the seven deadly sins?"

"Why are you asking me these questions?"

"Answer, *padre*, please."

"Yes."

"So, you know one of them is lust, correct?" I said.

"Yes," he said with indifference.

"The same lust you used to do unspeakable things to me and other boys."

"I don't know what you're talking about. Are you here for penance or not?"

"I'm here to listen to a confession from someone who's broken more than just commandments. Who has destroyed the lives of the innocent in the parish and continues to ruin them. Who's broken laws and never paid the consequences. Closure is what I seek during my remaining time on this wicked earth. You *will* give me that much," I demanded, slapping the thin wall beside me.

"Again, I don't know what you're insinuating. I've done nothing wrong. This church, my parish, and God. They are who I am devoted to."

"You've taken more than given. You've hurt more than loved. You've destroyed more than nurtured," I said, tremoring, spit splattering the webbing between us.

"I've done nothing of the sort. I love everyone and care for them all."

"You hurt me as a child. You took advantage of my naiveté. Even when I questioned you, you told me I was wrong. That I was imagining the devil upon me. That the nightmares were just useless fears. You lied. You deceived. You destroyed a part of me I can never replace."

"You are mistaken, my son. I did nothing of the sort." He slammed his palm against the grating. "I care for all my children. And adults. Speak. Don't converse in riddles."

"You care about nothing. You're a self-pleasing monster. You had me lay on the couch after feeding me vodka mixed with juice and then violated me. I'd wake delirious. You'd say I'd fallen asleep and nothing had happened."

"Nothing did happen. You always slept on the couch. It wasn't my fault you tired."

"Then how do you explain those times when I awoke disrobed, my underwear wrapped around my knees?"

"You probably did that while sleeping. A lot of children go through that phase."

"Liar. I learned much later in life what you did to me. Now, I sit beside you listening to your denials. My end is imminent and your audacity is repugnant."

"I did nothing to you or anyone."

"Then, why is it I know you have a birthmark on your inner thigh? Why is it you always had wipes to clean up after me? Tell me, *Father*. Or should I call you Satan?" He remained silent, breathing heavy, his outline shifting and shuffling within the chamber. I continued my interrogation, hoping for an admission. His denials broke my fortitude. I slipped a set of pills into my mouth to tame the raging heart. I heaved, swallowing the bile and continued. "Do you even remember my name, Father? Or is the list too long."

"I don't know what you're talking about. Things that happen in life are sometimes out of our control. We ask forgiveness and move on. Turn to God for forgiveness."

"I did nothing wrong to you. And, I don't believe in forgiveness. I believe in truth, in culpability. When we arrive at the point, then I'll consider leaving you and this horrible place. How many were there in your life? Tell me, dammit."

"Well…" He paused, thrumming his fingers against the mesh. "I don't know."

"You don't even have the respect to remember us after destroying our souls. You are worse than the devil. You stole a part of my life I can never regain. Why did you do that to me, to us?"

"It wasn't personal…" I glimpsed a smirk through the grille. "Things happen, urges have to be satisfied, voices have to be quelled, but I didn't do anything wrong to you or anyone else. It was mutual."

"What? You can't even admit what you did. You're beyond help. You need to die." I grabbed my cane and struck the wall ahead of me. He fell backwards with a thud. "Don't you want to know my name?"

"No," he said, disappearing within the cubicle.

"Don't think of leaving. I'll chase and flog you with my cane. The top is metal and it'll crack your skull. You'll die on the floor of the Church and others will come forward. I demand you stop lying and ask my name."

"No, I will not. End this. It's over. You've said your peace. I didn't do anything wrong to you or anyone else."

"Damnit. I'll tell you my name. It's Romano. Nicola Romano. The son of Luigi and Lidia. Do you remember now? Driving me home in your fancy car with your hand between my thighs. My parents helped bankroll your church filled with debauchery."

"My apologies, but I do not."

"You preyed on me and can't even remember my name. What is wrong with you? Have you no shame?"

"We all have diseases and some don't have a cure."

"That's the first truth you've told. I'm dying, but it's you who deserves to die. Admit the hell you thrusted upon me and I will leave" I said, massaging my trembling legs to remove the tingling.

"Fine. If I did something wrong, then forgive me, but you must understand, it wasn't my fault."

"I want to jump through this divider and strangle you. I'm dying and have nothing to lose." I rapped the cane across the mesh, then hammered the wood enclosure. "Or maybe I'll return and shoot you dead, even if it's my last deed. Promise you'll resign from the church and disappear, or you'll meet your maker soon. Tell me and I'll leave."

"Promises are easier said than kept."

"Don't play with the words. Tell me!"

"I can't leave the Church. No way. It's all I have."

"You should've thought about the penalties for ruining our lives. Tell me," I commanded.

"Fine... but you have to do me one favor."

"And, what is that?"

"Forgive me."

"Not a chance in hell, heaven, or whatever worlds you've invented for a false absolution. I'll leave that option to your god. Your best bet is to crawl into a cave and end your life because the future is grim."

"Don't do this to me. Please forgive me."

"Never. Walk ahead of the congregation and admit your depravities. Only then, you will be pardoned. If not, then end it with a rope from the rafters above the altar. I'm done with you. My life is more valuable than yours and you're wasting what little time I have remaining. To hell with you. *La morte è facile, ma la vita è difficile. Pezza di merda. Spero che soffra quando morirai.*"

The pompous bastard had no intention to come clean to me or anyone. Our back and forth had reached a pointless pinnacle. The idea of killing him spectacular at first thought, but could backfire, making him a martyr. Riled, I snapped the curtain open with the cane, gripped the edge of the booth, and escaped the confines of the box, setting another set of pills under my tongue.

As I approached the exit, he bellowed to wait. I ignored the request and turned, glimpsing his miserable countenance, alit by a series of votive tapers and sanctuary candles. The man pictured in the office far removed. Boils layered his skin like a pebbled road. Rotten teeth and a gum smile forced me to retreat, fearing the gargoyle could turn me to stone. Rushing from the church with unfettered, unexplainable strength, I burst through the mammoth doors to never return.

Steps from Abdi, I crashed onto the front fender. He ran

to my rescue.

"Are you okay, buddy? You seem okay before, like marathon man."

"I lost all my energy. Good the car saved me from the pavement."

"I help you," he said, lifting my shoulders and guiding me to the backseat. "How it go in Church?"

"I cleared a part of my conscience. Holding certain things inside for too long isn't good for the spirit. Now, I'm as free as I can be from his evil."

"If you wish to tell me, I listen. If no, not big deal. I am happy for you, Nico."

I firmed my brow. "I don't want to talk about it," I said, deadpanned.

He winked with a thumbs up. "No problem. Okay, buddy. Where we go next?"

"We're going to Alessio. My son. I'll bang harder on his door and won't leave until he answers or arrives. If I must, I'll die on his steps. But first can I borrow your cell?"

"Sure. What for?" he said, handing me the phone.

"Thank you. I have to tie up another loose end."

I dialed 911, and just as I was about to press the call button, I realized they would trace it to Abdi. I couldn't burden him. He'd already done more for me than anyone else in my lifetime. I returned the cellphone and asked him to take me to the nearest repurposed payphone. I dialed the operator who connected me to the Rochester Police Department.

Officer Michelle Gentry answered. I explained the importance of the call and that it involved sexual assault. After introducing myself, I gave her the assailants, Father Jerry

Dunnkirk and Michael Pollock. I explained I'd been to Precinct 13 and reported the crimes, speaking with Private Investigator Jasper Albatross and Detective Sonja Struthers, skipping the follow-up meetings due to fear and embarrassment. Instead, we spoke by phone and they assured me a file is open because other incidents were being investigated. I begged her to have them arrested. She advised she noted all the details and will forward the information to the appropriate personnel. They'd contact me as soon as possible. I thanked her, giving Ariel's number for further consideration. We ended the call and I returned to Abdi, setting off to visit Alessio.

GIANNI FRANCO

CH 25

"I have an idea, Abdi," I said as he bumped the front wheel of the car against the curb outside Alessio's apartment on Hemingway Drive.

"What's that, buddy?" he said, stretching his arm across the headrest and twisting his face.

"Since I'm weakening, will you help me knock on the door?"

"Of course, buddy."

"I wish I had one of those oxygen tanks. My insides are disintegrating and the pills keep working less and less. This idea to visit everyone was wrong. I should've waited or not done it at all."

"We move forward, but I understand. Don't worry, I help you, my friend."

He opened the door and pulled me to my feet, grabbing the cockeyed cane dangling from the edge of the seat, setting it into my hand, then slid his arm around my back, nudging it against my armpit. We shuffled to the apartment, pausing once for the two-pill regimen. Atop the steps, my legs surrendered. Abdi caught me with his shoulder and coaxed me to the porch. I firmed my soles against the concrete and propped my knees against the shingled wall. Raising the cane high, I whacked the door with the metal handle. Determined for a response, I continued banging as Abdi ogled, wincing with each thunderous thwack.

"Follow my lead," I said, smirking. "We're not leaving

until he comes out."

"Okay, buddy." He joined the onslaught, pounding the door with his fist.

I stopped for a breath, then reconnected like Joe DiMaggio. Well, at this point, more like a Wiffle ball batter. "Call his name. You have better lungs than me."

"Is it Al—ess—io?"

"You don't have to whisper. We're making enough noise. And, yes."

"Good. I want to make sure. No mistake."

"You got that right. No time for those."

We continued like wild animals thrashing a cage, ignoring the neighbors peeping between their curtains. A police car slowed by the cab. I grabbed Abdi's arm, ceasing the ruckus. The officers made brief eye contact, and as I whipped my head away, they sped off with sirens blaring. We were saved by someone else's misery. Jail, a bad option, whether dying or alive. We returned to the drubbing and within seconds stunned again into stopping. A man dressed in a dark t-shirt and jeans espied us from the sidewalk. His gait increased to a brisk jog.

"What the hell are you people doing?" he barked.

"We're waiting for Alessio to answer the door. Do you know him?" I said, hiding the cane behind my leg.

Abdi jumped to my side and raised his hands. "We want no trouble. Please, no trouble."

"I'm not looking for it either." He jumped the steps and planted himself ahead of us with a hand on hip. "And yes, I know him. I *am* him."

We glanced at each other, amazed at the coincidence.

He less, I assume, since he lived at the residence and we the intruders. I studied his gentle, youthful face for a bit with an uneasy stare. He furrowed his brow and narrowed his hazel eyes. A full head of hair rested over his collar, just atop his shoulders. For a brief moment, I imagined myself young again, he and Beatrice sitting upon a blanket on the lawn waiting for me to arrive. The vision short-lived as he interrupted my daydream.

"What do you want, old man? You damaged my door," he growled, fingering the marks.

Abdi turned with an abhorrent face, his lips parting without utterance. I slouched and frowned. My eyes moistened, and before a tear trickled, I stood as tall as my back allowed and pursed my lips. Any sign of weakness at this point might torpedo my chances to know or learn a bit about him.

"We apologize. I just want to talk. I've been trying to find you. I would've searched years ago, but I wasn't told about you. I'm Nico… Nicola Romano. Beatrice—" I cleared my throat. "—your mom and I met a long time ago. We shared amazing love and from our time together we had you. I'm your father."

"You're lying." His haughty laugh shook my bones. "Get out of here, man. My father died a long time ago."

Damn you, Beatrice. She lied, saying she explained everything to him. Funts and cuckers. Everyone lies.

"I'm telling the truth," I said with pleading eyes. "You have to believe me."

"I promise he honest," Abdi said, pointing at me. "He a very good man."

"Of course, I believe you both."

"Thank you," I said. The dread ephemeral.

"And I believe poodles poop peanut-butter cups." The laughter arrived once again followed by callousness. "No, I don't believe you. Two guys are banging on my door like lunatics. One of them looks like a zombie. You don't find this strange?"

"I see your point, but we wouldn't be here if it wasn't true." An idea popped into mind. "Look," I said, pulling the note from my pocket with his address written by Beatrice. "Your mom gave this to me. This is her handwriting. I'm not lying. Does it look familiar?"

He swiped it, scanned it, and shoved it into my hand. "It could be hers or anyone else who writes like her. It's not like she signed it."

"No, she didn't, but she wrote it. I wouldn't lie about a piece of paper. Why would I keep something like that in my pocket?"

"Probably because you and your buddy were going to rob me. Then, you saw me coming and came up with an amazing story. I know your kind, shady and always scheming for the next high or drink. I should call the cops."

"Please don't. I can't go to jail. I'll die there. I still have things to accomplish."

He crossed his arms and curled his lip. "Okay, I won't call them. Only because your appearance is unhealthy and wretched. How about I give you five dollars, will you leave then?"

"Thank you for not calling them, but no. I'm here to talk to you... about us."

"How about ten? Five for each. That'll get you a couple beers. I can't offer more because I'm low on cash."

He pulled out a meager wad and slipped two fives from the top, leaving the singles below. Abdi remained silent with a perplexing glance.

"We don't want money. We need to talk. About us. I'm not leaving until we do," I said with determination.

He retracted the money into his pocket, then with a scathing glare firmed his lips and massaged his temple. "Alright. If the only way I'm going to get rid of you is by talking to you for a few minutes, then let's do it. I'm only giving you a few. After that, you leave, and take your buddy with you."

"Good start, my friend," Abdi whispered, then proclaimed to our standing triangle, "I wait in car. Take all time you need. Good luck, buddy."

"Thank you." I nodded to Abdi as he walked away, then engaged Alessio. "Can we go inside and talk?"

"Let's start out here and we'll see how it goes."

"Fair enough. So… how have you been?"

"Good." He grunted with a grin. "I *am* young."

"Yes, you are. It's only a wish for me now." I paused, thinking about the precise words to keep him interested.

"Is that all you have to say? Are we done here?"

"No," I blurted. "Not at all. I want to spend what little time I have with you, and hope we can connect. I was robbed of those opportunities my whole life. All's I ask is that we try."

"I've already told you, old man—I mean Nico. My dad died. I don't know who you are and I can't give you what you're searching for."

"Let's go inside. Call your mom. Beatrice will tell you about us."

He shook his head. "No. I'm not a child. I don't need

to talk to her. The truth is he died. Long gone. My mom's boyfriends and that loser who beat her raised me." He hung his head, scuffing his polished boots against the pavement.

"But we share a bond, a blood bond. It's stronger than anything anyone could ever have. Look at my eyes. You'll see we're the same."

"Are you Dracula? Come on, man. Anything else you want to talk about?"

Our gaze met. He probably couldn't refuse the chance to prove me wrong. In that brief moment, his eyes widened and he seemed to believe me. Pressing the topic required patience.

"Are you dating?"

"Yeah. I suppose I do well for myself."

"Anyone serious?"

"There is someone. We've been dating for a few months. Her name is Eloa. She's from Brazil. Beautiful, exotic, and speaks like four languages. Anyway... that's none of your business."

"Very cool. Your mom and I dated. We loved each other. I think we still do. Or at least I still love her in a certain way. Every day we spent with each other was like frolicking in lavender fields filled with strawberries."

"If it was so good, what happened?"

"One day, out of the blue, she ended it. I learned later it had to do with being pregnant with you. She didn't want to tell me and felt better raising the child without me. I can't lay blame, since it's her body, but I wish she would've told me. If she did, then our meeting today would be much different."

"Assuming I believe you, then that's screwed up on my mom's part."

"You should believe me, but in the end it was her choice. It's not about fault at this point. By the way, your middle name is my first name. She did that on purpose."

"Coincidence is all it is." He dismissed my argument with a wave.

"No, it's not. She wanted to include me somewhere in your life." I sighed with despair. "Just not physically." Our back and forth useless. I could better explain the beginning of civilization to a cat, then Beatrice's motives for not involving me in his upbringing. I needed more time and another angle to convince him. "Do you mind if I use your bathroom?"

"Oh, come on, man. I told you only a few minutes. Now, you want to come into my place? I don't think so. Get your cabbie friend to take you to a gas station for a bathroom and beer." He retrieved his wallet.

"Please, no. Put it away. I won't take long. I promise. I don't think I can make it to Abdi." I squeezed my crotch and faked grimacing, hoping for a successful play on a sliver of emotion.

"Fine, old man. Follow me."

"The name is Nico. And, thank you."

"Okay, *Nico...*," he said, shaking his head.

He retrieved his keys and unlocked the door. "This way," he said, pointing in no specific direction. "Straight ahead. It's not worth writing home about, but it's better than a gas station. The bathroom is on your left at the end of the hallway. It's a little warm out there today. Do you want a drink?"

"Sure. Thanks. Greatly appreciated." The cane clomped between strides while I sidled the wall with my shoulder.

"Water, wine, or liquor?" he yelled.

"Water and wine is fine," I said from behind the closed door. A chance to share a drink with him worth more than winning the lotto.

"What did you say?—Never mind. I'll pour one of each."

Glasses clanged and bottles rattled. I stretched for a towel, dabbing the sweat stinging my eyes and soaking my brow, pausing for a moment at the reflection in the mirror; crimson starbursts filling the whites of my eyes, a wan face splotched with blue hues converging at my lips. I kecked, then gulped and blacked out, falling backwards, my tailbone striking the toilet seat, saving me from the floor.

"Everything okay in there, man?"

He should've came running, knocking on the door to check on me, but such utopias only exist in movies. Not even a follow-up question arrived. I murmured all's well as I struggled to stand, pushing from the toilet-paper holder, which flexed like a toothpick. Good thing it didn't snap or the sooty tiles would become my permanent bed. I lunged for the sink, spinning the faucet, and splashing cold water onto my forehead. Regaining some composure, I sipped from cupped palms to soothe my sweltering chest. A cracking spine guided me into an upright stance only to encounter cricking shoulders, which didn't respond to a massage. Just another problem to add to the never-ending list. Lowering my head, more for comfort than sadness, I entered the hallway and lurched to the kitchen. Clueless, he stood by the counter.

"You made it back, old man? I was thinking to call an ambulance, if you didn't return." He spanned his arms with a salesman smile. "Cheap wine and liquor at your service with expensive tap water on the side."

"Thank you, Alessio."

"Not a problem. You don't look so good. Rough time in the lav?" He chortled. "Do you want to have a seat?"

No point in explaining my bathroom woes. "Yeah, sure. I need all the rest I can get these days."

Four mismatched chairs surrounded an oval table with a battered surface. He placed the drinks on the areas without the particle board exposed. We sat silent studying each other. I, thinking what to say to bring us closer, and he probably thinking how to get rid of me.

"So… Nico. You have nice eyes, even with all that red and yellow."

"I suppose I'll take that as a compliment. Those eyes should look familiar. If I was a bit younger, they'd look like yours."

"Yeah, I suppose I can see it."

"Does that mean you believe I'm your father?"

"No. It means I can see the color resemblance."

"Come on, Alessio. You have to know it's true. Can't you feel the bond between us? Let's call your mom." I made an attempt to stand, but my hands slipped on an oil spot atop the table.

"Slow down, old man. Don't hurt yourself. And, we're not calling. I'll deal with her later. I'm intrigued by you. Tell me how you ended up this way."

"Might be easier to just call her. You're more important than my story. Plus, it's too long and not exciting."

"Give me the shortened version. I want to know."

"Did you know your great-grandparents on my mother's side are still alive?"

"I don't want to know about them. Just you. Tell me. I don't like to beg, but I'll say it. Please."

"Alright. Short and cropped. I was born in Italy and brought to America as a youth. Not many people liked the way I looked, or talked, or my Italian heritage. They couldn't pronounce my name, and some still can't, so I used different versions to avoid the never-ending questions, 'How do you say it? How do you spell it? Are you Italian? How come you're not American?' Your mom was the first to say it correctly and from that day forward I fell in love with her. We had more than just the name thing, but, I have to admit, it was the initial attraction because it showed her appreciation for me. After we broke up, I lumbered through life searching for love I could never find, although I have found it with Ariel, but it was different with your mom. Some days the bottle became my best friend, and at times, those days turned into months. It wasn't anything crazy. I still went to work at the deli. I had interviews at other places, but they turned me down because of my name or green card. It was okay. *Such is life* as your mom says.

"And now, after a hospital stay some time ago, they've told me my lab tests aren't good and that I'm dying based on some program called iLifeCheck. The timeframe is unclear, but it's soon compared to how long I've lived. I set out on this wild notion I had to visit those that mean something to me, which brings me to you. I've been trying for two days to meet and talk. One of my last wishes, since I don't believe in any of that afterlife mumbo-jumbo. That's it in a nutshell."

He closed his gaping mouth. "I was right to be intrigued, although I was hoping for happier, exciting times. Mom uses that saying way too often. It's annoying and odd that you know it."

"It couldn't be truer for me today. I have nothing left but to convince you that you're my son. If I could turn back time, I would've been there every step of the way. Will you allow me to be part of your life? A father to a son. Please."

My hopeful eyes welled. A lingering silence filled the space between us. Dispirited, I cleared the lump in my throat, interrupting the deathly pause. His poker face offered no clues to a response. A rejection certain to shred my psyche like paper and gluing those pieces together impossible. My inescapable end arriving soon. I wiped my cheeks, straightened my strained shoulders, and studied his every move, hoping for a hint. He took a deep breath and exhaled. I held mine. He extended his hands to the center of the table, exposing his palms.

"I think we can work something out," he said with reassurance. "Place your hands in mine."

"Come on. You're joking, right? I put out my hands, then you take them away and laugh at my demise." I unfolded my hands and inched them towards him, then retreated.

"No, Nico. I'm being honest. Place them in mine."

I moved my hands within a fingertip of his and he flinched as if pulling them away. "I'm just kidding. Come on, Nico." He smirked and nodded. I followed through, and his warmth heated my cold, pasty hands like a blanket.

"Thank you, son. What's stirring inside me is inexplicable. Positive, of course," I said, eking out a smile.

"You're very welcome, but I'll be honest, I'm not ready to use that other word for you yet," he said with a smile that reddened his cheeks.

"It's fine. I'll take what I can get. What made you change your mind? I thought for sure you were going to say no."

He paused for a moment, gazed at the window, then returned to me. "Three simple reasons: One, you knew Mom's saying; second, she always used to talk about a guy who worked in a deli. She said he was my father, but he died one day in the city, either by a mugging or got hit by a car. I really don't know that part too well. I never pried about the specifics, and at this point, I don't believe them. Third, why would a dying man want to find me? I think I'm important, more to do with ego, but in reality I'm not *that* important. Also, as a side note, I don't think you have the strength to steal from me."

"You're correct on all of the above. Smart kid, you are. I never believed dreams could come true until this moment," I said, awed, squeezing his hands with the strength of a sloth. "How do we continue? Son… I can't believe I've uttered that word more than once. Am I in a dream?"

"Dreams are realities for those who want them to be true. You've shown me that as well. I would never have chased someone like you did." He sighed and rolled his eyes. "That's a lot of work."

"As you get older, you realize when you want something, it's the hope in obtaining it that's worth more than any immediate pleasure. I would've found a way to locate you even if you lived on the other side of the world. I bet you would've done the same, plus you're still young."

"I guess you're right. Maybe if I was in your position and desired something, I would've chased it," he said, grinning.

"Well, we have the same blood, so I think you'd act like me. It's difficult to break those bonds."

"I understand now. I'm a little of you and a little of Mom. Where do we go from here? I don't know what to say or do. Flabbergasted might be an understatement."

"We don't have to go far. I just wanted to be in your presence and be accepted. Tell me what you're wanting to do. If I wasn't here, what are you pursuing?"

"Well… this is a little embarrassing. I want to be a writer. When I'm not scribbling dreams upon the page, I'm creating Italian and French cuisine at La Trattoria." He bowed his head.

"Cool for both options. Do you mean stories and such?" I said, enthused.

He jolted the seat. "Yeah! Fiction, nonfiction, poetry, short stories. My dream is to write a few novels like Hemingway or Bukowski. I'm not as good as them, but I have to try."

"Don't say you're not as good. That's all relative based on timing and who's reading. There are a multitude of popular authors who don't write well. You'll do fine. Only compare yourself to you. If you write it, someone will read it, even if it's just one person."

"Thanks for the positivity. I'm not giving up just yet. Haven't been able to shake the writing disease since I was a child."

"I know what you mean. I used to write as well. Being an immigrant and trying to perfect English, I studied dictionaries, thesauri, and read a lot of books. I gave up because I didn't have support. Eventually, I trained my mind to silence the urges. Since you have them, you better keep feeding them. I wish I could live long enough to read your stories. I'm certain Beatrice will love them. I promise on her behalf."

"You're funny. She doesn't really support me. I suppose she'll come around when I publish a novel." He drummed the table and flipped his hair. "Like you said, it'll be fine. I just need to trust myself."

"And you have cheffing as a backup plan."

"Second options are an excuse not to pursue one's dreams. Plan A is all that matters," he said with panache.

I paused to process his statement, realizing after repeating it to myself that it rang as true as a bell in a church tower. "You're correct and advanced in your age. Yes, that's the most important thing to do. Don't listen to any negativity and always pursue the things you love."

As he pondered his thoughts, I scanned the apartment. A quaint place with simple furniture scattered throughout the open space. A fireplace, which didn't seem operable, centered the living room, and above it, an empty mantle with a bare wall. The space perfect for my idea. I stood from the table and told him I'd return in a moment. Unfazed, he stared into the distance probably pondering his next novel, or short story, or how to throw me out. With cane in hand, I hobbled to the entrance at a good pace. As I opened the door, Abdi showed, holding the portrait.

"Abdi. Do you have ESP? How? Why?"

"I know…, buddy. A very weird shake came to me while I sit inside car and knew you missing picture. Make sure he take care of it for you."

"I will, but I have so many more questions."

"Don't worry about those. Take care of important things with son. Everything be fine. I be waiting for you."

"Thank you, Abdi. What would I have done without

you? You're beyond amazing."

"I'm not. I here to help. Go, my friend. Give to him."

He bolted before I could say more. I snugged the portrait under one arm and stabilized it against my body while the other negotiated the cane towards Alessio. Within a few feet of the table, the frame slipped from my body and burred into the floor. He looked at me startled.

"I'm sorry, Alessio. I tried to set it down, but fell short."

He rubbed his jaw. "No problem. What's under the sheet?"

"Just a picture of—me. It was just an idea to bring this to you. You know… for remembrance."

"I get it." He nodded to confirm. "Show me."

"Well, this a portrait drawn for me by my beautiful Ariel from when I was younger. When I was innocent. The chipper years."

He snapped the sheet from the picture like a matador. I stood in amazement, hoping he'd view the canvas as a Picasso or Rembrandt. He didn't, instead sighing and raising a brow.

"Looks good, but what do you want me to do with it?"

"Hang it." Simpering, I pointed to the wall above the fireplace. "You can remember me every day."

"It's an option." He studied the painting. "She captured you well. Your face glows in the neutral colors. You know… it could be perfect for that wall."

"Ariel, my love, is talented. All's I ask is that you consider it. We have something to share and this is all I have to give, excluding our bloodline."

"I understand and promise to think about it. By the way, you look good. I wish I would've known you prior to today's encounter. You almost look like me," he said, smirking.

"Of course. You're my boy, my son. Mount it whenever you like, so you can see me for what I was, not what I am."

"Pictures are worth more than a thousand words, so it's a possibility." He paused, then ran his fingers through his hair. "On second thought, this is all too much for me to process."

"Come on, Alessio. You must accept the portrait," I said, slapping the table.

"I think it's time for you to leave. I can't handle the stress from this, us. I need some time alone. Don't be offended. It is what it is. I have to pass on the picture."

"Us? That part is over. I'm dying. Thinking about the hows and whys will only waste more time, which I, we, don't have to spare."

He thumped his body against the backrest. "Look Nico, or Dad, or whatever we need to call you. You've been missing for all these years and you can't possibly expect everything to go your way like a fairy tale. This is real life."

He stood and leaned the portrait against the counter, pouring himself a tall whiskey, and returned to his seat. We sat silent. He, staring at the spinning cubes within the glass, and I, counting the stipples on the ceiling above. I adjusted myself in the chair while folding and unfolding my hands atop the table. He ignored me.

"I should go." I rose with the cane. "I have a few more stops. I hope I can make them. I'm tired and sick. If you want to find me, I'll be at the shore later. Call your mom. She'll tell you where. I'm sorry it had to be this way, Alessio. If I could change any of this, I would. I hope I see you later." At the door I stopped and turned. "If I don't see you, I wish for you to have a perfect life. Make sure you wake up every day and accept it as your last. Living with regret is unbecoming."

Abdi exited the car, tucked the cellphone into his front pocket, and welcomed me with a wide smile at the rear fender. I wanted to wail, but my mind demanded otherwise, telling me I'd visited my son and should be satisfied considering the circumstances. I obeyed, negotiating my body upon the seat like a blob of dough as Abdi kneaded me, manipulating my body upright and situating my feet and cane upon the floorboard, then tapping the door shut with his hip.

He turned towards me, flopping his hand atop front seat. "How it go?"

"Well… I left the portrait with him and dashed." I followed with a disheartening sigh.

"What went wrong?"

"I expected better, but I can't blame him for how he's feeling about me and the whole situation. It's horrible. I've missed his whole life."

"There's nothing you can do about it. Try to stay positive for whatever remains ahead."

"I'll do my best," I said with a twisted grin.

"Good, buddy. Keep smiling. Where we going next?"

"I don't have enough money to pay for the cab rides, but I do have enough to buy lunch. Do you want something to eat? Are you hungry?"

"Sure. Anywhere you want."

"We can go to a café. Something simple. My appetite is low."

"Perfect, buddy. I'm looking forward to it."

GIANNI FRANCO

CH 26

He turned onto Alexander Street, stopping in front of La Bella Vita Café. The sign, painted by a local muralist, showcased two, overflowing demitasses paired with sugar-filled teaspoons above the name denoted in yellow calligraphy. He offered I exit to find a table while he circled the streets locating an empty spot. I didn't want to enter alone, so I told him I'd wait with him in the car. He acknowledged with a wink in the rearview and pulled forward a few feet, then rammed the brakes.

"I see one, Nico. Hold tight," he shouted, followed by a cheer, cranking the steering wheel like a Formula 1 driver.

I whiplashed against the backseat like a lone rag in a washing machine as he negotiated a U-turn between oncoming traffic, stopping just beyond an empty space, then slapping the gear into reverse. Before the vehicle behind us could react, he smoked the tires, sliding the car into a tight space snug against the curb. My heart raced, and for once, I enjoyed the palpitations from the daredevil antics. I still had to swallow a set of pills, but it was well worth the Alexander Street rollercoaster ride.

Huffing, he caught his breath. "Are you okay, buddy?"

"Yes. Thank you for the rush. It's been a while since I experienced anything fun."

"No problem. If you want, we do it again," he said with exhilaration.

"It's alright. I don't want to lose the parking space." It

was the only excuse that came to mind. As much as I wanted another fervent spin around the track, I don't think I could handle it.

"Sometimes driving is fun. I be right there."

He rushed to the door as I pulled the handle. Leaning onto his arm, he yanked me upward, locking a wrist with one hand and the forearm with the other. Handing me the cane, he smirked and nudged me with his elbow. We laughed the whole way to the front door while he mimicked an exaggerated driver holding an invisible steering wheel, not withholding the guttural intonations and verbal squeals. Entering the café, we tried to tamp our hysterics but to no avail. Our outpourings continued and the waitress had to repeat her request to seat us several times. She didn't acknowledge my apologies, leading the way to a small table, then dashing to the bar and returning with two waters and menus. I set mine down, knowing my order while Abdi perused the three-page lamination.

"What can I get for you gentlemen?" she asked with docile eyes and a quirky smile.

I squinted at her name tag. "Hi... Beth?"

"Yes. Short for Elizabeth, but it's too long to fit." She shrugged.

"Cool. My vision isn't what it used to be. Glad I guessed right." My giggle went from a snort to a cough in a blink of an eye. I held my breath and sipped the water, hoping it didn't turn into another bout. Abdi stretched towards me, grasping my hand and the hacking subsided. "Please excuse the choking, Beth. I mean Elizabeth." I cleared my throat. "I know what I want."

"Great. And Beth is fine." We exchanged a subtle nod.

"How about you, Abdi?"

"I ready, buddy."

"Perfect. I'll have a slice of Tiramisu and three rainbow cookies."

"Great choice. And for you, sir?"

"Same as my friend. He know more about Italian food than me. His name is Nico."

"That's good to know. Anyway, great choice again. I promise neither of you will be disappointed. Did you want anything else to go with the pastries? Espresso, latte, or…?"

"I shouldn't, but I'll have an espresso," I said, glancing at Abdi. "You only live once, right?"

"Correct, buddy. I have mocha latte."

"Good idea. Can you add a splash of milk in mine and make it an espresso macchiato? Please."

"Of course. I'll be back in a few. Do you want everything served together?"

"Sure. Not a problem," I said. Abdi confirmed with a blink, then sipped the water.

"Perfect. Be back soon," she said, walking away, scribbling the notepad.

"This is nice place, Nico. I never been."

"It's a quiet café. Good place to bring a date, or write, or think to yourself. No one bothers you, even if you stay for a few hours. I used to come all the time when I was healthy. The espresso and cookies are so good you'll think you're in Italy. There's no other place like this in the city."

Exposed rustic trusses separated the copper ceiling etched with florals, complementing an array of murals depicting Roman and Greek architecture, as well as montages from the Renaissance representing the musical arts. The sporadically placed tables battered like they were taken from a thousand-year-old cantina. Those seated near us whispered, respecting the patrons reading on the couches and chaises, the classical music on low volume. Every so often, a wave of yeast and baked loaves drifted from the kitchen, traveling throughout the café, enticing a stomach rumble.

"Are rainbow cookies like…?" He pointed towards the sky.

"Not really. More like the colors on the Italian flag. So, pretend the tricolor is made with almond paste and topped with chocolate. They make them in long slabs, then cut them into pieces. My mom had a friend when I was young who baked them all the time. Her name was Mariella. Most of the cookies she created weren't good, but the rainbows flawless. I could eat a whole block in one sitting. They were a delicacy for me because, oddly enough, Ma could bake every cookie except those. You're going to love them. I promise," I said, rubbing my hands with anticipation.

"I can't wait. I bring my wife one day, so she can enjoy some Italian cookies.

"She won't be disappointed."

"If you have time, I take you to Somali cuisine."

"I wish, Abdi. One of a list of many things I didn't get to experience. It's odd…"

"What is, buddy?"

"You realize life is short only when you're told you're going to die, and not one decade, or year, or day sooner."

Beth interrupted our deep conversation at the perfect time. With tray in hand, she leaned across the table and deposited our orders. "If you need anything else, just holla." She beamed with a dimpled cheek and winked.

"Will do. Thank you for everything. You've been a great hostess."

"Not a problem, but I only brought you cookies and coffee. Pretty easy."

"It means a lot to me." I'm not sure she understood my comment or grateful grin, but I didn't need to get into the whole end-of-life thing with her.

"Okay... sir," she said with a perplexed glance. "Enjoy. Let me know if you need anything else." She hustled to the counter, then disappeared into the kitchen, the double-doors smacking the wall behind her.

"She nice," Abdi said, picking up the layered cookie. He gobbled a square in one bite and his eyes widened. "This is crazy. So good. How can cookie be so perfect?"

"Yes, they are. I told you. I wouldn't lie." With care, I slid a piece into my mouth, savoring the moment, the chocolate and almond paste melting on contact.

"I love this country. It have so many options. And most important, no war."

"True. I've been meaning to ask, but haven't had a chance. How were you able to get to America?"

"It difficult process from Africa. We seek asylum and find legal sponsor in United States. Then, we pay thousands of dollars with high interest to stranger who give me ticket for ship. I believe he part of government or military. In my country, better no ask. I not sure it real ticket because they put me on bottom of ship with many food crate and mice. The mice not mean or bad. Trip last almost two months. We arrive in Los

Angeles port. From there, I meet other immigrants who help me travel to other side of country, so I meet contact. Only place that hire me and other Somalians, All Day Taxi."

I paused, stunned and envious of his perseverance and courage. "What about your wife?"

"We no have money to get two ticket, so she stay in Somalia. She wait for me to find work. It take a long time, maybe two years, to save money and buy her pass. They raise price when we present money to man in Somalia. We beg for more money. Loan man agree but say cost triple now. Last week, we finally pay debt to him after many, many years."

"What if you didn't pay him?"

"Very simple. They go after family in Somalia. Maybe they kill them. That is life of immigrant coming to America. I sure you understand."

"I do, but my voyage wasn't like yours. I arrived on a plane. I know after we acclimated most people wanted us to leave. They didn't like the way we speak, or our looks, or our names. They accused us of stealing jobs, even though they didn't want the ones we worked. The streets are paved with gold, they'd say, but as I got older, I realized coal ash covered every road."

"You right, buddy. You need special tool for that kind of magic, and the one who have tool do not share." He scooped a spoonful of Tiramisu. "Cake is amazing. Let us enjoy goodness we have for we can do nothing to change past."

"Agreed," I said, raising a healthy portion to my lips. "Hey, in my opinion, Italians are better bakers than pasta makers. Don't tell them I said that or I'll never hear the end of it."

We chuckled in unison.

"You secret safe with me." He mimed zipping his lips.

I took a sip of the steaming espresso, then chugged it, which was no different than I'd done throughout my life, but this time it didn't go as planned. Seconds later, my heart palpitated and my breath escaped. Dreaming, I floated into the silence of the dark universe, observing the chaos erupting beneath me. Ants bustled in straight lines to their colonies while whirring bees maneuvering like jets whisked any stragglers, returning them to the congregation.

"Are you okay, buddy? Nico. Can you hear me?"

"Yes... Yes...," I said to the muffled echo, attempting to wave my hand lodged under my head.

"I don't know what happened. I must've dozed for a moment."

Abdi tugged my shoulder, leaning me against the backrest. "You faint, buddy. Strong coffee. Like whiskey, maybe." His high-pitched laughter brought some relief.

"Yeah, it is. Whoever invented espresso probably never thought this could happen to a person."

He dug into my pocket and retrieved the pills. "Please, take these."

I swallowed them with a splash of water. Abdi and the interior of the café came into focus with Elizabeth surveying me from the edge of the table.

"I'm sorry, Beth. I didn't mean—"

"You didn't do anything wrong. Are you okay?" she said, concerned, yet determined. "Do you need me to call an ambulance?"

"It'll be fine. They can't help me. I didn't want to bother

telling you prior, but considering, well, I've been given bad news by my doctor. I think I've overextended myself with this stupid, brash idea to complete a familial bucket list."

"Oh, my." Her hand rose to her mouth. "I understand. Is there anything they can do for you?"

"Unfortunately, no. Such is life. We can only go with the flow." I closed my eyes and lowered my head.

"Sorry about the bad news. I'll comp your meal."

"It's okay. You don't have to."

"Correct. I don't have to, but I want to. It's the least I can do." She sniffled and skimmed a finger over her eye. "Have a good day or try…" She turned and sprinted between the kitchen doors.

"You want go?" Abdi said.

"Let's stay for a few more minutes, so I can regain my sanity," I said with a hand pressing my cheek, the other patting my forehead with a napkin.

"No problem, buddy. Whatever you want to do is okay with me. Have drink."

I gulped the water, then we headed to the car. "We have to figure out where to go next, but I can't seem to think."

"My opinion is go to places you think most important. Even if for couple minutes. We figure it out."

"Thank you, Abdi. Have I said that before?"

"I think you have."

"I'm like a broken record, then."

"Yes, but you playing good song."

"Good to know." I nodded instead of thanking him again, pausing to ponder the next options. "I believe I have an idea."

"Yes. Yes. Tell me where and we be there."

"Are you sure I'm not inconveniencing you? You can be honest with me."

"Not at all. This your day, buddy, not mine. I know you do same for me, if reverse."

"Great."

"Well, on one condition."

"What's that?"

"As long as you no ask to drive off cliff or take you to big building to jump, then we be fine."

"What about a mountain?"

"That no too. Lucky, no mountain near here."

"I promise to not do either or anything like that. No martyr mission for me," I said with a throaty giggle.

"I trust you," then he mumbled, "I hope."

"My heart may be gone, but my ears still work. Don't worry," I snickered.

"Okay... Let's go, but to where?"

"I think the time has arrived for me to rest. I'm a bit tired. Let's go where there is peace. The open water of the Irondequoit Bay at the Marine Park," I said.

"Great idea. I would do same," he said, nodding with a warm smile.

"Plus, there's free parking and plenty of spaces."

"Here," I said, tapping the seat, then sliding a twenty upon the armrest. "Since Elizabeth comped the meal, I can give you this to cover some of the costs for driving me around."

He waved it away, but I insisted, then accepting the money after losing a brief back-and-forth. At least, I satisfied a portion of my enormous debt to him.

CH 27

During the jaunt, I drifted from consciousness, awakening multiple times to snippets of my life ending at the bottom of the bay or freefalling from a plane with no parachute. In each scenario, I died alone and not one person knew, except for the coroner at the morgue. Abdi stirred me from the torment with a series of slaps to my cheeks. Dazed, I swatted at him, contacting more air than skin. He garbled all would be okay and I needed to follow his lead. Surrendering, he grabbed my ankles and thrust them upon the sandy pavement. I bucked at his aggressive plan, plummeting my upper body onto the seat like a felled tree. Unrelenting, he latched onto my hand and yanked upward. Out of breath, he angled my limp head against the door jamb, cradling it as I searched for fresh air. I tried to stand, but failed, rolling my cheek over the fender, attempting to find the correct Abdi among the three floating before my eyes.

"Where are you?" I muttered.

"Here, buddy. Place your hand on cane." I did as he instructed after several missed attempts. "We be there soon. I promise."

With his arms tucked around my waist, he heaved me upright, my heels searching for balance, grinding the sandpaper pavement. "I can do this, Abdi. *We* can do this. Find me more pills. I'll make it to the shore."

"Yes. We do it together. Lean against door."

Panting, I obeyed his instructions once again because

fighting them is a worse option. He sifted my pockets and slid the pills into my mouth. I crushed them between my teeth and swallowed, regaining some semblance, the blurriness clearing. I firmed the cane against the asphalt and waddled forward.

"Great job, Nico. You can do it."

"Yes. We must."

"One foot at time. Careful," he warned, holding my elbow and bracing my back.

The expansive Irondequoit Bay resided on the outskirts of the city. I'd been several times throughout my life, some of the experiences great, and some not so much. We toiled along the cobblestones towards a partially secluded section, our steps raking in unison over the silty bricks splattered with tropical hues. In the distance, gulls squawked as they gained flight within the freshwater breeze, surveying the turquoise waters for their prey.

I envied the children ahead of us, cartwheeling with uncontrollable laughter. They quieted as we approached, probably frightened and appalled at my deterioration. Offended at first, I let it slide. I wanted to tell them not to fear what life brings, but disrupting their day at the beach with negativity seemed trifling. They deserved to be carefree, to live in the present, and remain ignorant about their dire future because when life is ending, there are no more tulips left to pick.

"We're going to make it to the sand, Abdi," I murmured, flapping my shirt and fingering my hair to clear the humidity, neither of which succeeded.

He led me along without responding, stopping for a breather at the coral, dressing rooms fitted with exterior showers. The less the onlookers, the better, saving me a barrage of rhetorical health questions from older folk who knew their outlooks wouldn't be much different than mine, other than age.

"Stay put, Nico. I be right back." He leaned me between one of the sheds and a handrail lining the walkway.

"Where are you going? Don't leave me," I implored.

"Don't worry. I be fast," he shouted, bolting towards the parking lot.

Slouching, I gripped the cane like a vise and squared my back against the wall, hoping not to list like a ship. I attempted to clear the dribbling sweat stinging my eyes and slipped, almost crashing to the ground with no one to assist. Fretting, I scanned the beach and parking lot with blurred vision, but couldn't locate him. The children had scampered off as well. I called to him between labored breaths. Perhaps he had decided to leave rather than deal with a wretch like myself who's more of a hindrance than anything else. He'd done plenty, and I couldn't lay blame. Without him, I'd be dead on one of the avenues or in hospital hoping for a magic carpet ride to Eden. I confirmed my hold upon the cane and gazed at the diminutive waves lathering the shore. The end could arrive, and it'd be fine by me.

"Nico. Nico."

His voice roused me from the aquatic hypnosis. "Abdi, you returned," I said, relieved.

"Of course, buddy. You think I leave you?" he said, scrunching his face.

"I wouldn't be mad."

"We come so far. I don't do that to you. Our people do not

leave friends behind."

"Appreciated. Where did you go?"

"To get blanket from trunk. You need to sit on sand."

"I won't say those two words again. I'm indebted to you. I hope there's an afterlife, so I can repay you."

"No need, my friend. Allah will thank me, in return everyone near me prosper, including you. Come, let's go. The water is calling to us."

Arm in arm, we lumbered towards the shore. He used the corner of the quilt to clear the moisture from my face, then, with cautious fingers, cleared the matted hair from my brow. At the edge, where the colored cobblestones ended and the beach began, we stopped.

"You want boots off?" he said, nonchalant.

I paused, contemplating the complexity of the offer, since I could barely walk, let alone stand. "I'm not sure I can. I don't feel well," I said, shaking my head, then mumbling several vulgarities.

"I help. Lean on my back with your hands. I remove them."

"No, Abdi. That's too much to ask. It's not right for you to do that for me. I'm a pauper not a king."

"It fine, buddy," he said with a high-pitched laugh. "We all paupers in world of imaginary kings. Follow my lead."

He bent over. I nuzzled the cane against his stomach while planting my hands onto his back. Like a magician he slipped, turned, and swiped the boots with socks in tow, tucking them under his arm. "Freedom. Feel good. Right, Nico? Now, you walk in gentle beach."

"Yes, it's amazing. It's been so long." I slithered my feet

into the sand, curling my toes and sifting the cool powder between their spaces.

"Me too."

"I wish the beach was closer to where I lived. I would come more often."

"Cities like to hide the best from the residents," he said as a matter of fact.

"Very true."

"In Somalia me and friends walk barefoot all the time. If the sand clean, of course. We do it to be one with Earth and her strength. You can be one with her now too."

"Yes, yes… to be one with her. I wish we met years ago. I could have learned so much from you."

"Learning never end until we—you know what I mean… Come on. Let us go."

"Yes. Let's find a spot for us to sit," I said, measuring each step in the calming powder.

He nodded, leading the way, pointing in various directions where empty beach existed. I suggested a remote location off to the side that had no stragglers. He agreed.

"Sit, my friend. I help," he said, ironing the corners of the quilt, then stretching his arm towards me.

"Perfect. I couldn't ask for anything more."

I wedged a shoulder against his chest, and as I adjusted my grip upon the cane, I slipped, twirling and face-planting onto the sand with a mouthful of grains. Abdi, quick to react, rolled me onto the blanket and cleared the airways before I suffocated.

"I'm not well, Abdi. I'm not well. Something's changed for the worse. Crying is not even worth the hassle anymore."

"You be fine. Stay positive. Evening approaching. Soon water be like glass. This best time to come to beach," he said, ecstatic.

I wanted to yell at him, curse him, as I lay soiled like a toddler, but even that served no purpose. "I suppose, Abdi, but I'm tired. I want to sleep. Just close my eyes for a few minutes."

"No. Absolutely, no. Look ahead. See the glory. Love the beauty."

The sun glowed a quarter turn above the horizon, allowing ample time to absorb the magnificent rays before they departed to illuminate those in darkness in other parts of the world. Awed, I hoped to etch its brilliance onto my mind. "It's as if after a long day's work the moonlight cradles the seas to sleep. Amazing."

"There, that better. You are happy now. Is anything more I get to make you more comfortable?" His face held a hint of sadness.

"Everything you've done is more than enough." I gazed at the purple and red hues drawn onto the sky. "My family could complete this picture, but in my current condition, it's best they stay away."

"You do all you can for them and make your peace."

"It's not enough because something is still missing. Inside, I'm empty."

"Maybe just part of process. It's okay, buddy."

"I don't believe it is." A shiver crawled along my back, ending upon my scalp. "There must be more. One last thing. Them. My high hopes always tumble to the base of the mountain." A painful tingle sieged my hands and feet, welling my eyes. "No one has ever cared about me. All they've done is lie to me, deceive me. It's better to die now. Alone," I cawed, sniffling, then cupped my hands over my cheeks. "Abdi, don't ever waste your time with bucket lists. They're a dumb idea."

"I'm sorry, Nico," he said, patting my back and stroking my shoulder.

"They should've have come to hold and console me," I said, swatting, attempting to remove the stings emerging across my skin like a swarm of gnawing red ants.

"You okay, buddy?"

"Yes—No. I don't know anymore. Everything is cloudy. I can't stop the pain. They should've..."

Frantic, I scanned the ends of the beach and the parking lot, turning to the bay and skies for reprieve, then lowered my head between my legs, gritted my teeth, and sobbed, the tears trickling upon the quilt, discoloring the rainbow squares.

"Look, Nico." He pounded the blanket and shook my shoulders. "There," he said, waving, "Behind you. They coming." He sprung to his feet and cheered.

I knuckled my eyes, cleared my throat, and swiveled. A lackadaisical, motley crew approached in a chaotic, single file. They plowed through the sand, the powder cascading from their shoes like waterfalls. My son, the only one with a wide smile, leading the way, holding the portrait. Behind him, Beatrice, then my parents side-by-side, their hands longing to clutch each other with each stride but settling for careful strokes. My stoic grandmother lagged with Ariel in tow, neither interested in scurrying with the pack.

"Abdi, this is amazing!"

"I step away now, so you have private time. I be back soon. Just in case, you need take more pills."

I did as told and watched him walk away. A shadow crept over me. "Son…" I stretched towards him as he approached the edge of the blanket. "You came." I paused. "For me."

"Yes, Nico—I mean, Dad. And I brought your picture, as well as a few other friends." He flicked his head and turned.

"I see. I'm not sure what to say to you, or them. I'm speechless, yet ecstatic."

"You don't have to say a word. We came to support you."

"Thank you, Alessio."

"No need to thank me or any of us. We will hope for the best and that all the predictions are wrong," he said, stepping away, resting the portrait atop the blanket.

"My beautiful son. *Bello mio*," Papa said, approaching. He leaned over me with a gentle embrace, as if he thought he'd break me or himself. Ma knelt and kissed my cheek, then parted several strands of hair from my cheek, clearing the sand. She opted not to say a word, or perhaps it was Papa who wouldn't let her get one in. "Are you okay? Is there anything Lidia or me can do—to make everything easy?"

"Yes. My arms and heart are weak. Can you reach into my pocket and grab the pills."

"Of course, son." I directed him to their location. He stood perplexed. "Do you want me to put them in—?"

"Sure. It'll be easier." I stuck out my tongue and received them like Eucharist. His eyes moistened, then waved Ma to enter the conversation.

She hunched ahead of me, her hands upon her thighs. "I know your father talk about us, your birth, the adoption. I wanna apologize for no explain the situation *complicata* before." Her lips trembled, teetering between a frown and a smile. "You maybe no believe this, but it harder to hide truth. Maybe, you forgive me, us."

"It's fine. What's there to do about it now? I suppose it wouldn't have made a difference growing up, but I'll never know for certain. This might seem weird, but I always knew something was a little off between us."

"I sure it have more to do with dad and me fight all the time. Imma sorry for that time too. All the day and night we fight, it not fair to you."

"Why didn't you get the divorce sooner to save us, I mean me, all the trouble?"

"Good question. Take me many years and many relationships to figure out. When two people meet we have wild feelings that never last. Then, as time pass, we keep try to make-a them alive again and it fail. Each time we fail, we dig another hole. Before you know, we have deep hole, too much dirt, and nowhere to put, so we die in dirt. Can't breathe." She sighed and rolled her eyes. "Well, that was then, this is now. You are important, not the past. Can I help you with anything? Make-a you more comfortable."

"Being here is enough. Thank you. I didn't expect for anyone to come."

"Well, don't forget to ask." She looked into my eyes. "I meet your son before. He very special, like you. I know his secret too, but be proud of him."

"Easier to say when you're looking through the window instead of inside looking out."

"Well, he is here. True or no?"

"I suppose that's better than not."

"Stop acting like that, Nico. *Testa dura.* Maybe illness is make-a you brain crazy. I know you want this from all of us. So, accept it." She stood with a glowering face.

"I understand and you're right. The pain from my heart and lungs is taking a toll on my being. Thank you for coming to visit. It's like a dream come true."

"That is better." She glanced beyond me. "More people waiting to talk to you. They love you, too." She stepped aside and Grandma Porto filled her space.

"Thank you for coming, especially considering Peter, Mrs. Porto—just kidding, Paola."

"It's never a problem. We are family. After all our time together, I'd come see you no matter where you are. But, before I continue, there's a sweet young lady who wants to say hello."

"Oh... Ariel. My everything."

"Yes, love, it is I, tagging along with the group. Beatrice called and invited me. A sweet woman."

"She is, but she's not you. You're irreplaceable. I don't know what I'd do without you."

"Oh, my love, you swelter my soul."

"Likewise. It's as if we are meeting for the first time every day I see you."

"Well, I don't want to interfere with your family. I just wanted to say hello and let you know I'm here for you just like everyone else. I'll be waiting." She pointed to the edge of the water.

"I hope I can meet you there soon."

"No rush, my love. I will never leave." She sniffled and dashed away.

"What a nice woman, Nico. Ariel is her name? How come you didn't bring her to my place yet?"

"I didn't want to intrude with Peter. Is he by himself? Will he be okay?"

"Don't worry about him," she said, waving. "Worry about you and Ariel. He'll be fine. I got one of those nurses to take care of him while I'm away."

"Good. I'd hate for something to happen to him."

"Life's bound to happen. As you know, Nico, we can't escape the end. It's just different for everyone, mine, your mom, your dad. It's coming for all of us. A roll of the dice or spin of the wheel decides how and when. Can't fight or beat it." She scooped a handful of sand and sifted it through her fingers. "Can you find a single grain that touched my palm?"

"I don't think I can," I said, squinting.

"Well... it was rhetorical, and exactly. Those are our chances in life. Everything's okay and even if it's not, then don't worry about it. Let's celebrate you now. Forget five minutes ago or five minutes into the future. Agreed?" She nodded.

"Agree to disagree," I said with an unsure tone.

"No. Agree, dammit. There are no other options. Your mom's right. Sometimes you *are* difficult." She simpered, neared, and patted my hair, separating the gritty, matted strands. "There's someone waiting to speak with you. I believe she's more important than me. And don't argue," she said, shushing me with a finger pressed to my lips. I didn't respond as she stepped away, replaced by Beatrice.

"Nico... Are you feeling okay?" She sat beside me, crisscrossing her legs.

"I could always be better, but that's not an option anymore."

"Oh, you're still funny, even with—"

"With death upon me. I'm not well. I can't even recall what anyone's said to me, and yet, I know there's nothing we can do to resolve any of this. It's sad and satisfying. The finiteness of life has brought us all together. I don't have to worry about the future and I have all of you here to complement my life. Anyway, thank you for coming."

"You're welcome," she said, wrapping her arm around my shoulders. "Do you remember making love under a full moon? I think at this very spot."

"I do. It was so bright we almost needed shades. I'm surprised no one saw us?"

"Maybe they did and just watched." She blushed, then giggled. "We may have conceived Alessio that night. I counted the days and they almost match up."

"Really? Wow. We shared so much during our time together. I loved you since I first set eyes on you. I experienced so many things with you. The newness of it all changed my life, my perceptions. You provided an escape from the hell at home. I wanted to impress you more than myself. The loss of innocence and demureness of love spun me into a whirlwind. Do you remember when we used to talk for hours?" I gazed at the sky, then her eyes.

"I do, Nicola. Our conversations just as perfect as when we sat silent. I longed every day to see you. Your touch and kiss created gusts of surprise and euphoria within me, but you have to admit as time passed they changed into hurricanes." She lowered her head and sighed.

"Yes, but hurricanes have some positives, don't they?" I hoped for agreement.

"Their rush is immense and unexplainable, but their destruction is irreparable. I wouldn't trade what we had for anything, regardless of the final ruin. In the end, we had a child. I may not have told you, but he is yours, ours."

"I'm glad you told me because it gave me added purpose during my struggles."

"Better to know, than die not knowing. I understand that's crude but—"

"It's fine, Beatrice. I know what you mean." I pointed at her, then myself. "We will always think alike because we learned from each other at such a young age. I wish we could've continued further together. But as you say, such—"

"Such is life. Such—is—life. Words to live by in any situation. Let's call over Alessio. We can sit together."

She screeched his name. He'd since removed his polished boots to walk along the water's edge and have the small waves roll over his feet. He stopped, turned, and gestured, increasing his pace into a jog towards us, globs of wet sand flinging from his toes with each stride. A few inches from the blanket, he attempted a leaping pirouette, which almost ended in a tumble. He dug his heels like skates, splashing the grains across our thighs. I envied his exuberance.

"Slow down, Alessio," she barked, wiping the residue from both of us. "Be considerate and respectful with those around you. Your dad is sick."

"I'm sorry, Mom." He hesitated for a moment, then lowered his head. "Dad."

"It's okay, Beatrice. Let people be. And you can call me Nico, if it's easier. We don't have to be formal. Come. Sit."

I scooched over, leaving just enough space for his seat.

My hand brushed Beatrice's, and for that brief moment, I recalled the warmth she filled me with many decades ago, evaporating our time spent apart. She then slid her hand into mine and squeezed, her watering eyes steadfast at the setting sun ahead.

"Do you want me to get your portrait and stand it up?" Alessio said, solacing with his hand atop my shoulders. "It'll cheer you up."

"Leave it for now, but thank you for offering. Make room for yourself and sit. Let's enjoy our time together."

He lifted the portrait partially covering the blanket, searching for a spot to set it. As he lowered it upon the sand, Abdi showed and scooped it before it touched the ground, carting it to the car. We waved at each other, I beaming with thankfulness.

With my breath laboring, I motioned towards the horizon. Alessio situated himself upon the blanket and nuzzled against my body. He followed my direction to the sky with a quivering lip. Between gasps for air, I caught the calming swoosh of the rolling waves, setting my mind at ease. All the thoughts of dying alone wiped from memory. To my left sat Beatrice, to my right sat Alessio, and ahead of me, Ariel. We were never a family, but in the end a family we are.

Scanning the beach through a haze, I attempted to recognize those who came to see me, including Abdi. I closed my heavy eyes as the yellow orb reddened the sky to signal its departure from the horizon. I laid my head atop Alessio's shoulder, then held his hand. The ebb and flow of the water in unison with my slowing heart. The option always exists to amend any situation while you're alive. Such is life. Such—is—

life.

"Nicola!"

"Dad. Nico."

"Help us. He's not moving or breathing. Help. Help."

"Dad!"

"Love! Come on, love. Come back to me."

"Our child. What are we to do, Luigi? We're helpless. No, please, no. *Figlio mio. Non morire. Ti amo, figlio mio.*"

"Nicola. Nico. Help! Help. Call 911. Please… get an ambulance. Help… Please…"

GIANNI FRANCO

CH 28

I awoke from a medically-induced coma three weeks after that day at the beach. One morning, Doctor Gordon visited my hospital room and explained what had happened. Even though my mind was clouded by morphine and whatever else they had dripping into the IV bag, I understood most of what he described. He explained I flatlined twice, several minutes each time. They revived me with a defibrillator and multiple injections of epinephrine. I don't recall anything from the trauma, nor did the white light so many religious fanatics talk about appear. The cardiac department had an emergency meeting to discuss my options, and although the procedures carried great risk, which they assessed as too dangerous during my last hospital stay, they decided to proceed to give me a chance at living. In essence, I was dead either way. During the thirteen-hour surgery, the cardiothoracic team performed a coronary artery bypass graft, which Doctor Gordon referred to as the cabbage procedure, repaired the aortic valve, replaced the mitral valve, and implemented seven stents. He kept rambling about tests, procedures, the iLifeCheck programmers wanting to meet me, cardiac rehabilitation, and taking medications, but I'd reached my threshold for storing information, so I waved him away.

"Stay well and get some rest," he said, before exiting the room.

"Ariel will take care of me," I mumbled. And, she has like a drill sergeant, ensuring I follow the regimen.

With the exact date of death unknown due to iLifeCheck glitches, I've spent my time bonding with everyone I encountered during my bucket list escapade, excluding any enemies, of course. The trek through the neighborhoods wasn't so bad after all. Ariel and I approached a pinnacle in our relationship where I professed my love to her on the beach in front of several onlookers, asking for her hand in marriage. Neither of us believed in that controlling sacrament invented by some sadomasochist eons ago, but we succumbed to peer pressure and faked a wedding for our friends and family during a small gathering. She ditched the overalls for the day, wearing a fitted, black dress, and I donned a new pair of jeans, dress shirt, and boots. To complete the sham, we downloaded and doctored a marriage license and found someone to administer our vows who lacked the proper certification. The highlight of the charade occurred at the Woodcliff Hotel and Spa where we spent our false honeymoon. That night the thought of our finality propelled us to intimate levels I never foresaw.

Beatrice befriended Ariel at the wedding after catching the bouquet. Beatrice ran in the opposite direction of the throw, but somehow it ended up in her hands. We decided to call it the immaculate reception. I met with Beatrice and Alessio every other week to talk and have a small lunch or dinner. Ariel suggested the idea first, saying a closer relationship with my son and her mother would be healthier for all those involved. I agreed, delighted with her understanding of the situation and giving us space to rebuild. I never thought my first love and current love could harmonize.

Alessio turned out to be more accepting of our situation

than I envisioned. Sometimes, sans Beatrice, we'd chat for hours by phone or in person. Not as frequent as I hoped because love, work, and writing took precedence, which I understood and supported.

He invited me to Papa Joe's, the restaurant where he works, and cooked me the most amazing Spaghetti Carbonara, sending me home with an equally awesome Chicken Parmigiana. He even paid the tab, including drinks. That same night, approaching morning, he knocked on my door as I watched *The Late Show*. Well, actually Ariel's home, since I had moved in with her after our fantastical wedding. Mico, the beautiful kitty from the pet store, prancing behind to the entrance. Ariel promised to take care of him if and when my time arrived, a win-win for Mico.

"Nico. It's… been a long night. Dad," he slurred, flipping his long hair with a head flick.

"Hey, Alessio. Thanks for treating me tonight."

"Who is it, love?" Do I have to call the police?" howled Ariel from the second-floor studio, painting another masterpiece.

"It's all good. Nico's here. He's a little tipsy."

"Good to hear, love. Have fun. I'll be up here for another hour or so. If you need anything, let me know."

"Will do, Ariel. Love you."

"Love you, love."

"What's up, Alessio?"

Alcohol oozed from his pores. Considering my health, I was sober for the most part, sneaking a glass of wine or a cocktail here and there, including this evening.

"Not much. I'm drunk and wanted to talk about us."

"Sure, come in. I'll get you another drink. Liquor or wine?"

"Liquor... Vodka, whiskey, whatever," he said, stumbling towards the kitchen.

I hobbled to the refrigerator with the cane still on loan from Papa. I filled a tumbler halfway with whiskey and added some ice. With my back turned to him, I snuck a sip, then slid him the glass upon the table.

"Thanks, Dad."

"Not a problem. Least I can do. Wish I could join you for a full one. Man, I miss those days. What's on your mind tonight?"

"I know it's late and won't take up too much of your time. I want to talk about us, separate from mom. I've been thinking these last few days, weeks."

"Go ahead. I'm always here to listen."

"Exactly what I meant. Like you read my mind. You're not *always* going to be here and that's going to suck. Well, I don't mean that in a negative way. It's positive. I promise." His head swayed, eyes chasing the swishing liquor within the glass.

"I understand. Continue."

"Our time together has been short. And, when you came to the restaurant I watched you from a distance. The staff commented on how much we look alike. I told them our story. They were awed and enamored by it. I realized as you finished your meal that I didn't want you to leave. Ever."

"Thanks, Alessio."

"There's more. I want to say, I—love—you, Dad... Nico. And I don't want to see you go anywhere, but I know that's out of my control. While we're both here I want us to be as close as possible and share all we can, just like you did when you gave me the portrait. I look at it every day. That's it in a nutshell."

"I love you, too."

He slugged the drink and doddered to the counter for a refill, tipping chairs during the short trek. He chugged that one as well, then called it a night, leading himself to the exit. By the time I reached it, dragging the cane behind me, he was at the sidewalk. I waved, which he didn't notice, and locked the door. We never spoke about that night again. I appreciated the follow up to my dinner, regardless of his inebriation, and didn't mind our love wrapped in silence.

The following day I divulged the loving news to Abdi. He visited me at the hospital with his wife a few times, even bringing a bouquet of flowers and a card. I didn't thank them while they stood bedside because of the sedation. I did swarm him with gratitude during our ride for dinner at the Blue Nile, an Ethiopian-Somali restaurant; his wife not in attendance because one of the children had the flu.

Our food tasted better than any Italian cuisine I ever sampled. We shared a spicy meat platter, combined with Bariis Iskukaris, Sambusa, Injera, Tibs, Doro Wat, and Salata. He said that even though Ethiopia and Somali had warred several times during the last century, not everyone hated each other. In America, especially, they combined their forces to create exquisite dishes not found at many places across the globe.

To settle the dinner, he suggested we drink Ethiopian coffee. They served it in a metal pot, leaving it at our table for additional pours. I limited myself to one cup due to its strength. He drank a few since he had to drive the cab all night. The roast just as good as any espresso, clearing the knots caused by my overindulgence of food.

He dropped me off at Ariel's shortly thereafter, wishing me the best from Allah and success to living forever. I reciprocated with just as much good fortune, expressing the weirdness of how all of this came to be. He pointed to the sky without uttering a word, smiling as confident as the sun rising from the east, reiterating the prediction he made about Alessio. I responded with an assenting grin, then exited and headed to my love.

She welcomed me with open arms as I entered, storming down the steps from the studio. Her overalls loose, covered in a hodgepodge of colors, one shoulder strap dangling to her elbow. She swooped me around the waist and led me to the bedroom. The other strap fell to her waist as we stood, our gazes locked, lips quivering before our kiss.

I interrupted the moment of bliss. "Ariel... I could never have imagined this. Us."

"Well, it's real, love. You have to accept it and delve into all the beauty it offers. Don't think about it. Just go with the flow like a river from a burst dam and let it swallow you."

"I was dead not too long ago." I sighed with a welling eye.

"Love... *You* will die. *I* will die. It's part of the curse to be alive. All we can do, every single day, is to hope, to love, to kiss, to hug."

Within her genius I surrendered, hypnotized. She took the reins, leading me onto the bed. Fervid fondling and kissing continued onto the silk pillows and under the satin sheets, our undulations culminating with intemperate ecstasy. We lay beside each other, our bodies intertwined like lace. I knew if I died tomorrow, I wouldn't have any regrets. All I could do is wish for more days not to rue and to dream before time stole my ability to dream. Such is life, a life I hope never to lose.

THE END

ACKNOWLEDGEMENT

Thank you to my parents, Lidia and Luigi, who brought me into this world, and to my immediate family abroad in Celano, Italy, the Contestabiles, Agostina (Linda), Rita, Lina, Agostino, Domenica, Linda Rita, and many others too numerous to list. *Ti amo* and hope to see you again. They, as well as all the Italians in Rochester (Gates), NY, shaped me for this novel, supporting me as a child and dealing with me as an adult.

Thank you to those who supported me when my parents passed away, Paola Bianchi Grieco, Lina Colaprete, Michelina DiGirolamo, Concetta Melfi, Maria DiRenzo, Pia Palozzi, and Agostina Contestabile.

Thank you to everyone whom I ever encountered from all walks of life who fed the additional experiences into this book, helping it move forward. Thank you to Corey Morgano, the Professor, Dimitrios Manou, the CPA, Mario Colaprete, the Chef, Domenico Colaprete, the Artist, Filippo Colaprete, whom I have known since his birth, Antonio Napoli, the Promoter from Catania, Brian Keeler, the Guitarist from high school, Abdi, the Cabbie, Mark Witt, the former Coworker, and the Loves who loved me and those that broke my heart.

Such is Life. Cheers to all.

ABOUT THE AUTHOR

Gianni Franco

Contact info:

Website: https://giannifranco.com/

FB: https://www.facebook.com/authorgiannifranco/

IG: gianni.franco

Amazon: https://www.amazon.com/dp/173662170X
https://www.amazon.com/dp/1736621742

BOOKS BY THIS AUTHOR

Stained Mirror: A Serial Killer Memoir (Frank Stark, The Life Of A Serial Killer)

Frank Stark is losing his grip on sanity, his mind a battleground for the demons that torment him. This psychological thriller invites you to witness his descent into madness, a terrifying journey into the heart of a fractured psyche where he also wrestles with the duality of his existence, including his complex sexuality. Prepare yourself for a macabre exploration of the human mind at its most broken.

Excerpt: "The birds no longer whistle. Love equates hate. My dreams are all nightmares. The sky is no longer blue. If there's no other side, then to sleep forever will be better than to stay awake for one more minute in this life. I am the Alpha and Omega."

Ramblings From A Broken Mind: Anthology

Gianni Franco, the mind behind the chilling Stained Mirror: A Serial Killer Memoir, returns with a powerful collection of poems and short stories. These unflinching works explore the darkness within, touching on themes of horror, young adult struggles, LGBTQ+ lives, the scars of PTSD, and the enduring power of love. From the deeply personal "A Mother's Dying Breath" to the politically charged "Freedom Weeps," and the immigrant reflection "The American Supermarket" to the haunting "The Willow Tree," this anthology offers a raw and unforgettable journey into the human condition.